LGBTQ FICTION AND POETRY

FROM APPALACHIA

LGBTQ
fiction and poetry from
Appalachia

edited by
Jeff Mann & Julia Watts

West Virginia University Press
Morgantown 2019

First edition published 2019 by West Virginia University Press

Printed in the United States of America

ISBN

Paper 978-1-946684-92-9

Ebook 978-1-946684-93-6

Library of Congress Cataloging-in-Publication Data

Names: Mann, Jeff, editor. | Watts, Julia, 1969- editor.

Title: LGBTQ fiction and poetry from Appalachia / edited by Jeff Mann and Julia Watts.

Description: First edition. | Morgantown : West Virginia University Press, 2019. | Includes
     bibliographical references.

Identifiers: LCCN 2018040196| ISBN 9781946684929 (Paper) | ISBN 9781946684936
     (Ebook)

Subjects: LCSH: Gays' writings, American—Appalachian Region. | Bisexuals' writings,
     American—Appalachian Region. | Transgender people's writings, American—
     Appalachian Region. | Gays' writings, American—Appalachian Region—Literary
     collections. | Bisexuals' writings, American—Appalachian Region—Literary collections.
     | Transgender people's writings, American—Appalachian Region—Literary collections. |
     Appalachian Region—Literary collections.

Classification: LCC PS508.G39 L43 2019 | DDC 811/.00902664075—dc23

LC record available at https://lccn.loc.gov/2018040196

Book and cover design by Than Saffel / WVU Press

In loving memory of Okey Napier Jr., aka Miss Ilene Over, a ferocious Appalachian drag queen, West Virginia Wonder Woman, and courageous champion of LGBTQ rights.

For the ones who stayed.

CONT

ENTS

CONTEN

TS continued

EDITORS' NOTES

In the mid-1970s, a book was the catalyst for my coming-out. I was sixteen, a high-school student in Hinton, West Virginia, when my favorite former teacher, Jo Davison, confided to me that she was a lesbian and lent me a paperback copy of Patricia Nell Warren's 1974 novel, *The Front Runner*. As I read Warren's tale about the love affair between a track star and his coach, I was finally able to understand and name the feelings I'd felt for years about attractive local men, male teachers, and a handful of older students. It was same-sex desire. I was gay.

This revelation was a relief—I understood some profound part of myself I hadn't understood before—but it was also alienating and complicating. I lived in a small mountain town of around three thousand people, many of them conservative Christians, few of them likely to approve of my homosexuality. Young as I was, I sensed some hard truths: were I to be openly gay, I'd be shunned, or I'd get my ass kicked . . . or worse. I didn't think of myself as an Appalachian then, only a queer kid stuck in a hostile, potentially violent environment from which he needed to escape as soon as possible.

My escape was a scholarship to West Virginia University, where I made gay and lesbian friends and frequented Morgantown's gay bar. My mountain roots meant little to me then; indeed, they felt like a handicap. All the gay novels I read depicted life in San Francisco, Los Angeles, and New York City. There was, as far as I knew, no LGBTQ Appalachian literature. The two identities seemed mutually exclusive.

Two events began to change my attitude toward my native region. In graduate school at WVU, as I worked on a creative thesis, writing passionate gay love poems and hoping to become an author, I read Maggie Anderson's first book, *Years That Answer* (1980). Not only were many of her poems suffused with Appalachian imagery, but friends in the know informed me that Anderson was a lesbian. "So you *can* be a homosexual poet from West Virginia," I thought. "You can even *write* about West Virginia."

Then, in the fall of 1985, I lived in the suburbs of Washington, DC, and taught part-time at George Washington University, hoping to achieve an exciting gay life in the big city. Despite my housemate's many kindnesses— he was from the Mountain State too—I found urban and suburban existence intolerable. I was homesick. I missed my native region: its customs, its dialect, its manners, its food, its landscapes. Another uncomfortable revelation: I was very much both a southerner and an Appalachian. So being a mountain boy made me unfit for city living, and being a gay guy made me unfit for existence in Appalachia? There was nowhere I entirely belonged.

Disheartened, I returned to West Virginia. I taught as an English instructor at WVU and then moved on to Virginia Tech. There, a friend introduced me to the work of Dorothy Allison. Another southern Appalachian lesbian writer to admire! Occasionally, my teaching assignments included introduction to Appalachian studies or Appalachian literature—both fields I had never studied before—and learning that material, teaching those classes, I began to come to terms with my mountain roots and became defiantly proud of them. I grew determined to balance my Appalachian and gay identities, in my life and in my writings.

What affirming pleasure, then, to stumble upon other mountaineer queer authors over the last few decades, to discover how varied we are but how much we have in common. I've often said that I'm too selfish to edit a book, because I want to focus on my own writing, but when Abby Freeland at WVU Press proposed this book to me, I knew that this was a collection I'd be pleased and privileged to edit. Julia Watts has been a real delight to work with, and it's been exciting to compile such fine work from so many LGBTQ authors. Let's hope that Appalachians struggling to reconcile mountaineer and queer identities discover this book and find that balancing act much easier as a result.

—JM

As a teenager in southeastern Kentucky, I struggled with how my identity as an Appalachian could peaceably coexist with the other identity I was just starting to discover. It seemed that being LGBT was something you had to go Somewhere Else to do, as in the story of my mom's high-school classmate who Moved to the City to be a Lesbian (I'm not sure why I always thought of these things as needing capital letters, but I did). That being said, there were always Open Secret gays in Appalachian small towns—the two spinster high-school teachers who lived together, the florist who took such good care of his mama and played the organ at the First Baptist Church. No doubt there were more who were so deeply closeted nobody noticed them. And even with the gays who went Somewhere Else, it was usually the nearest decent-sized city. They were still Appalachians living in Appalachia; they had just traded a rural or small-town life for a more urban one.

As a young adult, I read Appalachian literature and what was then called gay and lesbian literature, but the two identities never overlapped in the same work. And so a few years down the road, in grad school, it was a thrilling, transformative experience to discover authors who wrote not about being LGBT *or* Appalachian, but LGBT *and* Appalachian, writers who, as a friend of mine is fond of saying, "don't put an *or* where God puts an *and*." Some of these touchstone LGBT authors are included in this collection: Lisa Alther, whose first novel *Kinflicks* featured a witty bisexual East Tennessean heroine; doris davenport, whose poems celebrate Black Lesbian Appalachian identity; and Dorothy Allison, whose fiction and poems ask tough questions about sexuality and social class in the voice of the region.

The 1990s ushered in vital new works in LGBT Appalachian fiction, among them Fenton Johnson's *Scissors, Paper, Rock*, a novel which brings the AIDS crisis home to Kentucky, and Dorothy Allison's groundbreaking *Bastard Out of Carolina*. In our current century, we have been blessed by my brilliant coeditor Jeff Mann's Appalachian gay memoir/manifesto *Loving Mountains, Loving Men*, and as we embrace the full spectrum of gender and sexuality, we hear a cacophony of young, exciting voices: the frank yet lyrical poetry of Nickole Brown, the insightful and moving fiction of Jonathan Corcoran and Carter Sickels.

A few people, when I told them about this project, asked, "Are there enough authors to make a whole book?" Obviously, the answer is *yes*. But really, there are enough for more than one. This collection is not meant to be exhaustive; Jeff and I lacked the time and ambition to create the equivalent of a *Norton Anthology of LGBTQ Appalachian Literature.* I know that there is worthy work by dozens of LGBTQ Appalachians that does not appear in these pages as well as eloquent writing about LGBTQ subjects by straight allies. For this book, though, my coeditor and I decided to invite only established Appalachian authors (with at least one book under their belts) who identify somewhere on the LGBTQ spectrum. We wanted to show that there is indeed a contemporary Appalachian LGBTQ literary canon—an assortment of authors of different ages and styles in different stages in their careers—who consistently give voice to what it means to be both Appalachian and LGBTQ.

Are there enough authors to make a whole book? You bet your boots there are. And a damned fine book, too.

—JW

INTRODUCTION

At the time of this book's release—Spring 2019—this collection is unique. For decades, heterosexual Appalachian authors have been depicting LGBTQ characters in their fiction. Some notable examples are Denise Giardina in *The Unquiet Earth* (1992) and Lee Smith in *Fair and Tender Ladies* (1988): both novels portray characters who express same-sex desire. At the same time, LGBTQ-identified Appalachian writers—most of them included in this collection—have published queer-themed work in literary journals, anthologies, and individual-author books. Despite this array of voices, until now no compendium of queer-identified authors from the Highland South has existed. This collection is the first of its kind to gather the work of LGBTQ writers from Appalachia into one volume of poetry and fiction.

What do we mean by *LGBTQ*? Though the abbreviation means different things to different people, and those meanings shift over time, for the purposes of this collection we've defined LGBTQ as lesbian, gay, bisexual, transgender, and/or queer. For some, "queer" serves as an alternative to L, G, B, or T. For us, "queer" serves as a catch-all term, shorthand that includes the previous categories.

Writers who define themselves as both queer and Appalachian often find that juxtaposition of identities difficult, confusing, and conflicted. Helen Matthews Lewis, in *Living Social Justice in Appalachia* (2012), described Appalachians as bicultural, possessing an Appalachian identity and valuing their subculture while at the same time being able to navigate mainstream culture. Add queer identity into the mix, and one must deal with the complications of being tricultural.

It's rarely easy, this identity-juggling, this balancing act. Some folks, to make their lives simpler, renounce their regional identity, refusing to define themselves as Appalachian and fleeing to a queer-friendly urban area outside of the region where they might attempt to forget their mountain roots. Others renounce their queer identity, remaining in the region but doing their best to live a heterosexual lifestyle, often at the insistence of whatever conservative religious doctrines with which they grew up.

For those of us who determinedly and insistently claim both queer and regional identity, life is complicated. However, it's those very complications that fuel most Appalachian LGBTQ writing. Virginia Woolf claimed in *Moments of Being* (1972) that making sense of shocks is why writers write, that the "shock-receiving capacity" is what makes a writer.

What in particular makes queer Appalachian experience full of shocks and conflicts? In Loyal Jones's well-known essay, "Appalachian Values," he lists what he considers the positive traits shared by most inhabitants of the region. Among them are "Independence, Self-Reliance and Pride," "Love of Place," "Familism," and "Religion."

The former is a godsend for nonconformists everywhere, giving us the strength to fight convention. In this regard, Carrie and Michael Kline's reader's-theater piece, "Revelations," focuses on the life-saving resilience that self-reliance can provide LGBTQ hillfolk. The last three traits, however, are quite often problematic for queer-identified Appalachians, as much of the writing in this collection makes clear.

What if you love your place, but your place, or, rather, the fellow inhabitants of your place, object to honest expressions of LGBTQ identity? Perhaps you grew up in a rural area, learned to garden, to savor the quiet, the wooded hillsides, the spring wildflowers, the grazing livestock in the fields, but can only enjoy the companionship of other queer folks by driving an hour or two to the nearest gay bar. Perhaps you still live in the same place where you were raised, a small town set amid a scenic convergence of mountains and rivers, but you know that being honest about your same-sex attractions would make you the object of jokes, gossip, threats, or even violence.

What if you love your family, but your kin are less than pleased to discover your attractions to the same sex or have serious problems with your expression of gender? Perhaps your mother and father, after meeting your same-sex love interest, refuse any contact with you in the future. Perhaps your grandmother, who has baked biscuits and pies for you since you were a child, sits you down to share her passionate belief that "morphodites" are hell-bound abominations. Perhaps your favorite cousin remains polite to you after you tell her that you're queer, but she makes clear that she's voting in the next election for a candidate who wants to rob same-sex couples of the opportunity to adopt children.

What if you were brought up in a fundamentalist faith that taught you that homosexual desire was sinful, only to recognize those same desires in yourself as you entered adolescence? What if you choose not to adopt any of the conservative faiths of your native region, only to find yourself surrounded by people who did, people whose religious convictions cause them to shun you and other members of your LGBTQ subculture, to stereotype you, and to crusade on both social and political levels to isolate you and deny you your basic human rights as a US citizen? As political theorist Cynthia Burack makes clear in *Sin, Sex and Democracy: Antigay Rhetoric and the Christian Right* (2008), "it is undeniable that traditionalist religious belief motivates most antigay bias and activism." Perhaps, in such a climate, you simmer with self-doubt and self-hatred. Perhaps your friends and kin strive to save your soul by demanding that you repudiate your same-sex attractions or modify your gender expression. Perhaps you grow suspicious of Christianity altogether, bristling at the packed-full church parking lots on Sunday morning, the ichthys "Jesus-fish" bumper stickers on local cars and pickup trucks.

These are some of the deep-rooted conflicts that queer Appalachians face. Many LGBTQ hillfolk, in working through them, achieve, with luck, some sort of self-awareness and emotional maturity. We writers wrestle something more out of these "shocks," these adversities: we deal with them by making art.

A few words on the organization of this book: as its contents attest, LGBTQ Appalachian writing nearly always concerns the ways that sexuality, gender identity, place, and family converge, interweave, and complicate one another. As we contemplated ways to position the authors' works, we considered a thematic structure, perhaps one that grouped the entries under such headings as "Desire," "Gender," "Place," and "Family." Eventually, we decided on the present egalitarian organization, listing the authors in alphabetical order by their last names. Appalachian literature is rife with fabric metaphors, but we'll risk one more: segregating the writing in this collection into thematic sections would be like pulling out the threads and separating the panels in a complex quilt. The way those threads are woven together and those panels are juxtaposed is the point of LGBTQ Appalachian writing.

So, for instance, we have attachment to family intermingling with same-sex desire in poems by Maggie Anderson, Dorothy Allison, Anita Skeen, and Nickole Brown, and in fiction by Rahul Mehta, Charles Lloyd, and Mesha Maren. We have painful conflicts between sexual orientation and religion in Jeff Mann's "Three Crosses." Savannah Sipple, in contrast, plays with those same conflicts in humorous, whimsical ways in her WWJD ("What Would Jesus Do?") poems. Region, family, and transgender identity collide in Carter Sickels's "Saving," and the convergence of lesbian desire, gender identity, and place causes suspenseful conflicts in Julia Watts's "Handling Dynamite." In Fenton Johnson's "Bad Habits," Silas House's "How to be Beautiful," and Jonathan Corcoran's "The Rope Swing," Appalachian small-town and rural settings make honest expressions of gay desire difficult, if not downright dangerous, and place-based homophobia informs Ann Pancake's "Ricochet."

We've done our best to make this collection as diverse as possible, as much as the limited number of published LGBTQ writers has allowed. The authors included vary in age, race, and ethnicity. Some have left Appalachia; some remain. Some are Christians; one is pagan. One identifies as a trans man, another as a member of the leather and bear communities. Some are single, some are partnered, and some are parents. Some are academics; some are not. Some are known nationally, some are known regionally, but all of them are well published.

The settings of these stories and poems are equally diverse. Some are urban areas like New York City and Lexington, Kentucky. Some are real small towns like Hinton, West Virginia, or fictional ones like Hawk, Kentucky. One setting is a Walmart, another a Tennessee coal camp, another a tobacco farm, another a fishing cabin on the banks of the Little Kanawha River.

Finally, we'd like to point out that the timing of this publication is important. In the last few years, conservative politics, religion, and the homophobic attitudes and policies they breed have burgeoned, both in the Appalachian region and on the national level. In such an atmosphere, writing and publishing queer literature is more important than ever. Most LGBTQ people in the United States are feeling uneasy at best, besieged at worst. To publish a collection like this one is a way of giving Appalachian queer voices—members of a double minority—an opportunity to be heard at a time when many people in power would prefer to silence or ignore us. It's becoming more and more of a political necessity for queer writers to continue speaking about the truths of our lives, to continue expressing our rage, passion, sorrow, and hope with honesty and with defiance. We need to create literature that demands a place for us in our communities, our regions, and our nations. Thanks to West Virginia University Press for giving us the rare opportunity to release this collection at such a critical time in our country's history.

—Jeff Mann and Julia Watts

DOROTHY ALLISON

Dorothy Allison is the bestselling author of two novels, *Bastard Out of Carolina* and *Cavedweller*; a memoir, *Two or Three Things I Know For Sure*; a collection of short fiction, *Trash*; a collection of personal essays, *Skin: Talking About Sex, Class, and Literature*; and a volume of poetry, *The Women Who Hate Me*. The recipient of numerous awards, she has been the subject of many profiles and a short documentary film of her life, *Two or Three Things but Nothing For Sure*.

Roberts Gas & Dairy

....

Forty minutes north another decade . . .
Chevy Cavaliers, Toyota Tercels and Ford Flatbed pickup trucks
Gas a dollar eighty-nine, milk fresh and day-old doughnuts

Nights she cannot sleep my sister
drives forty minutes north
she borrows her girlfriends' sedans
her ex-boyfriend's convertible
Corvette, Mustang, Cherokee Jeep

Different vehicles to lure the man
out of the bright lights to the dim island
where she waits
cigarette stink squint
sour metal grimace
at the far pump

He has to walk the whole way
before she puts the window down
honks long and shouts loud

"You're still a stupid son of a bitch!"
and peels away

burnt rubber rage
on black sugar tarmac

Once he threw a garbage can after her
sonofabitch
son of a bitch
says the bitch
his daughter, my sister
redeemer, haunt, and scourge

survivor and proudest relation
forty minutes south.

Careful

....

I dreamed for years
of a highway going north
a skinny-necked girl
with scared eyes, tight chin
a New York accent

she was walking in my footsteps,
talking in my ear
saying "you wait,"
"You wait"
I am coming for you

Who was she?
Is she waiting still?

I have known women with skinny necks
Girls with tight chins,
New York exiles and
Yonkers matrons

Black girl from DC called me a Staten Island kind of woman
Said them Staten-island women were too careful
Like me.
Too careful,
Too prone to whisper when we should shout

I learned to shout.
I learned to kick

I learned to bend my neck and lift my eyes

I learned the weight of women's hearts and men's fists
All right I am too careful.
There's not enough of me left to waste.

Butter

....

I am my mama's daughter
biscuit's butter, calf moon wailer
textile honey, low-life
low-life

"Your work
I like your work,
it's your person
I can't stand."

Can't tolerate
that kind of stuff
that kind of
pinch and tickle
wink and wiggle
mama's taste
for honey & meat
biscuit butter
welling up in the crack
running down the
spread of thighs

the shame of it
all of it.

I come with all of it,
all my parts
sex
blood
shit
and rage.

Honey & meat.
Butter. Butter.

Domestic Life

....

Peppers and carrots and quartered
green beans
I stand in the kitchen
cut vegetables
chop greens
slice everything down to
manageable size
a pepper, a carrot, a misshapen red tomato
the memory of his hand going back
the image of her body falling forward
a cup in her hand
vegetables rolling off the table
peppers
and carrots and
quartered
green
beans

LISA ALTHER

Lisa Alther was born in 1944 in Kingsport, Tennessee. She has published six novels, a novella, a collection of short stories, two memoirs, and a narrative history of the Hatfield–McCoy feud. They have been translated into seventeen other languages, and four were *New York Times* bestsellers. She has taught southern fiction at East Tennessee State University and at St. Michael's College in Vermont.

Swan Song

....

I

You've come undone, dear one.
Your shoulders show their scars.
So zip yourself up and march out my door—
Grit your teeth, clench your fists, hide your flinch.

Or else shrug those silk straps off your arms,
And stretch out beside me right now.
Let me tend to your wounds, soothe them with salve,
Bathe them, and bind them in balm.

I'll touch you so softly tonight, my love,
That you'll scarcely recall all that gall.
You'll cry as before, but this time for joy,
In the red through my window at dawn.

I know your chagrin. It's my own.
Hope guttered and gone out.
Promises scorched, trust turned to dust,
Ashes and soot, smoke on the wind.

But bloodroot can sprout in charred forests,
When swallows swoop home from the south.
As sun thaws the frost, mauve buds swell and burst—
Until snow spreads its shroud in the fall.

So stay with me now.
Hand me your pain.
Look in my eyes.
Let love live again.

II

I know the time must come, sweetheart,
When you and I won't be attuned—
Photos in your memory book,
Borrowed shirts that weren't returned.

My finger will forget the code
I punch to dial you on the phone.
My hands won't remember how
To stroke you so you moan out loud.

But let's pretend our current bliss
Will never start to feel banal,
And let's agree to face its death
Like warriors who have dared it all.

III

I will soon be leaving
This place where poppies bloom
In rose and ocher soil
By rocks from the dark side of the moon.

I plucked wildflowers in that field
That was spiked with asphodel.
I clutched them tight while you just smiled
And said they'd wilt by night.

Of course I know that blossoms fade
And autumn storms must rage,
But I had hoped two birds in flight
Could soar above a plague.

I'll try to erase that shadowy room
By the river that drifts to the sea,
And the chasm that gaped between us
When you turned your back to me.

I'll press this poppy in my book,
And think some wishful thoughts,
And hope they help me to forget
What might have been—but is not.

Yet, life is long (unless it's short),
And friends who last are few,
And since love first starts in one human heart,
It might just as well end there too.

MAGGIE ANDERSON

Maggie Anderson is the author of five books of poems, including *Dear All, Windfall: New and Selected Poems, A Space Filled with Moving*, and *Cold Comfort*. Anderson has also coedited several poetry anthologies, including *A Gathering of Poets* and *Learning by Heart: Contemporary American Poetry about School*. Her awards include two fellowships from the National Endowment for the Arts, as well as fellowships from the Ohio, West Virginia, and Pennsylvania councils on the arts. She served as the director of the Northeast Ohio MFA in Creative Writing (NEOMFA) from 2006–2009. The founding director of the Wick Poetry Center and of the Wick Poetry Series of the Kent State University Press, Anderson is professor emerita of English at Kent State University and now lives in Asheville, North Carolina.

Anything You Want, You Got It

....

And what will I say to my friend who is
twenty years younger than I am and who slows
her pace to walk with me along the path
the pines rained down on all afternoon?

Twenty years is everything –
your whole life, each leaf and fallen branch,
every random pile of stones. Tell me
what you want to do, your shapely plans,
and I will listen to your bravado. Everything
I have imagined was for you, for this hour
we rested in the warm meadow with the drowse
of bees and watched thin clouds rush over.

What I want to do with you is dance,
to saxophone and heavy bass, fast and easy,
the way ferns shift and lean toward sun,
or the way a thought starts up in pulse
and limbs. When the music slows and fades,
I will put my arms around you,
as I have in the dream from which
my own sounds woke me to gray morning,
and then, my dear one, you will turn
away from me, or I will let you go.

Biography

....

Born, I was born.
    In sweat and tears I lay on a flowered blanket
before a chrome bucket of ice and a bladed fan.
    My mind is clear as polished glass,
my hair a tangle of black moss. I fall down
    on the grass in my harness, laughing.
Father is doing his skits and antics,
    running and sliding, dropping his trousers.
His starched shirts are strict and ghostly,
    they hang on a line over the bathtub.
Dying, Mother is dying, pale in her housecoat.
I am learning to run faster and faster,
    I can feel the blood in my ears.
Great-aunt Nell is large as a boat with her
    slick jersey dresses and embroidered handkerchiefs.
Flying, dust motes are flying, in a caduceus of light
    between the studio couch and the radiator.
Family arrives on the train in the rain
    carrying leather grips and hatboxes.
The self blooms,
    a chrysalis of sorrow.
Patricia, the soft reticule of her mouth
    pulls me from my dry cave.
I drink Father's gin with Robert,
    suck sweet smoke from a plug of blond hash.

The police are shoving into the crowd with tear gas and rifles,
    we do a day in a cell with no window.
I eat rice from a red lacquer bowl,
    green tea singes my tongue.
The riderless horse leads the procession.
    Fever carries me out of my body.
Father: "Listen at this;
    I have written it down."
Mother: "This is the table they have laid before me.
    I am not afraid."

Cleaning the Guns

....

The deer heads were bolted to the wall in my uncles' houses
stuffed & mounted on a plaque. As a child, I was sure
the body of the animal must be behind the wall, as if
it had just poked its antlers through a curtain. Every fall,
two days off from school for the start of deer season
& then dead deer were hung to cool in backyards
from heavy ropes, their eyes still open.
My uncles were all white men who chewed
Mail Pouch tobacco & spit into coffee cans
& all of them were hunters.
I liked to sit on the cement back porch
with my Uncle Ike & help him clean his guns.
We started with his revolver, then the rifles
& last his shotgun—it took all afternoon.
Ike had a white blanket to put the parts on
so they wouldn't get lost & old undershirts I cut up
in little pieces to wrap around the rods. Ike was a machinist
on the railroad & he knew parts. He taught me the names
of each one & it was my job to do the final buff.
After we worked awhile,
he might tell me how he got his deer
this year, or another one from some time back –
the one whose head now hangs over the TV set.
Of course, in a few years he taught me to shoot
& I wasn't bad, but I never went hunting.

Too much trouble I told everyone & by then
I had grown a little scared of him,
but really it was the helplessness
I couldn't get around. The deer absolutely still, alert,
one shot & death. I couldn't do that.
But I did like cleaning the guns,
all the tiny parts—heavier than they looked –
& the requisite precision, the art of it.

In Real Life

....

One's real life is often the life that one does not lead.
—Oscar Wilde

I've been napping in my chair
and have wakened just in time.
Sleeping in the daytime sharpens me
for night life, as if it were my job
to get up and wet down my reeds
to play the clarinet in a small ensemble
where the first set doesn't start till half past ten.
My nap was the color of a moss agate,
gray green and striped, buffed to sheen
and sweat, the usual nightmares:
the house burns down with all my writing in it;
a famous and successful writer friend offers me her dregs,
Here, take these, I don't need them anymore.
My editor ransacks my closets. His shirt is ripped off
by my faithful and beautiful, half-vicious dog.
In real life, I am planning a new career. I imagine
for myself a small congregation of gay Episcopalians
somewhere in the Midwest, in a town not known for
tolerance, but respectful, even a bit in awe of
anything that passes for style. I am their priest,
their good shepherd, and all my flock play

musical instruments and give amusing dinner parties.
Or, there is the life I seem to have imagined myself into
in which I am cleaning my reeds and shining my shoes
for the band that doesn't exist, in the town I never lived in,
playing the instrument I don't know how to play.

My Father and Ezra Pound

....

I drank iced tea with whiskey in it,
    smoked Salems and read small poetry books
    on the cement slab we called a back porch,
wedged into a chair made from a broken barrel
and painted bright orange.

Pound had just died
    and also my father.
I could trail a silly thought for hours;
for example, when I first read Pound he was alive,
    silent in Saint Elizabeths
and then I read him dead.
    Did this make any difference?
And what about Dad?
The year before he died
    he wrote fifty poems and six plays,
collaborating with his lover,
    the college business manager,
who had AIDS, though we didn't know it then.

My glass of tea was dark and didn't show the liquor
    but my breath did when she kissed me.
I was writing my early poems
    of vegetables and grief, reading the *Four Quartets*
    and Algernon Swinburne for my exams
mixing martinis in a chrome shaker

                      from my father's house.

All those years it took him to work out
        whom he loved, and he waited
                until the end to break his silence –
envelopes of blue mimeographed pages—his legacy.
Once a week, my uncle called to see how I was doing.
My father was his only brother, so
        Pretty good, I always said.

I listened to the Doors and Joplin.
This was the seventies.
I was 23 years old, turning
        the thin pages of *The Cantos*.
No one came to visit.
        We had two dogs.
        We needed nothing then except each other,
                and that we needed all the time.

NICKOLE BROWN

Nickole Brown is the author of *Sister*, first published in 2007 with a new edition reissued by Sibling Rivalry Press in 2018. Her second book, *Fanny Says*, came out from BOA Editions and won the Weatherford Award for Appalachian Poetry in 2015. The audiobook of that collection became available in 2017. Currently, she is the Editor for the Marie Alexander Poetry Series and teaches at the Sewanee School of Letters MFA Program, the Great Smokies Writing Program at University North Carolina–Asheville, and the Hindman Settlement School. She lives with her wife, poet Jessica Jacobs, in Asheville, North Carolina, where she volunteers at four different animal sanctuaries. Currently, she's at work on a bestiary of sorts about these animals, but it won't consist of the kind of pastorals that always made her (and most of the working-class folks she knows) feel shut out of nature and the writing about it—these poems speak in a queer, southern-trash-talking kind of way about nature, beautiful, damaged, dangerous, and in desperate need of saving. A chapbook of those poems called *To Those Who Were Our First Gods* recently won the 2018 Rattle Chapbook Prize.

My Book, in Birds

....

A book of birds. A story in birds. Each breath
a bird, each dream slipped from my ear

to my pillow out the window a song:
cardinals laughing at me—*birdie birdie birdie*—

on a lonely Valentine's. Then robins swarming
the last bits of red another February day,

so many of them on the holly tree the branches
tick with their picking and I stop

the car. But I was so cold, I had to get to the store,
and in the fluorescent buzz of the freezer aisle, I swore

I heard, *A flock of larks is called an exaltation*,
but thought, *No, that's too pretty, that can't be*

right. I bought my frozen pizza and peas and tried to
remember warmer days:

the surf shop with the parrot, big and green with a beak
full of fingers, my hair a dread of salt and seaweed

so I would run home
to wash the sand from my scalp. In the shower,

on the sill of the window made to crank tightly closed
to hurricanes, her porcelain bluebird—

all those years, Fanny swore she'd die and come back
red-breasted, blue-winged, and singing,

but when the time came, it was only morphine
talking: white beasts stalking the hospital room,

with tails long as a Cadillac and tail feathers flowing like new
curtains, she said, *and faces, they've got faces bright and sharp as a fox.*

There was nothing I could do. The reincarnation
I used to believe in became a drag queen named Phoenix

on Saturday nights at the bar where a girl leaned in
to me with both thumbs cowboy-hooked

to the pockets of her jeans, nothing more.
When she asked for my number, I made for the door.

There was nothing I could do and so I traveled
to Brooklyn where birds sing louder, competing

against sirens and cabs and ice-cream trucks.
I tried to find a woman there who made me forget

the woman before, the one who took me
to a red barn, swallows knifing

the air between rafters. I left her,
I always left, my heart a young hummingbird

that learned hummingbirds land
but never really stay—only fledglings

hesitate at the red plastic feeder. I said, *I just can't,*
I said it, then left, said it,

then made my way to that stone marking
the death of my grandmother. Her ashes are not

there, but her name is, and because I still believed
in some words, it was enough. I went there to seek

permission, to cool my face against the granite and ask,
Is what I have become okay?

After, I fed the cemetery swans dandelion greens
and thought their beauty not unlike the hissing

swan of Lake Bled, the tidal swan of Galway, all
water the same drowning, no matter how far I go.

Once I had the courage, I took another woman
to my bed but woke on the porch

to a cathedral of sunrise singing, the boards splintered
hard to my back. I walked with her

to the park where a yellow bird followed alongside
in a sine cosine rollercoaster of flight.

I argued with her—*It's not possible, a canary
in Kentucky*—but thought, *Why not?*

What's lovely in this world is no more impossible
than what's not—when I was married

to a man, three sparrows trapped themselves in that porch light
and cooked against the glass; later that first summer

as a wife, a mother jay—again, say it—*trapped*
in the garden pond, my face reflected in that fish-shit water

dashed bright
with blue feathers and golden koi.

I never did grow old enough with him
for the pink plastic flamingos to decorate the front yard,

never did see that hokey sign—*Lordie, Lordie,*
look who's forty!—and it made me cry like a peacock and shred

my flesh in strips to the black tower
beaks—*Take it, dear raven. Take it,*

clacking black crow. When there was no meat
left, I threw strands of hair and bits of cheap bread

to fast-food sparrows, ate for years on the bland sorrow
of grease and plastic and frustrated men

until I traveled to a lover who had a lilac-eyed
cockatoo who beat its head against my collarbone

to rush up a serving of hot fruit and seed, a vomit offering
meant for another with a beak to guzzle it

back down. I say, *I'm sorry, but I think your bird*
is sick, but the woman simply cleaned

off my shirt, put her pet softly back
in the cage. *No, baby, that's her way of saying*

she loves you, she said. *Can't you tell*
love from sickness?

To My Grandmother's Ghost, Flying with Me on a Plane

....

For if there's nothing then
        nothing. And if there's something
            then there's something. Say it
                again: if there's nothing, then
nothing, and if something,
        something. This is ablution:
            a curl of a cousin's hand
                into a blackened fiddlehead,
the mirror shattered on your
        closet door. This is the detritus
            left behind: something, something,
                nothing, nothing, nothing, nothing.

I try to steady myself, say the Lord's
        Prayer as the wings crest above
            the city's capillaries of false light
                so crowded this morning when I followed
a beautiful woman to the square.
        She stepped into the subway stairs
            and before disappearing turned,
                said, *Come step into this dark*

hole in the ground with me?
        Fanny, she did not mean to be
            morbid. She only meant to say,
                Follow me. And what I mean

is that I love her and did not
   follow. Fanny, the stewardess
      has nothing on her rattling cart
         to quench this thirst and the Sky
Mall does not comfort me tonight.
   Worse, I can see death either way:
      the velvet black of anesthesia, count back
         and you're nine, eight, seven, six, five,
gone, or something better, peacock-feathered,
   smelling of leather-bound books and you baking
      cornbread. I mean, will you come for me? Will you
         come get me, your hair piled high and white, when
it's my time to go? Or will I find
   you another kind of mother,
      the one who knows the dyke
         I've become? Will you be cross,
your face a streak of all my
   desire, telling me I was a fool
      to yearn to follow her? Or ashamed,
         will you turn away your face and hold up
a shard
   of that mirror,
      showing me
         I'm going to hell?

An Invitation for My Grandmother

....

When Mama called to say you were
gone, I was in New York and climbed
the impossible top of a brownstone to talk
myself down. *Don't get sentimental; dying is what*
grandmothers do, was what
I told myself, but what I should have done
was invite you there with me. You'd never been
further north than Cincinnati, and the view—
the spatter and fleck of all those lights—
you'd have to see to believe. So now that you're

on the other side and got your knees working
again, a proposition: Come, lace up your Keds,
walk with me a while. I won't say the world's better—
it's not—since you left, I've seen a pelican
stretch her wings to dry, the dripping
petrol making her into a bent crucifix of oil,
and the penguins have dropped their proud
eggs into melted ice, and this spring, yet another wind
bulldozed my neighbors, all their homes razed
to slab foundation, their trees now
splintered bone. But we can take a train

out of Arkansas—Come, sit next to me,
because out the window
a girl on a horse jumps a junkyard fence.
She wears a shirt the color of poppies, of bright
soda cans, and I bet you'll agree: blurred,
it is a brown pony with red wings.

And three years ago: Can I take you there?
My sister, sitting up during a contraction,
how she reached inside
herself to touch the crown of her son
not yet born. I want to show you the look
on her face and that cord
cut, a rich earth of blood, a joy in
black. And please, take off your shoes now,

stand with me last October when
I took a wife, barefoot in the grass.
We made our vows, and after, when she held
my jaw with both hands, I could feel
the bones of my skull
rising up to make a face finally
seen.

Ten Questions You're Afraid to Ask, Answered

....

1.

The first time? I thought myself an infant, rooting the breast for dinner.
You too may feel the seamless press of your body to a mirror,

the smudge of your own skin a ridiculousness that needs
Windex, and quick. Embarrassed, I asked to be taken home,

but in the car was the bright green of her dashboard lights burning
the clean color of *go*.

2.

Years before. I even admitted it once to a woman that later sent me poems
about hummingbirds

dipping their beaks into feeders full of cocaine dissolved in sweet,
red water.

3.

Finally came summer, my summer of plain clothing—
unironed and cotton and bland—nothing afraid

to get dirty, nothing afraid to be slicked with mud, the forest coming off
in a happy heap on the tent floor.

It was the summer I allowed myself to be bitten
enough that the welts rose but dissolved back by bedtime;
it was the summer I finally said,

come, mother mosquitoes, my reddest blood is ready for your young.

4.

Stupid things, mostly. That's how I wasted most of my worry—
dumb-ass questions that do not matter: Who should open

the door? Who to pay for dinner? Who to lean in first with whose hands
braced strong to the jawline? Who in the tie, who in the dress, and what
about all this long, long hair?

5.

Consider this: a woman's pH is between that of wine and bread.
An imperfect leaven, the kind of crust that betrays the softness

inside. Cooled to the heat of your mouth, its sweetness
dipped in a dry red, the aftertaste of that one oyster you had

from the other coast. You were slightly repulsed, but then the fisherman
pulled it straight from his bucket for you, cut it free

with a small, curved knife.

6.

You will miss it. Not the man but the normal
the man brings.

7.

Unfortunately. All the time. In the grocery, a mother swung her arm to
corral her daughter behind her, protecting her from us—
the contagions behind.

We were hurt, but we stayed in line; we waited our turn. We smiled at
the child peeking from behind the thick coat, and because it was a good
day, we felt a little sorry for the mother. In our basket was red tomatoes
and yellow peppers, a riot of greens, the unbelievable brightness of

all we had chosen.

8.

The strawberry is a fruit unshamed of its seeds. Make no mistake how it is
textured as the tongue.

9.

Thirty years old.

10.

Too late? Perhaps, but only when you think of evening, the song full
and crickets volleying the trees,

the sound from one side then the other, a saturation that can carry
the young down the black river of who they think they should be.

Think instead of morning. Not the thin monotony of weak light,
but that low, constant pleasuring of the air

that doesn't try so hard but simply tips your ears
with light.

JONATHAN CORCORAN

Jonathan Corcoran is the author of the story collection *The Rope Swing*, which was a finalist for the 2017 Lambda Literary Awards. His stories and essays have been published and anthologized widely, most recently in *Eyes Glowing at the Edge of the Woods: Fiction and Poetry from West Virginia* and *Best Gay Stories 2017*.

The Rope Swing

....

The drive to the river takes Christopher along the old highway. He passes vacant gas stations at the edge of town, then seemingly idle farmland with lonely rolls of hay, and, finally, miles of unfettered green forest. The old highway consists of two small lanes that rise and fall with the contours of the mountains—steep grades of sudden change, marked by big yellow signs that indicate the climb or descent of the road with a percentage point. The road at times angles sharply and frighteningly around steep cliffs. When he looks out his window, he sees that beyond the tiny gravel shoulder, the land falls precipitously away: a hillside of boulders, some half-buried by moss and wild grass. On the other side of the road, the worn mountain face towers upward. Poplar, pine, and sycamore somehow find patches of soil on these steep surfaces. Christopher, though, trusts in the roots of these trees. He does not worry about them losing their grip on the soil and falling onto his car as he drives past. He trusts mostly in the simplicity of such a life, in which the main concern is against leaning too far in one direction.

The new highway, on the other hand, just two miles to the east but out of sight, has four level lanes paved into the bombed-out heart of the mountains. The ledges that frame both sides of that highway bear the jagged marks of explosives—artificial striations slicing across the once-impenetrable rock. Miles of metal netting hug the bodies of the carved cliffs to prevent the crumbling limestone from dropping down onto the passing drivers. The falling rocks gather in big piles at the bottom of the nets so that the metal at the base is stretched out toward the road: a reminder, Christopher thinks, of both safety and sadness; one thing created, the other destroyed. And the seeming impermanence, too, the constant erosion of what seems so solid.

Last spring Christopher's geology teacher said that in those crumbling rocks he could find evidence of the prehistoric world. Fossils. Impressions.

Living things weighed down and immortalized by mud and silt. Aquatic beings, from when the world had been more ocean than not. But no one stops to notice, the teacher said. People just drive right by, unaware of the treasures literally spilling out onto the shoulder of the road.

People can't get to the river from the new highway. They can get to the mall in a half hour or to DC in three. This, to Christopher, is a small comfort. It means that the river will always be a secret of sorts. As time passes and the old highway is used a little less each day, he imagines that his slice of river, the spot he shares with his friend, Greg, will become forgotten by all but himself. He imagines growing old and building a cabin down at the riverbank with a deck that hangs over the water. There are two chairs on the deck: one for himself and one for Greg. Nights of peace and no one around for miles. An unthinkable touch of the hand, rendered acceptable by the privacy of the forest.

Just as soon as he imagines this life, he wills himself to forget it. The more time he spends at the river with Greg, the more he feels himself floating away from the things he understands. This is both exhilarating and painful. A moment of bliss, and then an evening of aching. He is a split self: his visible body and his hidden blood. The guilt pounds in his gut, especially when his mother lingers at his bedroom door to say goodnight; he's a year away from adulthood, and she no longer kisses his forehead.

Imprisoned rocks, metal nets rusting toward disintegration, a once-booming rail-yard town that no longer has any trains. Extinct creatures swimming toward immortality. A mother hovering a second too long at his door in the darkness. He leaves behind all of these images as he rides down from a mountain peak into the narrow valley below. He thinks only of what he must say to his friend—the words that he's been rehearsing since the summer began. Will he be able to utter the words aloud? He tells himself—just as he did yesterday and the day before—that today will be different. Today he will leave that other version of himself behind. Today he will let his blood flow freely. He inhales the crisp air of the mountains. He feels the burn of the sun on his hands that rest on the steering wheel. Coming down the hill, he lifts his foot off of the pedal and coasts.

He rolls downward, and as the road levels out, Greg's car comes into sight: the sagging bumper, the dented body, Greg himself splayed across the trunk, basking in the sun. A figure that even from fifty feet makes his throat tighten. He tries to speak the words—the ones he has practiced alone in his car—but only his friend's name comes out. "Greg," he says, like an enchantment. And again: "Greg."

He eases in behind Greg's car, which is parked in a bend in the road, along a wide, gravel-strewn shoulder meant for big trucks to stop and check their brakes. But few trucks come here now, thanks to the new highway. They are safe, then, the two boys. They are alone. His tense body loosens.

Greg slides off of the trunk and walks up to Christopher's window—his blond hair is matted to his skull, damp with a fresh summer sweat. "I thought you weren't going to make it," he says, and by his heaving chest, it's clear that he's frustrated. "I've been waiting for over an hour."

"I'm so sorry," Christopher says, and then Greg's face softens. Christopher could stop there. He could say nothing else and all would be forgotten. But he continues anyway, because he needs to talk, he needs to press forward with any intelligible sentence. He feels that his time is running out. The summer will slip away, and as school begins again, this secret life at the river will have burnt up and fallen like the turning autumn leaves. The freedom their bodies feel here, at the river, could never be possible in the halls of the high school. "Something's wrong. It's my mother again. She was in one of her moods this morning. I didn't want to leave her alone in the house. I was afraid to leave her. I was afraid to stay."

Christopher knows that Greg understands this. It's their river ritual to speak of such things. Then the water washes over them and rinses their skin of all the unpleasant residue. It's like a daily baptism, like going to the altar at church and being born again, reset to zero, over and over.

"It's fine," Greg says and looks down the road. "At least your mother speaks to you. I'm just happy to be here, and not there."

"I drove as fast as I could," Christopher says.

"I know," Greg says. "Let it go. Let's catch the sun while we still can."

Christopher grabs a towel and his swimming trunks from the passenger seat of his car. He takes them and walks with Greg down the steep path from the road into the forest. The walk, along the trampled dirt, underneath the dense canopy of the trees, frees him from all the chaos, the remaining conflict in Christopher's mind. Behind is the town, his mother, the road. At a certain point the whirring of passing cars stops. At a certain point, he can no longer see the road at all. For a while, he cannot see the river either: only the green leaves above, and the tan, dry leaves on the ground below.

The sunlight pierces through the forest in spots, almost cinematically, so that what normally seems invisible—individual beams of hot white light—appears suddenly tangible. Christopher reaches out to touch that white light, beating down on a bush of rhododendron. The sounds of trickling water become audible, and then the trickle becomes a rush—the current beating over smooth rocks. As the sound of the water grows louder, Christopher sees the thinning edge of the forest and then the sparkling river itself. This, to Christopher, has begun to feel like home.

"She's coming to the show tonight," Christopher says as they walk down the path along the river's edge.

"Are you nervous?" Greg asks.

"Yes and no. I guess I find myself caring less every day. Or I wish I could care less. I don't know. I'm just going to pretend she's not there. How do you do it? I mean, with the two of you the way you are."

"I don't do anything. There's nothing to do anymore. You just keep moving. You just stop thinking."

Christopher falls back and watches his friend walk ahead. He looks for Greg to shrug his shoulders, to tense his neck—a gesture to indicate a fear of the unknown. But his friend marches forward, shoulders straight, unhindered by his reality.

"I think she's afraid of me," Christopher says. "She's afraid of whatever it is she thinks I'm becoming."

Greg stops walking, turns his head toward Christopher: "And what are you becoming?"

He hesitates only a moment: "I don't know." The words are as true and blue tinted as the summer sky above.

They hadn't really known each other before the show, though they were the same age and attended the same high school. Christopher came to the theater like an asylum seeker—a last act of survival, a way to make it through his final years as a teenager with some kind of hiding place—from the kids at school, from his mother. He thought of the old brick building like he thought of a cathedral—a place with history and safety and dark crevices for praying to a God that often felt more like an enemy.

Their conversations began in those dark spaces, backstage while they ran lines—Christopher, the Tin Man, and Greg, the Lion—the roles, like their lives, in search of one missing element. Soon they were standing next to each other during vocal warm-ups. Soon they were goofing off in the costume closet. One day Greg asked Christopher to come with him to the river before rehearsal.

The way their friendship developed felt like a dream—the movements blurred, the reality of the situation questionable. It had been so long since Christopher made a new friend; he had so few to begin with. And here they were now, every single day before the show, stalling at the river, reaching for a feeling that couldn't yet be acted on.

"Do you know where this river flows?" Christopher asks his friend as they walk along the bank, opposite the current. "All this time, and I've never really thought about it."

"The water comes down from the mountains—it actually starts right up there," Greg says, pointing up at a mountain peak off in the distance. "It joins with a bunch of streams—this is what you see here—and then it flows down the valley until it meets its sister river—the one that goes through our town. The rivers meet up, they join as one, and then they flow down south—the Ohio, the Mississippi—until the water we're swimming in goes through New Orleans and out into the Gulf of Mexico—the Atlantic Ocean, really."

"I've never been to the ocean."

They walk along, Christopher leading ahead. He's afraid to look Greg in the eyes. He's afraid that he'll cower into himself again, like every other day, and then say nothing at all when he really wants to say everything—to speak his body and his heart into existence.

Christopher pauses when he notices something attached to the big sycamore tree that leans over the water. "What's that?" he asks.

They step closer, and Christopher sees that tied to a high branch is a long, corded rope. The rope hangs out long and limp, the end dangling just a few feet above the river's surface. A low breeze pushes the rope back and forward over the river—the hempen fabric glowing golden as it touches the edge of the sunlight, then the dull tan of dried mud as it slips into the shade of the tree.

"It's a swing," Greg says excitedly. "Someone's put up a rope swing."

Christopher has no desire to test the rope's weight. He senses something menacing about its hanging there, barely disturbed in the breeze, wanting only a body. "It wasn't here yesterday. That means someone's been out here, either early this morning or last night. Do you think they're out here now?"

Christopher searches around for evidence of teenage mischief. He looks for a beer can, a smoked-out joint, or the cut line of a fishing pole. He's convinced that the intruder must be someone they know, one or more of the boys from school, no doubt, that he'd tried to forget about over the past few months.

"What are you so afraid of?" Greg asks. "Besides, if anyone were here, there'd be a car parked back up at the road."

Of course this is logical, but the presence of the rope persists. Christopher pulls his arms into his chest, and sits down on a damp log. He feels the moisture soaking through his pants onto his skin. Greg sits next to him.

"I ran into someone from school this morning," Greg says. "Matt Boone, of all people."

"I hate that guy," Christopher says.

"I was at the gas station. He was sitting in his truck at the edge of the parking lot. Waiting for someone, I suppose. Or fucking around with nothing to do, like they all do. I was filling up my tank."

"You just have to walk away," Christopher says, his throat tightening—the images of what's to come causing his pulse to quicken.

"I made the mistake of looking in his direction. Do you know what he did? He pointed a gun at me. He had a goddamn shotgun in the cab of his truck, and he pointed it at me and pretended to shoot. And then he just laughed."

"Greg, I can't go back there."

Christopher watches the rope swing gently over the water. And suddenly, he's no longer in the forest, but inside a classroom, with the teacher's back turned. First the gestures. Then the words. The situation escalating. The rising fear of harm—bodily harm—forcing him back into the most instinctual form of a human, thoughts only of self-preservation.

"It's going to be alright," Greg says, but his words don't resonate. He grabs Christopher's hand and squeezes it. "We'll make it through the year. We have each other now."

Christopher allows himself to feel his friend's touch for only a second before pulling away. He turns his gaze away from his friend and out toward the river.

"I'm seventeen and I've only swam in rivers," Christopher says. "Everyone says how easy it is in the ocean, how in the saltwater your body just floats. If I could just ride this river all the way down . . ."

They sit on the log, listening to the calling birds and flowing water until Christopher has calmed his nerves. He looks around. There are no beer cans. There is no evidence of seventeen-year-old boys hiding in the bushes waiting to sabotage them.

"We're really alone," Greg says. "I promise. Can we enjoy ourselves a little bit?"

Christopher looks down at the sun-reflecting river, through the shadowy forest, trying to imagine how many secrets have been imparted under the protection of these trees.

Greg drapes his towel over the roots of the big sycamore tree. He takes off his shirt and begins to strip off his jean shorts. Christopher quickly turns his head, his cheeks reddening.

"Do you want me to hide?" Greg asks, laughing. "Haven't you seen me do this a hundred times?"

Christopher turns back around. He forces a smile—the easiest smile he can manage. "I'm sorry," he says. "I know I'm weird."

He pretends not to watch as Greg lowers his shorts and underwear. He pretends not to notice his friend's strong legs as he pulls on his swimming trunks. Christopher looks to the river but sees only, in his peripheral vision, Greg's large birthmark, round and chestnut brown, at the spot where his back meets his buttocks.

Christopher knows this is his signal also, to participate in the show that's not supposed to be a show. How many times had they played at this? He pulls down his jeans first, because he's never grown used to walking around without a shirt. He's never grown comfortable with the dark hair sprouting on his chest. He doesn't dare look at Greg, to check to see if Greg is looking at him. He wills it, Greg's vision on his body, but he also knows that to catch Greg in that moment would be to open the floodgates. If Christopher saw Greg staring back, he would have to let Greg in.

Christopher takes off his shirt. Just as he pulls the cotton fabric over his head, he sees a vision of Greg running down the bank, pummeling his way into the water.

"It's freezing," Greg shouts. He grabs the rope swing and drags it back to the shore. He begins to climb up the slanted trunk of the sycamore tree.

"Don't you think that's a little dangerous?" Christopher asks. "What if the water's not deep enough? What if you hurt yourself on the rocks?"

"The water's plenty deep. I won't hit the rocks."

Greg pulls the rope taut, testing its ability to hold his body. Before Christopher has time to dissuade him any further, Greg jumps from the tree. He shoots out over the water, and as he flies, clinging to the rope, a wild sound issues from his mouth—a joyous yowl, a primal scream, an explosion of self. As the rope passes the center of its pendulum, Greg lets go and floats through the air, arms extended. The flying form and the creature howl make Christopher jealous of his friend's courage. They also make him want to run and jump into the river, to find his friend and dance with him, to join together and hold him in the weightlessness of the cold current.

Greg drops from the rope and sinks, leaving a splash and a spray of fast, white bubbles. Then the bubbles are gone. He does not rise.

"Greg?" Christopher calls. "Greg?"

Christopher scans the surface of the water for the shadow of his friend's body. His stomach is a brick. His jaw clenches. "Please, come up! You're scaring me." His eyes begin to well with water. He wants to save his friend, but his body is frozen in place. "I'm so sorry," he murmurs—a summer's worth of unspoken words weighing down his speech.

But of course Greg surfaces—laughing first and then coughing, spitting water. "Now you jump," he says. "What are you afraid of?"

Christopher wipes his eyes in embarrassment, hoping his friend doesn't notice. He looks at the rope swinging in small, tight circles over the current. He sees the mottled trunk of the sycamore tree, Greg treading water. His gentle smile, his warm, brown eyes.

Most of all, he knows that when one jumps, one must also fall. He fears that if he breaks the surface, he might never find the air again.

"Someday," Christopher says. "But not today."

"Your choice," Greg says, "but summer's almost over. If you wait much longer, the water will be too cold."

DORIS DIOSA DAVENPORT

doris diosa davenport: i am a sixty-nine-year-old performance poet-writer-educator; a lesbian-feminist bi-amorous iconoclast from northeast Georgia, with a PhD in literature from the University of Southern California. i have published eleven books of poetry, reviews, articles, and essays. My most recently published book is *rectify my soul: poems* (2018). Contact: zorahpoet7@gmail.com.

verb my noun: a poem cycle

....

erroneous assumptions abt people wth vaginas that a large part
of the more ignint (ignorant) general public seem to hold (and act upon) &
need to quit, really: lesbian-feminist political manifesto for the day

1. That having a vagina means having breasts (called, in the mostlymale
   vul[gar]nacular,
tits, hooters, udders, melons, etc.) & there to suckle anymale anytme
   anywhere

2. That vaginas always need something in them

3. That babies can come out, crawl out, slide out or be yanked up from
   there

4. That, after they out, babies between birth & 5/6 shld cause vagina-
   carriers to swoon & regress into baby-speak babble

5. That all males, 2–92 & beyond death should be treated as babies, since

6. Wimmin (women) are responsible for (all) kids b/c—vaginas & clda or
   shlda
had some (babies) crawl out of up there, at any time, metaphorically

7. That a vagina is unpredictable, dangerous, uncontrollable & so lots of
   nasty old (mostly white) males gone tell you how to control yours.

8. That these holes between our (often copious, succulent) thighs are
   gateways to alternate, new, alien, wondrous, magical dimensions of
   space/time (Wamint. [wait a minute.]Wait. THAT may be true. For
   some of us.)

After the Villagers Go Home: An Allegory

....

(inspired by and a tribute to the old, classic b/w horror movies)

At closing time the bar shuts out normalcy & the thickly
accented East European suspicion-laden, ominously intoning voices
under curious starved voracious eyes drill the foreigner's soul saying
stay here and be our IT forever / stay & fuk me /
stay let us fuk over you / RUN that one soft
compassionate telepath whom you ignore. Yet
all slowly gradually lingeringly eventually

absolutely leave wafting behind
clingy vestrals (air currents) of soft good nights
promises 2 return 2 send for a pint &
goulash for their version of lunch the
village drunk then recalls to mind the
innkeeper's ailing ancient parent(s) who will
be 101 next fortnight, *Inshallah*, which the drunk
begs to be remembered to, then he

slips from the Inn into total darkness
with a howling wolf or raucous thunderstorm,
saying *goodnight loser* in that guttural language
the American foreigner cannot
comprehend yet whose universal bodyspeak no
one cld not understand and the scene shifts
to black & white & the host locks the door.
And floorboards creak as something heavy scrapes itself
against a wall. Invisible footsteps drag

across the floor. The host hides
the key with a smirk we
all know. And the candles flicker.
(And yr cellphone battery's dead.)
And u think u are seeing things
or a little tipsy (drugged). U think this
is a dream. U think u ought 2 maybe
scream but no this ain't that movie
& u r not *that* foreigner. And yr
choices come at u in 3:
Pray. Roll over & play dead. Or
(inevitably)
"Bring it. Now."

Halloween 2011

....

One year in Asheville with dyke
buddies Pat said it's the Witches'
New Year; we could stop smoking
that night or at least the next day.

Many years in Cornelia (GA) on the hill
trick or treat or just out walking, crisp
apple-scented fall air
sharp tang of possibly

Doors between worlds open
pleasures might pop thru a monster mashed,
a one-eyed snaggled tooth flying
purple people eater
grinning *gotcha*. the realm

of suspended beliefs
in carnivals, the circus,
identity politics in sweet-colored air
tinted red gold orange yellow red.

pecans drop heavily ripe
red apples become wine (again)

Halloween 2017

....

Haunted by what
might have been
driven by what was
terrorized & stunned & stupefied &
outraged
by what is (real title:
Halloween *Political* Poem 2017)

for Cheryl D my first lover, 41 years later

....

Rain and rain and rain
today i stayed inside,
grieved and mourned Kay
my latest loss and
thought of you, Venice Beach,
us in 1976.

Three days after the 2017 Solar Eclipse

....

still glowing
in the bliss of being in the
Path of Totality and glad i
told my niece Addie so she could get her
some of that in ATL too
still, knowing what i have newly
relearned, yawl, we have a major
Eclipse twice a day:
sunrise. sunset.

Sept. 1 Invocation

....

Let me sit here
in wonder of this day
of cloudiness, breezes, hills

mountains early leaf fall, in joy
(can't i sit here and witness)
i submit this request to the Universe,
The Multiverse, the OverSouls the
Goddess of All That Is may i just
BE in peace, in joy, in you.

a conversation with an old friend

....

worn out by this contentious,
hard explaining
aggressive exchange, i
long for gentle
conversation
like a tall glass
of sweet iced tea,
on the front porch,
in deep summer

Upon realizing

....

what i really want to do is
sing with a dulcimer and recite poems too—
i might have done that years ago
but when somebody keeps pushing
a broom in your hand instead of a
guitar; telling you you a mule instead of giving you a horse;
trying to take your space, your place, your beauty and joy
you pick up a pen
write it down and wait
for the fragments to whole
wait for the return of my soul
wait for that broom to
turn into musical strings
morning twilight
misty rain, fog, falling leaves.

                                     Miraculous days
of sun, sunshine, clouds
trees that stay in place
and do not walk away from
this abomination, although
coast to coast, the Earth
is on strike . . .

——

Freedom is
knowing that
at the end of the day
or in late evening as
the sun sets freedom is
knowing that [within the
restrictions & constraints
& chains of Living in Amerikka]
Knowing that you did ([as much as
possible, inside the parameter
of what is allowed or permitted])
That you did—pretty much &
pretty well—(well, within the mental
curfews, restraints and real
terrorism) you did what
you wanted to and almost (almost)
accomplished

something.

"The Black Atlantic"

....

Covered in mystery made
of bones blood spirit
each day we make
the Crossing, stand &
testify. Witness. Rise.

——

In the orangeness of October
fingertips eroded
cuticles inflamed and
thumb spasms inside wrist braces
i write.

——

i still want a dragon

and on nights of the
Full Moon we will ride
singing into the sky
my dragon and me
        and my dragon

and

Verb my noun
why doncha just verb
my noun. That's (almost)
all i got ta say

VICTOR DEPTA

Victor Depta is professor emeritus at the University of Tennessee at Martin and the publisher of Blair Mountain Press, which focuses on Appalachian issues. His works include thirteen books of poems, four novels, two books of essays, two collections of comedic plays, and a memoir.

The Desmodontidae

....

They let me be, Caleb and Judith.
I can sit on the porch for hours
peaceful, writing, and they never ask, never bother me
though I sometimes wish, when I'm finished
that they would ask
that I could share with them what I do

but that's impossible
at least it is with the project at hand.
A gay friend is writing the music for an opera about, of all
clichéd subjects, gay vampires, and he asked me for
a libretto, which I refused to do, so then he asked
for lyrics, some arias, anything.
Rather than offend him I said I would try.

1.

To be so far away from the sun
on that side of the moon made black by nothingness
and never to know the grace
gold dappled on a face
and the green shadows of an afternoon
which ease the lines about the eyes
and which the wine and the fluted glasses
make sublime the harsh sun in the sky
and all reminders of oblivion

while we are not so doomed
and never suffer the extinguishment of the self—
nonetheless
we cannot see beyond the false dawn
and never before twilight the subtleties of the soul
the sun-riffled shadows, half-awakened longings
the nearly spoken, the nearly beyond a sigh of what is meant
by a kiss

but are violent at it
knowing the blood we gulp
gluttonous for the sun's warmth in the veins
is a rape of the sun—
the body we hold, the arms possessing us

go slack, slipping to the black of what we are
even as we drink and deny and curse
we know that our desire, our destiny
is not to know what they guessed at

in the green shadows of the afternoon
that love is the sun
short-lived and ecstatic
and never won
by the immortality of the will

though we are immortal
we are the Eve, the Adam

who weaved beneath the serpent's tongue
well before he spoke
the story of what becomes of us
of those whom God ignored
when in his wrath he destroyed
the immortality of the guilty pair
and made them sweat and cry out
in their despair, *I perish, I will die*
while we, beneath the phallic jaw
the female coil of hip, and of thigh
became one, sunless and immortal
and witnessed their grief in the moonlit night
their wailing after twilight and before the dawn

while we, although they die
wish for such a death in the sun
and lie quiescent
pausing and waiting in the darkness of the moon
for our deliverance
our moment in the sweet warm blood
when everything that's green and dappled
everything that's various and sunlit
and intensely longing for immortality
fills our veins.

2.

O Florida, venereal soil . . .
I loathe the moon
when it's pale in the afternoon and weak as Griselda

suffering the brute sun while I yawn
petulant as an infant for the feast of breasts
the dunes and sea grapes and the salt of tides
when she my mother is the bride
and understands
as the yellow beast descends to the horizon
to the scrub palmettos and cypresses in the west
her child's need
his longing for the suckling feast

the *O* moon
the golden mouth, the golden aureole
glimpsed among the mangrove and banyan trees
their hueless leaden forms and silvery shadows—
the golden navel-stone of the sky
the sensuous tug on the ovate and fluted shapes
on the poinciana and jacaranda
the purple and scarlet of the blossoms indistinct

which the sun made vivid
and the moon made dreams
silhouettes on the sky
forms without substance or sustaining blood

the fluid on the breast
black almost in the moon
moist sea-salt tinged with nectar
with the fragrance of the frangipani
the dream flesh, the unreal
the violence which the moon knows nothing of
serene and indifferent to the Atlantic
which yearns for her
the seas which lean, continent after continent, with desire
while I, small moon
draw continents of the heart and limbs
though my own *o* mouth and throat
into myself

the self they long for
the self forbidden by the sun
the self I allow, dark shape and form
moonlit, leaden and color blind
to dream
helpless before images
swooning, half-dead

as I ease them to the sand

as I let them live to see the orange bulk
rise watery and be
the golden bully of the day
their master.

3.

Darkling I listen . . .
and in the too warm, humid night
the mockingbird, as if restless for dawn
trills pensively, uncertain as a lover would
in the dark haze of his passion
plaintive, charming, for his beloved, the sun I will never see
though the moist rings of the moon
the light fog, the luminous pale vapors veiling the trees
the crepe myrtle and the honeysuckle
assuage me, ease my fury, my longing

more absurd than the robin, spring drunk, delirious with desire
repeating in the darkness before dawn
its sweet, requitable song
though what I sing, whisper rather, is the mist
the dew on the tips of leaves, on the grasses
silvery, small globes, my rage calmed
and my longing for the sun—

my beloved
pale rose in the east, ruddy, cloud tinged
among the raucous choir and wings
in the cacophony of dawn
I will wrap myself in downy, supple wings
and will, in a lyric beyond hearing
in a realm where even pity dwells
conceive of reality, once again, as it catches fire
while I glitter as the dew, suspiring
in the golden consummation of desire.

SILAS HOUSE

Silas House is the nationally bestselling author of six novels, including his first, *Clay's Quilt* (2001), and his latest, *Southernmost* (2018). His work often appears in the *New York Times* and *Salon* and has been published in *Oxford American, Time, Garden and Gun, Newsday*, and many other periodicals as well as being anthologized in *Best American Food Writing* and *New Stories from the South: The Year's Best*. House is a winner of the E.B. White Award, the Nautilus Book Award, the Appalachian Book of the Year, and is a member of the Fellowship of Southern Writers. He is a native of southeastern Kentucky and serves on the faculties of both Berea College and Spalding University's MFA in creative writing. He lives in Berea with his husband, Jason Howard.

How To Be Beautiful

....

for Carla Gover

I told my parents I couldn't get off from work that night and Erin feigned sickness. Getting out of church and its various functions was one of the best things about my job at the Cinema Two. Erin's widowed father was easier to manipulate and all she had to do was hold a hot-water bottle to her face, then hide it under her pillow once she called him in to see if she had a fever. So, Erin lay piled up in bed like Melanie Wilkes and I stood out on the porch dressed in my work uniform, waving like a mad man when the Hawk Holiness Church van struggled up the hill to fetch our parents. The van would carry them three hours away to Louisville, where they'd watch, enthralled, as Jimmy Swaggart evangelized to the gathered masses.

Erin and I had lived next door to each other since we were born. Our parents were best friends so it made sense that we were, too, even though she was a year older and it wasn't deemed acceptable for a boy and girl to be that close unless there were romantic inclinations. We did a great job of convincing our parents that that might happen eventually. Erin was my *beard* before we knew there was a word for such a thing. Much later she would prefer the term *fag hag* or the more elegant *fruit fly*, but we didn't know any helpful names for the ways we were different from everyone else. All we knew is that we had to lead secret lives.

Whereas the church made the bond between our parents unbreakable, being different was the key to my and Erin's relationship. Ever since I was about eleven I had known that the sight of the Hawk High School basketball players in their gold-with-black-trim short shorts made me gulp a swallow. And even if I could keep that part secret, I still became suspect to everyone at school by simply existing. I was the only boy any of us knew who pegged his jeans, wore Eastlands, or carried novels like *Gone with the Wind* or *Wuthering Heights* on the school bus. Later my peers would emulate the first two elements but would never get onboard with reading anything, much less sweeping literary romances. Erin was different in every way a person could be in Hawk, Kentucky, in 1986. She cut her own hair to look like John Taylor's in Duran Duran—long bangs in her eyes, sides very short, the rest a rat's nest. While every other girl we knew loved Bon Jovi or Poison, Erin worshipped Van Morrison and Joni Mitchell. She wore trench coats that she wouldn't take off on the hottest days, flipped off cheerleaders, beat up boys who messed with her. Once she knocked Wesley Bates into crying after he called her a *nasty dyke*. One tightly clenched fist to the nose, then she loomed over him as he lay on the ground, tears popping from his eyes, and thundered: "That was for calling me *nasty*." She wasn't gay, but she was weird, and that was almost as bad.

We had been telling each other everything about ourselves for as long as we could remember.

As soon as the church van hustled away, I ran into the house, put on a David Bowie album as loud as it would go while I changed clothes, and Erin—who had been watching through the window from her sickbed— threw aside her covers and globbed on thick layers of eyeliner. Not long after, she leaned in my bedroom door watching as I struggled to settle on the correct outfit for our night out.

"Oh my God, just wear any tight pair of pants and any tight shirt," she hollered over the music.

"It has to be the *right* outfit," I said. "It's easy for you to get ready since you cover everything up in that big-ass trench coat."

I finally settled on a pair of black Levi's, black cowboy boots, and a white dress shirt.

"Jesus God, I thought we were going to a drag show," Erin said when I stepped out from behind my closet door. We might not have had any attraction to one another, but I still had my modesty. "You look like an extra in *Urban Cowboy*."

I changed again, switching out the boots for black penny loafers and going more casual with a Tom Petty and the Heartbreakers shirt that showed off not only my forearms—the only part of my body I liked—but also my good taste in music.

Erin drove us around the winding curves toward the interstate in Darrell's squat, green 1980 Pinto. She had paid her older brother ten dollars in exchange for one night's use of his vehicle and his silence.

"You got the IDs?"

I had bought the fake licenses from a classmate who worked in the fishing department at the Kmart where he had access to a laminating machine. He was an artiste and there was no way any doorman could tell they were forgeries, even though I was four years younger than my ID's stated age of twenty-one.

"Light us a cig and get us some music going, son," Erin said. Despite being a rebel in all other respects, she was a meticulously careful driver who wouldn't take her eyes off the road or her hands off the wheel.

I put in a cassette and as soon as the music came on we started dancing in our seats and singing every word to "Stand Back" along with Stevie Nicks. I rolled down the window and hung my body outside in the pummeling September wind. I raised my arms above my head and sang the song and kept my eyes on the night sky, well-lit by the white stars of late summer. In those days I was looking for freedom anywhere I could find it. I had been deeply moved by the explosion of the space shuttle a few months before and still couldn't look up without thinking of Christa McAuliffe and the other astronauts who had perished there.

Erin was pulling at my leg so I thrust myself back into the car just as the song ended.

"I said light me a cigarette."

We rarely ever smoked our own cigarettes, opting to share a Marlboro Red instead. We passed it back and forth, Erin's eyes latched to the headlights as she coasted onto the interstate and we were firmly on our way to Lexington. We had never been there on our own before. In fact, we had rarely been to any city, period. Our parents were not people who found much cause for leaving our little town. The fact that they had climbed onto the church van to go all the way to Louisville was a big deal and they would have never traveled so far for anyone except an evangelist. Jimmy Swaggart was their favorite. But tonight, Erin and I were on the biggest adventure of our life. She had found out that there was a drag show every Saturday night in Lexington, and we were going. We had never even seen a drag show or a gay bar in a movie and we had no idea what to expect. For the only time in our lives thus far, our parents were actually going to be out very late—they had announced they wouldn't roll in until around two in the morning— and we had time to do what we wanted.

"What do you think Melinda would do if she knew where we were going?" Erin asked, talking about my mother.

"Have me admitted to the psycho ward, most likely."

Erin laughed. "She's the one who belongs there." Erin never minced words about my mother. She had spent too many hours of her life comforting me after my mother had pushed me too far, bullying me into getting girlfriends or berating me because I wasn't good enough at basketball. Something in my mother must have known I was gay from the time I was little. Otherwise, there was no reason for her weekly declarations that all the queers should be rounded up and sent to an island. "They could just all give AIDS to each other until they were all wiped out." Once, when I couldn't take it any longer and feebly attempted to defend gay people without admitting I was one myself, my mother knitted her eyebrows, leaned in close to me, and said: "I'd rather you be dead than a queer. You know that, don't you?" Erin could never forgive her for that, but I always forgave her for everything. In all other areas she was a good mother. She adored me. She worked fifty-hour weeks at the only department store in town—Don's Ready-to-Wear—bending over to slip shoes onto the feet of my wealthy classmates who could afford the latest Air Jordans. She came home and cooked huge meals and made sure we all sat down to eat together every evening. While we watched television she scratched my back, always pausing to cap her hand over my head and cooing "my baby" before she turned in for the night. I knew that if she figured out for sure who I was she would never, ever adore me again.

"Well, she'll never know where we went," Erin said. "And tonight we're going to dance our asses off and not even think about anybody in that shit-town." Erin couldn't wait to get out of Hawk and was counting down the days until she went away to Berea College. My future wasn't as well mapped out, but I was pretty sure I'd never be able to leave my parents to go very far away to college. Ever since I was little they had been laying the guilt on me to stay close to home, so I'd probably end up going to the satellite campus of Eastern Kentucky University, which was located in a shopping center overtop the Winn Dixie. Most people from Hawk did as much those days. Once they got their diplomas—usually in education or business—they'd pull a trailer into the yards of their parents until they had saved enough money to build a little house on the family property.

"Not me," Erin would say. "Soon as I get out of high school the only thing this shit-town will ever see of me is my taillights."

I wished I could be as dismissive. As much as I longed to be able to dance in night clubs and kiss boys, the hills around Hawk had a stronger pull for me. I couldn't imagine ever leaving that little town or the army of cousins I loved despite the fact that they would have beaten me had they known the way I talked angrily about Ronald Reagan and lovingly about Andrew McCarthy when it was just me and Erin together. But the only person besides me that Erin had ever really cared about was her mother, who had passed away the year before after ten months of being devoured by breast cancer. I had stood beside Erin at the grave, holding her hand. Tears dripped off her chin but there was something magnificent about her refusal to wipe them away. She and her father had always been at odds with one another, and since her mother's death he was always onto her to assume more of the household responsibilities he deemed "women's work." Erin was not the vacuuming, laundering, dishwashing sort and every day was a battle royal between the two of them.

Once we were off the interstate I read the map to Erin and directed her right to Main Street where The Oscar was located. There was no sign out front but there was a small rainbow flag in the front window. I was good at reading maps because that had been one of my father's major roles in Vietnam and he had made sure I had this ability, which he said would always come in handy. As worldly as Erin longed to be she was still trembling by the time she had parked the car. She had never driven in a city before but she would have died before she let on she was nervous. I had no such qualms about admitting as much, though.

"I don't know about this," I said while she peered into the visor mirror, applying more eyeliner, as if it had faded between here and Hawk.

"What the hell are you talking about?"

"What if they figure out they're fake IDs and call the police and then our parents have to come get us and they figure out where we were going and—"

"I just drove all the way to Lexington mostly for you," she said, flipping the visor up. "So either we're going in there and dancing all night or I'm going to kick your ass all the way back home."

The doorman barely looked at our IDs. He motioned for us to put our arms forward so he could latch paper neon bands around our wrists. He was a huge black man with a shining bald head and muscles that threatened to rip apart his tight black T-shirt before our eyes like the Incredible Hulk. Yet he was wearing diamond earrings in each ear, fake eyelashes, and pink lipstick.

Erin walked on into the club as if she owned the place and I scurried in behind her. Prince was singing "Raspberry Beret" over the speakers. There was a bar crowded with folks lobbying for a spot where they might catch the bartenders' eyes. Two of the bartenders were working frantically, mixing and pouring drinks in elaborate and exaggerated ways. Behind them an entire wall of liquor bottles was lit up. Our home county was dry, so we had never been around alcohol sales of any kind. But Erin pushed her way up to the bar, parting the crowd. I held onto the back of her trench coat, then squeezed in beside her. Immediately a man who didn't look much older than us glided over and I realized he was wearing roller skates, along with a pair of red running shorts and nothing else. "What'll you have, baby?" he drawled.

"Two Tanqueray and tonics with lemon, please," Erin said.

"Classy choice, baby," he said, and made a big display of holding the gin very high while he poured it, glaring at the lemon as he gave it a lavish squeeze and using a little hose to spray in tonic water.

Erin held out a ten-dollar bill, folded in half lengthwise, between her two fingers just as he told her we owed five dollars. "Just give me three back, honey," she said.

He blew her a kiss.

"How'd you learn to do that?"

"Everything I ever needed to know I learned from Hitchcock movies," Erin said, as if that settled that. "Here's mud in your eye," she said, and tipped the side of her plastic glass to mine. "Clink."

"Cheers," I said, also emulating the movies, and we both took a drink of our very first cocktails. We had sneaked drinks from Darrell's Jim Beam he kept hidden in his room but this was different. The gin, the lemon, the fizz—all worked together for a perfect combination. I had never really liked alcohol before and had only drunk it to impress Erin and hope for a buzz. This was delicious enough to be dangerous. We had already agreed Erin would quit after two she'd have early on so she could safely drive us back home. Nothing enraged her more than drunk drivers.

The Oscar was split into three elements that we would figure out by night's end. First, there was the big bar that welcomed everyone in to immediately participate in the commerce of buying a drink. Next were the double doors that led to the room with tables and chairs and a small stage for drag performances. And in the back was a wide spiral staircase that led up to the dance floor walled by gold-streaked mirrors and ceilinged by strobe lights and disco balls. Our first order of business was to see a drag show.

Nowadays I can look back on that moment of walking through those doors into the drag room and see that nothing was ever the same again. The synthesizers of "Think About Love" started playing as if the music had been waiting to usher us into the room. The stage dimmed to hazy blue lights just as a drag queen came out dressed as Dolly Parton, pantomiming the song. This was Dolly to the extreme, though: huge blond hair even bigger than the real Dolly's, enormous breasts even larger than the real Dolly's, the white gown squeezed tight around the perfectly round rump that the queen was using to great effect, hips swaying to the music as she sang along. Immediately folks rushed forward, dollar bills held out in the hopes that she might take the money in exchange for a moment with her. All of the tables had been taken but Erin sailed across the room to a table that sat center stage, occupied by a tiny woman sucking furiously at a long cigarette and a boney man—his face all gaunt angles—who was squirming around in his seat with his eyes closed, singing every word of the Dolly song at the top of his lungs, arms moving out from his body in long, elegant lunges and curls.

"These taken?" Erin asked, gesturing to the two empty chairs at their table.

"No, darlin', take 'em, take 'em," the woman said, six puffs of smoke expelling.

I would have never dreamed of sitting with people I didn't know but this seemed to be perfectly acceptable behavior so I slid into the seat and watched the drag queen as she made her way around the stage collecting dollar bills from her adoring fans. People were singing along with her and swaying in place, excited when she leaned down to kiss their cheeks or the tops of their fingers after taking their money. They adored her as if she *were* Dolly. As if she were even better than Dolly herself. There was all manner of people: lesbians and gay men, gaggles of straight women, even a few men who looked a lot like burly straight men would've dressed and moved back home. And then I saw that many of the tables were occupied by couples: men leaning into each other's embraces, smiling and whispering to each other; women kissing; straight couples watching the queen as if mesmerized. Some people danced in their seats. Groups of three or four had their arms laced around each other's shoulders, singing along with the song. "When you think about love, think about me." Others stood near their tables and danced. The man at our table continued to sing along with his eyes closed, and he had a beautiful voice. The woman next to him continued to smoke, and when my eyes fell on her, she smiled widely. She had very long red fingernails and a great pile of dyed black curls teetering on her head. "Hey there darlin'," she mouthed, her words lost to the noise. She wasn't judging anyone in the room even though she was a few years older than my mother. No one in this room was judging anyone else. I had never seen anything like it. Everyone was being themselves. Everyone was free in a way I had never seen people be before.

In the pause between songs, the woman shook our hands and said her name was Flora Mullins and where were we from, and when we told her she let out a little yelp and clapped her hands and said they were from eastern Kentucky, too, and didn't it always just happen that eastern Kentucky people ended up together no matter where in the world they went? "And this is my boy, Caleb."

"Charmed, I'm sure," Caleb said, and put out his hand as if I might kiss it instead of shake it. I caught his long fingers sideways and gave them a little shake. He was not nearly as old as I had first thought, maybe only six or seven years older than me. "You are *real* pretty," he said, and brought the back of his hand down the side of my face. "How *old* are you?"

"Caleb!" Flora slapped his arm playfully and let out another yelp, which I now understood to be her way of laughing.

"Brought him out for his twenty-first birthday tonight," Erin offered, a perfectly capable and confident liar.

"Shit, ain't no way this boy here is twenty-one," Caleb said, not unkindly. "You're a butch little queer, though."

I was trying to process so many things in this moment: openly being called a *queer* by someone who seemed to love the word instead of hate what it stood for, the possibility of being caught underage in the bar, Caleb cussing in front of his mother—but mostly the fact that Caleb was here *with* his mother. Not only that a man was at a bar with his mother, but at a *gay* bar.

"Caleb has been pretty sick," Flora said. She lit another cigarette to hide the tears that had popped into her eyes as if out of nowhere. She must have looked like Lauren Bacall as a young woman, and she still smoked much like her, elegant and tough all at the same time. "Now that he's feeling a little better I wanted to get him out of the house."

"You're okay with—" I began, but was cut off not only by not knowing how to ask what I wanted to but also by Erin pinching the meat above my waist so hard I almost hollered.

Flora knew exactly where I was headed, though.

"He's my child," Flora said. She smiled at me and covered Caleb's hand with her own. "I want him to be exactly who he is."

I pictured my own mother: hands raised over her head, lips trembling with the Holy Ghost while Jimmy Swaggart strutted back and forth across the stage, hacking and condemning, preaching down hellfire and brimstone.

Then the music started again and the curtains were thrown aside and some unseen entity came over a microphone to introduce a queen named "The Delicious and Delightful Miss Pearl Clutcher." Whitney Houston was pumping out of the speakers and the place exploded just as Pearl Clutcher thrust herself through the curtains in a glittering evening gown that was split up to the crotch from the bottom and down to the navel from the top. Pearl threw her hair over her shoulder, stuck out her breasts, and jutted out her hips, floating around the dance floor and mouthing each word to the song, which the entire crowd knew by heart. "How will I know if he really loves me?" they all sang as loudly as they could. Even Erin was singing. Flora was, too. Flora had put her arm around Erin's shoulders and they were swaying together, rocking to the music. And of course Caleb was in full performance mode. This time he had jumped in his chair and was using his arms to full effect, elegantly accentuating each word in the song with a hand thrust forward or a sway of his fingers like birds gliding before him. The crowd surged forward, dollars held high, the scent of cologne and perfume and sweat and alcohol washing over us, the music swimming over the crowd like salvation.

But I did not dance or sing. I sat amongst them, watching them all, overcome.

A cigarette-scarred voice came over the loudspeaker to announce there would be a one-hour break between the drag shows but we could entertain ourselves upstairs on the massive dance floor. "Go dance now, you bitches," the voice prompted, and then "Let's Hear It for the Boy" blasted out of the speakers. One group formed a conga line to make their way out of the show room and Caleb squealed and grabbed his mother's hand, forcing her to join. Flora put her large purse on her arm and grabbed hold of Erin's fingers, who glared back at me when I didn't join right away. "Come *on*," she said. "Now." Everyone was twisting and doing kicks and throwing their heads back in laughter as the conga line snaked its way through the club and up the wide stairs. I had never seen Erin like this. She always refused to participate when there were dances at school, choosing to lean against a wall and shoot murderous glances at all the preppies who were out there trying to emulate Madonna. But here in front of me, Erin was not only moving her hips but throwing one hand out into the air while holding onto Flora's waist with the other, laughing at the top of her lungs, throwing her wild hair around, part of the energy. She had even left her trench coat thrown over the back of her chair, allowing her body to be on display for the first time I could ever remember. Flora took short little steps and moved her shoulders more than anything, her moves as prim and proper as she was not. Caleb was in front of her, completely lost to the music, and he lost control when the song filling the entire building segued into Janet Jackson singing "Nasty."

Once we got to the dance floor we made a little circle of the four of us and I could completely see him, strangely elegant with his arms moving languidly before him, his movements a combination of modern dance, ballet, and straight-up rocking out. He moved more like a woman was expected to and he seemed completely confident in a way I had never seen anyone be. There was one boy back home—Dwayne Miller—who twisted his hips and put one foot in front of another, one hand always hanging limply before him. "Here comes the *woman*," a knot of rich boys had howled one day as he swaggered down the hallway. Dwayne had stopped abruptly, thrown his shoulder and face around to them, and drawled, "I'm not a woman; I'm a *mothafuckin' lady*." But they beat the confidence out of him. He didn't change the way he walked except that now he didn't march flamboyantly down the hallways of Hawk High School. Instead he cowered as closely to the walls as possible during the breaks between classes, books held firmly to chest, head down. They had broken him, but he would not stay that way. As we danced there at The Oscar with everyone free and celebratory around me, I thought about Dwayne and wished that I had gone out of my way to be nice to him. Instead, I had just ignored him, trying my best to fit in, while Erin did everything in her power not to assimilate. She was the only person who ever even talked to Dwayne. Caleb kept his eyes closed the whole time he danced and I realized that this was probably the only place he had the luxury of not constantly looking over his shoulder. People like him had to always be on the lookout.

So there we were in a circle and I marveled at how we had only just met these two people but they already felt like old friends. My first lesson in the quick power of created families, of clans who are joined not only by the hope for safety but by the comfort of understanding one another without explanation.

The gold-streaked mirrors surrounding the dance floor made it seem four times as big as it actually was. Some of the dancing skinny boys pulled off their shirts and watched themselves in the mirrored walls. One of them saw me watching him and winked with exaggeration. I looked away, reddening.

Erin danced away and Flora smiled at me. I knew I should stay and dance with her since Caleb seemed lost to the music in such a way that would have left her completely alone there. Now Wham! was singing the song about jitterbugging and suddenly Flora shoved her purse into Caleb's arms and grabbed hold of me, one hand in mine, the other on my back, and we were fifties-dancing although I had never really danced like that except when they made us learn some dance steps in gym class in ninth grade. I guess old Flora had actually lived back when people danced together like this and knew exactly what she was doing. She twirled me and swung me around the dance floor, and the others moved back to give us more room, clapping to the beat. I followed her, messing up along the way, but getting the moves quicker than I could have ever imagined. I gave myself over to it, caught up in how happy Flora looked as she managed to direct me by a simple flex of her wrist or a whisper of "move under now" or "twirl out, darlin." When the trumpets played the song to its end, the crowd erupted in applause for us and Flora did a little curtsy, beaming. The crowd forgot us as soon as "Everybody Have Fun Tonight" came on, but Erin was suddenly there, holding out two gin and tonics for Flora and Caleb. She turned behind her to a woman clad completely in black leather who had carried the other two for her. "Thanks, honey," I watched her mouth say, and the woman winked at her and sashayed away. Erin handed me one and Flora hoisted hers in the air before us. "To us!" she cried out, and we clicked our glasses together and drank. When I brought the plastic cup back down the gin was already rushing to my brain.

We danced and danced. Without thinking about anyone else. Our little circle there on the dance floor of a night club named for Oscar Wilde in the very middle of Kentucky, where it was still illegal to act on being gay and could get you a year in jail if convicted. Where only twelve years ago the sentence could be up to five years. Where people still wouldn't go to a hospital that was rumored to be harboring AIDS patients. Where the worst insult at school was *faggot* or *queer*. Where my mother said it was better to be dead than gay. But there we were, four people apart from all of that, and part of it, too. In the middle of the dance floor, eyes closed, eyes watching, every part of us moving. Two underage teenagers; an old woman with her purse on her arm like Queen Elizabeth; her skeletal, vamping son; and all the others. Drag queens, queers, straight people, positive people, trans people (although I didn't know that at the time), weirdos, freaks, the other, the hated. Just human beings dancing as hard as we could to The Pointer Sisters. But more than that. It seemed to me that everyone in the room was loving everyone else without any questions. There we were, dancing.

"Are you about to *cry*?" Erin was suddenly in my ear, whisper-yelling over the music. "What's *wrong* with you?"

I hadn't realized that my eyes were wet but I took a deep breath and gathered myself. "It's just that everyone is so beautiful," I said, right when the song ended and a brief silence bloomed.

"Everyone's beautiful when they're being themselves," Flora said, leaning in close and running her hand down the side of my face. I wondered if my mother would ever touch me that way if she had known who I really was.

My favorite song by Eurythmics came on and the gin was singing through my limbs and I was about as happy as a person can be, I reckon. I was eyeing a smooth dancer—about ten years too old for me—across the room and he had just started eyeing me too when Caleb folded down toward the floor like a deflated accordion. Flora tucked her arm around his back before he completely collapsed. "Help me get him outside, right quick," she said, completely calm, and she swung him around so that one of his arms capped over my shoulder. I put my hand on his back to steady him and the boniness of his spine was as shocking as his lightness. He weighed no more than a child, but somehow seemed even lighter. Erin was close at our heels as we weaved our way through the undulating dancers. Some of them laughed or offered good-humored faux pity because they thought Caleb had simply had too much to drink but I could tell from the way his mother was reacting that it was more serious than that. We glided down the staircase and Flora led us to a back door that opened onto an alley where several other people stood in tight groups. A couple of them were making out. I could smell the skunky burnt-cloth scent that I would later know as the aroma of people smoking pot. The night had cooled off enough to feel exhilarating when it hit our sweating bodies.

No sooner than the September air had greeted us Caleb pulled away, swatting at us dramatically. "Let go of me Jesus God what is wrong with y'all I'm not a cripple."

"You've pushed yourself too hard," Flora said, and in her voice I could hear the nearness of crying. "I tried to just let you have a good time and not say anything, but—"

"Oh, Mommy, *hush*," he said, and wrapped her up in his thin arms. It wasn't unusual for men from our region to call their mothers this, but coming from Caleb it seemed like a term of endearment. I knew that they had only ever had each other to depend upon, that they had been alone in the world, just the two of them. I had wondered earlier if he knew how lucky he was to have a mother who not only accepted him but seemed to even encourage him to be himself. Now I saw that he absolutely knew.

He drew back from her and wiped at his eyes with the backs of his hands, then fanned at his face like a beauty queen who has burst into tears and is afraid her mascara might run. "Take a picture, honey, it'll last longer," Caleb said, and put his hand on his hip, staring me down.

"I'm sorry—" I began, but Erin cut me off.

"I hate to say it, but we better head back," she said, and gave me an eye-widening look that meant *If we don't go soon they'll beat us back and then there'll be hell to pay.*

"Curfew. *See*," Caleb said to his mother. "I knew it. No way these kids are old enough to be here."

"Oh, Caleb, leave them alone," Flora said, and took a deep draw on a newly lit Virginia Slim. "Who cares?"

"What will you do when you go back to little old Hawk, buddy?" Caleb asked me. He clearly couldn't remember my name. "What will you *be*?"

I didn't know how to answer him. The honest reply was that I was going to go back to my parents' house and hide who I was, and on Monday I'd go back to school and hide who I was, and I'd keep on doing those things until I graduated high school, and I still didn't know what I'd do after that. The world seemed bigger now. I knew that much. But I still wasn't ready to leave everything I had known my whole life, no matter how glimmering it all seemed to be that night.

"Listen, y'all," Caleb said, his clammy skin shining and the circles under his eyes suddenly darker. "You get the hell out of that town. You get *out* of there and never do look back."

"You let them find their own way," Flora offered, meekly.

"No. You get as far away as you can from this place."

"A lot of good it did you, didn't it, Caleb?" Flora said, stepping toward him. Angry. "You went off to New York and they beat you. Your face was so swollen up I didn't even recognize you when I got to the hospital." She threw down her cigarette, ground it under her heel. "At least nobody ever did that to you down home. And if you had stayed home—"

"But at least there was a time when I could walk down the street and be completely myself. At least I had that," he said, his voice rising now. His words slurred as he poked a finger at his own chest and I saw that he was drunker than I had thought. "At least I got to be *me*, for a little while at least. Before I had to run back home."

Caleb had more to say but he wasn't able to. He put a clenched hand to his mouth so that I thought he was about to burst out in tears but instead he coughed violently. A silence stood around us for a few moments as he gathered himself.

Flora turned to Erin and took both her hands. "I can't tell you how nice it was to meet you both," she said. "You are just the sweetest two I believe I've ever seen." Then, to my amazement, I saw that there were tears in Erin's eyes. I had never seen her shed a tear except at her own mother's funeral. These days when she talked about her mother, she didn't cry. She just got angry.

Flora hustled her purse up on her hip and rummaged around in it until she had lit on an ink pen and a silver gum wrapper, where she carefully wrote out her phone number. "And listen, if you ever need somewhere to go, you can call me." She thrust the gum wrapper at Erin but she looked at me when she spoke: "Promise me you will." As if she was some kind of clairvoyant who knew exactly what my home was like. Like she could see my mother holding court at the supper table as she went on about welfare queens and drug addicts and child-molesting queers while I sat there, clenching my jaw, while my father sat there, afraid to talk back. "Hear me?" Flora asked.

"I promise," I said.

The alley was nearer where we had parked than the front of the building so we didn't need to go back into The Oscar, although I remembered that Erin had left her trench coat in there. I didn't bring it up, even though I wouldn't have minded one last look at the bar and the pretty people dancing therein. It would be a long time before I'd be back. Years and years before I was able to free myself. Erin and I walked away in silence, our shoe heels clicking in the quiet night. About the same time, our parents were climbing back onto the church van more than an hour northwest of us, worn out from the Holy Ghost that had been conjured by Jimmy Swaggart. In less than two years Swaggart would be found with a prostitute and would make a tearful plea of "I have sinned" to his fans in the hopes of holding onto his ministry. Before long his followers would largely forgive him and move on. Some things were pardonable. Other things never would be. That night we were all driving back south at the same time, but since they were farther away we'd beat them back home with plenty of time to spare.

"Get out the *Veedon Fleece*," Erin said as she maneuvered the one-way streets, trying to find our way back to the interstate. She was talking about her favorite Van Morrison album. I unclicked the little silver buckle on the front of her cassette carrier, which looked like a small brown briefcase, and ran my fingers down the spines of the cassettes until I found the right one. I put in the tape and I didn't even have to ask which one she wanted to hear. I fast-forwarded to the third song on the second side and there was the piano, there was the guitar, there he was singing "I want to comfort you." We sang along with him, sharing a cigarette, our hands floating out the open windows on the cool September air. I rewound the song and we sang along with him a couple more times, in love with the wide world as we sailed down I-75 toward the soft blue hills of home.

FENTON JOHNSON

Fenton Johnson is the author of three novels, most recently *The Man Who Loved Birds*, and three books of literary nonfiction, most recently *Everywhere Home: A Life in Essays*. *Geography of the Heart: A Memoir* received American Library Association and Lambda Literary Awards, while *Keeping Faith: A Skeptic's Journey among Christian and Buddhist Monks* received Lambda Literary and Kentucky Literary Awards. He is a regular contributor to *Harper's* magazine, with four cover essays, most recently January 2018 (available, along with other writings and media, via his webpage: www.fentonjohnson.com). Johnson is on the faculties of the University of Arizona and Spalding University.

Bad Habits

....

(1984)

This time of year, which is November, Nick Handley drives his older sister Frances to her job at the county hospital, then stops to pick up a tying crew at the old L&N rail yard. Where his father tied tobacco by the weather, Nick ties by the calendar—tying on days toward the end of the month, when his crew's unemployment and food stamps have run low and they're desperate enough that they'll take farm work.

They sit on a stack of abandoned cross ties. On top sits Paul Carter, engaged for a few months to Frances some ten years ago, and Nick's occasional back-lot lover before and since. At his feet sit Leon Hughes and Hambone McCugh, black men old enough to be Nick's father.

Leon and Hambone climb to the truck's flatbed. Paul Carter sits in the cab. "Got a cigarette?" he says, before Nick can put the truck in gear. "Or have you let Frances rag you into quitting?"

Nick pulls a pack from his pocket. "So where were you last night. I waited, under the bridge. *Two* hours. You promised."

Paul pulls cigarettes from the pack, tucking extras in his pocket. "I got busy."

"You know how cold it was under that bridge?"

"Hey. You wait for the likes of me, you're asking to be kept waiting." Paul punches in the dashboard lighter.

"For Christ's sake, you could let me know. You got a phone."

"You want to quit meeting me under that bridge, just say the word," Paul says. "I got other fish to fry, in better places."

The lighter pops. Nick pulls it from the dash and holds it out. Paul Carter pulls out matches, to light his cigarette himself.

At twenty-six, Nick has never lived with a lover, but he imagines this must be how lovers fight: the first blow, then the silent treatment, then maneuvers, and the making up. Crossing the cattle guard, he takes a pack of Camels, his last, from the glove compartment. "Support the local economy," he says, tossing the pack in Paul's lap. Paul rolls the pack in his sleeve.

The crew breaks at ten, filing outside. They line up, backs against the side of the barn, each propping a foot against its gray-weathered poplar planks. Paul Carter pushes himself away from the wall to light a joint. Nick bums a cigarette from Leon and lights it. When no one is looking his eyes take in Paul Carter's thick-muscled arms, the low autumn sunlight skating off the flat, smooth planes of his chest. Hambone takes a leak around the corner, where he keeps a pint stashed behind the baling twine. He is of the old school and believes in hiding his vices.

When Hambone comes back, Leon pulls a pack of dog-eared cards from his pocket. "Ante up," he says, "I'm calling. Follow the whore."

They crouch to a sawed-off stump and put up quarters. Leon turns the cards over, one by one. They bet after each overturned card, while Leon patters through each round and over the betting: "One-eyed john to the Handley man, Old Dog Tray comes knocking at his door. A savanna to Hambone, pair of savannas, looking good, maybe this man is a winner, maybe this man is California bound. Split-beard kings to the man with the plan, kings up, bound for glory Carter. Dealer four, dealer eight, dealer folds, no inside straight."

"California," Paul Carter says. "It's been known to happen."

He is looking at Nick's sister Frances in her hospital whites, picking her way across the mud, and behind her, this scarlet BMW. Leon sweeps up the cards and the quarters and tucks them in his coat. Nick drops his half-finished cigarette and grinds it beneath his heel.

"Resident pothead," Frances says, talking at Paul Carter. "I smelled you halfway down the hill."

Paul stands, leans against the side of the barn, one foot propped back, thumbs hooked in his pockets. He cranes his neck to look beyond Frances, out over the farm. "Poke your nose in the feedlot and you're going to smell shit."

"Some car you got there, Frances," Nick says. "Where'd you get that car?"

"Some sugar daddy," Paul Carter says.

"Who makes enough money to be a sugar daddy," Frances says. She turns to Nick. "I borrowed it from George Sikes, he's back visiting family. Came in for a sprained wrist. A *tennis* wrist. I'm wrapping it up when he starts telling me how he's in real estate now, in Lexington, how I can borrow this car anytime I want, long as he's staying at his mother's."

"I'm curious as to what his wife would say to that offer," Paul Carter says.

"He's getting a divorce," Frances says.

"And here's his nurse to help make it final," Paul Carter says.

Frances takes up a rake to poke at the abandoned mud dauber nests under the eaves. "He's got money to throw around, I think, so I figure I'll bring him out to the farm while the crew is working, make a good impression, you know, make him think this place might be a break-even enterprise, maybe get him to thinking a little about buying some cheap land back in his old hometown. Or maybe buying the barn, anyway. This old barn lumber is worth its weight in gold, according to George." She digs a large nest from its niche, knocking it to the ground. "Good thing I stopped by first. Boss Man."

"So you're thinking about selling," Nick says.

"It's my place," she says, and this is true: twelve years older than Nick, she had the job and the salary and the nest egg to buy out the farm and so allow their mother to keep up appearances through her long and expensive dying.

"Boss Man turns around, his sister stabs him in the back." Paul levers himself from the barn. "Won't be the last time, neither."

Frances pauses, the rake poised like a spear. "Lot of tobacco left, Paul Carter," she says pleasantly.

She stands in the barnyard muck in her hospital uniform, clean and white as the angel of God, until Nick takes the rake from her, to jab at the nests. "Don't do that, Nick," Paul says. "Let the lady finish what she started."

Frances peers up into the eaves. "Paul Carter, you never were one to leave well enough alone. I expect that's what turned you into a pothead. Among other bad habits."

"I leave good habits to those that can afford 'em." Paul steps over to the car, runs a tobacco-gummed hand over its scarlet finish, leaving a long brown stain.

"Back to work, guys," Nick says. "We got half a barn left. We wasted enough time."

Frances pulls a rag from the trunk of the car and wipes at the stain, but this only spreads it around. She wads the rag into a ball and drops it in the barnyard. "Next time I come I'm bringing George Sikes," she calls. "See if you can make this crew pretend like they're doing something that turns a profit." She climbs into the car and drives off.

"Good thing she stopped by first," Hambone squeaks. "*Boss Man.*" He pulls Leon into the barn. Nick hears them laugh: Hambone, *haw, haw, haw,* Leon's high-pitched cackle, Paul Carter's low snorting that outlasts them all. Nick crouches to the stump, watching the scarlet BMW until it disappears into the oaks and hickories that crowd the ragged limestone lip of Strang Knob.

At supper, Frances waits until they finish eating before she brings up the subject. "I saw Hambone McCugh after you dropped him off," she says. "If he had been any drunker you could have poured him in the tank for fuel. And I hope you're not paying Paul Carter a full day. I saw him riding around with some girl."

"Hambone might drink less if I let him smoke in the barn," Nick says. "But then he'd burn the place down." He glances at the clock, pushes his chair back, pulls a cigarette from his pocket.

"I wish you wouldn't smoke," Frances says. "I quit. *You* can quit. It's like any bad habit. I had a long talk about this very thing with George. He quit himself, right before he left his wife. You just choose to give it up and pick a day and then stop."

"I think I'll go shoot some pool," Nick says, but he tucks the cigarette behind his ear and picks up a knife, turning it over, bouncing it against the edge of his plate.

Frances pulls the plate from under his stuttering knife. "You're going to meet Paul Carter. You can't fool me."

Nick takes the cigarette from his temple and strikes a match.

"Living in a dreamworld," Frances says. "Surely you can wait until you get outside."

Licking his thumb and forefinger, Nick pinches out the flame. On its quick hiss Frances stalks out.

Nick drives the pickup to the Gaddy's Ford Bridge, where he douses the lights and sits in the dark, smoking. Then he crawls around the pilings, under the bridge, to where he has rigged up a shanty at Paul Carter's direction. Its walls are fashioned from surplus parachute silk and an American flag, and its roof is the bridge itself.

Since Nick was twelve, since before Frances dated Paul Carter, Nick and Paul have met here. Paul smokes his pot and they drink Nick's whiskey and sometimes after they are both loaded Paul lets Nick paw at him, no kissing allowed.

On cold nights Nick brings a Kerosun heater, and he lights it now. He huddles before its orange flame: chest hot, back cold; back hot, chest cold. He smokes and waits and finally breaks into the Wild Turkey. Sometime after eleven o'clock he stumbles up the pilings, to drive the pickup home and park himself in bed.

The next day, and the next, Paul Carter is not at the rail yard when Nick fetches the crew. Both mornings a smart little sports car with Fort Knox stickers is parked outside Paul's trailer.

On the third morning Paul shows up, stoned and thick and blond. Riding to the farm Nick tries to say, Hi, how are you, getting any. "You're just slumming" is what comes out.

"That is no doubt the may be of it," Paul Carter says. "But I am slumming in a fancy car. A trick I learned from your sister."

At the cattle guard Nick floors the gas, throwing gravel up the drive and spinning the truck sideways into the barn lot. From the flatbed he hears Hambone and Leon cursing. "Shit-fire, Boss Man, watch out," Hambone says when Nick climbs from the cab. "I ain't got no more lives where this one come from."

Paul rounds the truck, to pull a cigarette from Nick's pocket. "You think I give a goddamn," he says. "Well, think again. Just a way to pass the time." He taps it down on Nick's chest. "Boss Man."

Nick turns to Hambone. "Sorry," he says. He does not speak to Paul Carter for the rest of the day.

Now the house is filled with her wanting, so strong the knowledge of it wakes Nick long before sunrise. He lies in the graying darkness, hoping that she will get what she wants: the phone will ring, George Sikes will call, to ask her for a date, to ask her to go away with him, to Lexington, to Fayette.

The first of the month comes. Hambone and Leon pick up their food stamps, Paul Carter picks up his unemployment. The crew disappears from the rail yard. A night comes when it gets late, then later, and Frances does not come home. Drifting off to sleep, Nick tells himself this is what they have wanted.

The next evening Frances pulls Nick from the barn, where he is working alone. She has signed a contract to have the tobacco barn torn down and its lumber sold to a friend of George Sikes, who sterilizes it for sale to city people to panel their living rooms.

Nick pulls out his cigarettes. "Not now," Frances says. "This isn't a cigarette break. I want your mind on business."

"Then lay off me," he says, but he tucks his cigarettes back in his pocket.

"Lord, Nick, I'm not laying *on* you. I'm just trying to help you break a bad habit, which in this particular case is farming." She waves the contract at him. "Nick, talk sense. You know how city people are. This year barn lumber will bring as much as the whole damn farm. Next year it'll be nothing but how tacky barn lumber is. I'll give you this money, to do with what you want. You could use it to train yourself to something useful. Look at Jenny Beams, she's computers, or Danny Mason, he's arts and crafts, he learned how to throw clay pots and the last I heard he was doing all right, selling them at Christmastime in Lexington. You could learn something like that, get out of tobacco."

Nick stares over the ridges. Fencerows have grown up in honeysuckle and sumac. Paint peels from farmhouses. Barn roofs are caving in. Stories are making the rounds about coal miners, a few counties to the east, who are back to working homestead seams with picks and mules. "Why are you so hell-bent on selling the farm?" Nick asks. "Why is it so important for me to leave."

"Because I don't want to sit around watching my brother growing old alone. Why would a woman take up with a man with no money and four hundred acres of knobs dragging him down? So she can watch what that does to them both I guess. Wait until you're thirty-eight. See how you feel about it then, only then it'll be too late." Her voice changes; she might be pleading her cause. "Nick, there's any number of women would love for you to ask them out. Ask somebody special out to supper some night. Just let me know. I'll fix a big meal. We'll have a little party."

"Ask George Sikes out to supper," Nick says. "Get him to pay to keep the farm afloat and take you off to Lexington."

"Don't think I haven't considered that angle," Frances says. She thrusts the contract into Nick's hand, folds his fingers shut around it. "Nick, I'm moving to town. Maybe farther, I don't know. George told me they need good nurses in Lexington. I should have done it a long time ago, made that move, I should never have bought this place from Mother. I should have taken that money and made something with my life. Well, better late than never. You figure out a way to make this place make you a living and you can tear this up. I'll sign the place over to you, barn and all. Otherwise, it's got to go. It's the only thing I can see my way to do. I won't watch you waste your future and my money on Paul Carter. Me helping you make a failure out of yourself."

"People in glass houses," Nick says. He stands with his back to her, waiting to hear her walk away. When he turns around, she is sitting on a hay bale, her knees drawn up, her forehead bent to her hands. He drops the contract in the mud and walks back to the barn.

That night Nick slips out the kitchen door, to walk the Handley farm. He picks his way across the rough clods of the moon-washed barnyard. His boots and pants and shirt are black, and in the barn's black shadow they disappear, leaving his head floating free. He strokes the barn planks, the splintered whorl of a knothole meeting his palm's callused ridges, and the splinters breaking off against his calluses. He smokes one cigarette after another, careful always to deaden the butt's fire against his palm's thick callus: he has done this since he first smoked, he is proud that he can do it, the coal's heat not so much as scorching his hand's hard flesh.

When he was younger and his father lived, Nick thought of killing himself, after doing what he does with Paul Carter under the bridge. But his father died and Nick took over the farm and since then it has been easy to deny himself time to think of such things. The unflagging demands of the animals and the crops are consuming him. What he does under the bridge is a small enough sin to ask in return. So he reasons, in the few silences he allows himself.

In town, in the city, this would change. Any job he found, if he found a job, would turn him loose at five o'clock, free as a jaybird, nothing to live for but himself, nothing but time and conscience on his hands. He is afraid of losing the Handley farm, okay. More than this, he is afraid of himself.

Back inside, he pulls the phone up the hall stairs and into his bedroom. He calls Paul Carter. He steadies himself for a woman's voice, but Paul answers. "Can't work, Boss Man. Not tomorrow."

"I figured that. I was just wondering if you'd want to come to supper. Next week, at our house. Frances asked if I'd like to have you over."

"You're shitting me," Paul says. "Sure, I mean, yeah, I'll come. A free meal is a good meal. Why not?"

Later, Frances asks why Nick took the phone into his room. "You'd think you were talking to some girl. Or up to no good, one."

"One," Nick says.

Nick has told Frances that he is bringing home somebody special. She leaves work early to cook. When she sees Paul Carter she leaves the kitchen, not to return until the biscuits have burned.

Then she makes a hard, bright entrance. "Burnt biscuits make rosy cheeks," she says. She seats them for supper: Nick to one side of the table, herself at the head, Paul Carter at the foot.

They make it through highballs and ham and biscuits and candied yams. Frances talks, about nothing that matters or even makes sense, but talking, talk. Then the words run out. She casts a dark look at Nick. He lets the silence grow.

"So Nick tells me you're bailing out on him," Paul Carter says.

Frances squeezes her lips together before answering. "That's family business. Nick had no call to go spreading it around."

"I wouldn't call talking to me the same as talking to just anybody. More like talking it over with a member of the family." Paul Carter pulls a Camel out, strikes a match on the underside of the table. He lights a cigarette and hands it to Nick.

Frances stands. "Nick Handley, this is my house. I have no need to put up with this man."

"Oh, Frances, sit down and have another drink," Nick says, exhaling to the ceiling. "It's not like this is war."

Frances lowers herself to her chair, knocking her knife to the floor.

"Expecting a gentleman caller?" Paul grins past Nick at Frances.

"And to think I used to wonder if I was right to leave you," Frances says.

"If *I* was right to leave *you*," Paul Carter says. "Let's get our history straight."

"If that's what you need to believe," Frances says. "But I know a few well-placed facts, if it comes to history."

"Yeah, let's talk history," Paul says. "I got nothing to lose but your family's reputation. Which means I got nothing to lose at all." He lifts the cigarette from Nick's fingers, takes a drag, stubs it out. "How 'bout it, brother? You were old enough to know who dumped who."

Frances's neck flushes bright up one side, and her voice trembles. "In him I can understand it. He's a Carter, he has his excuse. But you're a Handley, Nick, you're from good family, good blood. You're my brother."

At the table's center sits an antique bud vase, holding a single dusty stem of dried teasel. Nick takes the teasel from the vase, to stick a sharp spine into the ball of his thumb, but his callus is too thick for him to feel its pricking.

"I'm telling you, you can do it, Nick," Frances says. "Whatever it is that has got to be done. You just do it, is all. You give it up, whatever it is. And it works. You pick a minute out of any day and you say, 'Today I'm taking control of my life,' and then you do it."

"That's what I am planning," Nick says. "That's what I am going to do."

Paul runs his finger along and off the table's edge, to rest his hand on Nick's knee.

The teasel spine snaps, leaving a splinter buried in Nick's thumb. He sticks the stem back into its vase and turns to Paul. "From what I can remember, it was Paul that left you, Frances."

"That's right," Paul says.

"You think I didn't know what was going on underneath the Gaddy's Ford Bridge!" Frances cries. "Why do you think I left him!"

Nick will not look at his sister, but he sees her all the same: sitting on the hay bale in the barn lot, her forehead bent to her hands. "Leave the barn standing and leave me to manage the place. I'll make it work," he says. "Now's your chance. Take up with George Sikes. Clear out of this place."

Paul stands. "Nick, I would surely appreciate a ride back to town," he says. "If it's not too much trouble, that is."

"Don't keep the porch light burning," Nick says to his sister. She picks up the knife. She is still wiping at it with her napkin when Nick eases the door shut.

On the road, Nick pulls a pint from under the seat. He sucks on the whiskey until the blacktop whines beneath his wheels. Paul reaches for the bottle. "Give 'em hell, Boss Man."

Nick caps the bottle and tucks it under his seat. "I want to stop at the bridge. Right now."

Paul steers his outstretched hand to the dashboard lighter, punches it in, pulls it out to light a joint. "I might have somebody waiting at my place. I don't plan my dates. I just give 'em a key and wait for 'em to happen."

"So are they going to keep happening?"

"Never can tell," Paul says, smoke leaking from his lips. "I never known a single woman to turn me down."

"Frances Handley turned you down flat," Nick says. "Which you know as good as anybody. You think it can't happen twice?"

Paul stubs the joint out against the dash, then pinches the tip and tucks it away. "You couldn't do it. You don't have the guts."

"Times are tough all over, Paul Carter." Nick dodges small golden-eyed animals, a possum, a groundhog, frozen by the headlights against the road's graveled asphalt. After a mile or so he clears his throat, a quiet cough. "You heard what you wanted to hear."

"That's right," Paul says.

"She's moving," Nick says. "I'll bet she follows George Sikes. Maybe she'll move in with him. I'll have the place to myself. You could move out there, save on rent, help me make a go of it."

"George Sikes went back to Lexington yesterday morning, probably to his wife, knowing George," Paul says, his voice flat and cold. "Which Frances knows as good as anybody." He rolls down the window and spits into the wind's roar.

They sail up and over the bone-white flank of Strang Knob. The loose planks of the Gaddy's Ford Bridge rumble beneath their wheels. Paul says nothing. Nick slows, then drives on, to park under the blue hum of the mercury vapor lamp outside Paul's place.

The road is empty, his windows dark. They sit in the truck's cab, Paul silent, Nick sucking on the pint, until the windshield fogs over and Nick's feet are numb. He has promised himself that he will not speak first, but the words crowd his tongue and they force their way out. "So how about it."

"Maybe tomorrow night," Paul says.

Before Paul can climb the stoop to the trailer door Nick pulls away. He drives to the Gaddy's Ford Bridge, where he sits smoking and drinking, gripping the steering wheel, working the splinter in his thumb. The smoke curls before his eyes. He sucks it in, waiting for the little blood-rush to his temples; building a vision of himself, Nick Handley, a man without wanting and so without weakness, a man in control of his life, a man of power in the lives of those he wounds.

The sky above Strang Knob is paling when Nick gets home. Frances is sitting at the dinner table, smoking his cigarettes. The dishes are untouched, her own plate is littered with butts.

Nick longs to lay his head on his sister's shoulder, to take comfort from the only person he knows who might give it freely. His wanting grows and it is a hole in his heart that he feels himself falling into.

"You were with him all this time," she says. "The whole goddamn night."

"That's right." Nick takes the pack from the table, but it is empty. "They're all gone. I smoked every damn one."

Nick pulls a pack from his pocket, shakes a cigarette free for himself.

"I've changed my mind, Nick. I'm not tearing down the barn."

"Fine."

"I couldn't leave you here alone."

"Leave if you want. I'll get Paul Carter to move out here." Nick takes an empty pack from the table, tosses it at the garbage, misses by a long yard. "Don't stick around just to do me favors."

Frances stubs her cigarette into a spoonful of candied yams. "So what am I supposed to do? If I don't do you favors."

"Do what you want to do."

"You wouldn't say that if you knew what I wanted to do." Her hands roam the table, picking up a pepper grinder, a saltshaker, an empty highball glass, the antique bud vase with its single dusty stem of dried teasel.

He bends to strike a match on the underside of the table.

On its scratching flare Frances hurls the vase at him. It sails past his head. Nick hunches his shoulders for the crash, but the teasel spines catch in the lace curtain's tatting. The vase hangs there, tangled in the curtain, suspended above the Formica. "Who do we have, except for each other?" she cries.

Nick touches the flame to his cigarette.

On the slow sigh of his exhale Frances crosses the room to pick at the teasel spines. The lace is old, and she works the tatting free slowly, loosening the spines one by one. When she has freed the vase from the curtain, she retrieves a doily from the sideboard and sets the vase on it, at the littered table's center. "Leave the mess," she says. "I'll clean it up in the morning." She turns to climb the stairs, then leans her head against her brother's chest.

So this is how you do it, Nick thinks, how you keep them close: not with kindness but with pain, like a choke collar on a willful dog.

Over his sister's head, through the delicate tracings of the window's frost flowers, he watches the sun rising above the lumpy knobs. He stills his breath, the better to feel this triumph. He tenses, waiting, expectant. He feels only his wanting, flowing through his veins like the morning's first nicotine.

He rests an arm around her shoulders, stroking her hair. He takes her hand, kneading her small, smooth fingers with his thumb, until the teasel's splintered thorn works through his thumb's hardened callus, to pierce the tender flesh beneath.

AFTERWORD

I published this story in the mid-1980s, in the dark years after President Nixon's Secretary of Agriculture Earl Butz promulgated his "get big or get out" policies, which favored corporate farming and encouraged small farmers to go into debt to buy expensive farming equipment. Subsequent surpluses drove down commodity prices, bankrupting many small farmers. Farms were consolidated; farmers relocated to urban areas, leading to widespread economic and cultural dislocation and fueling the rural shift toward growing pot and dealing drugs as the only economically feasible means of remaining on the land. As a land of small farms, Appalachia was especially hard hit.

The tobacco farmer Nick Handley reappears in *Scissors, Paper, Rock,* my novel-in-stories about the scattered members of the Hardin family, reissued in 2016 with a foreword by Pam Houston and an author's afterword.

CHARLES LLOYD

Charles Lloyd is a retired classics professor at Marshall University who has published on ancient Greek "sexuality" and rural and urban attitudes. He coauthored the biography of a 1920s pop singer *Ruth Etting: America's Forgotten Sweetheart* (2010). His novel on ancient Greece, *The Walls of Sparta*, will be published in the near future.

Wonders

....

The twelve-year-old boy occupied the concrete step behind Mr. Benson's cabin on the Little Kanawha River. He was oblivious to the porch's clutter behind him: three minnow buckets of varying sizes, a pair of wading boots, a kerosene lantern, and a box piled high with jackets and tarpaulins—his father's fishing paraphernalia. He wore a white T-shirt with a hunting dog's head printed over his heart. His blue jeans were new for vacation, but they wouldn't ever shrink enough to wear without the four-inch cuffs, fastened in place by big safety pins that looked like shiny decorations. He had on his old red-top Keds, requisite shoes for the whole summer, including these two weeks of July. He bent his head down to look at Jake's brown face and black eyes and was stroking once again the solid sable of his back. His father's hunting dog, a blanket-back beagle, had his front legs on the step to be as close as possible to the boy. As he sat there, he kept thinking of the first night when Daddy brought Jake home. The boy had sat on the upside-down rowboat in the front yard with the new rabbit dog there beside him, petting him for two hours until the sun went down behind his back and it was time for Jake to try out his new house.

Click. His dad had captured Jason's preoccupation with Jake. The Argus C3 was a real camera, unlike the Kodak Brownie his mom had bought him at Haberhoff's Drugstore. It was more than a *click*, it was a *whirr*, as the camera's eye opened and shut. It happened so often Jason didn't bother to look up.

"That's a good one," his father smiled. "You about ready to check the trotline?" This duty was one of the few occasions when his father needed him for something. Jason's daddy was the most masculine man he had ever seen and entirely independent when it came to most things. Carrying stuff didn't count because everyone in the family did that when ordered, even seven-year-old Sam, Jason's brother. But he could feel that his father wanted him to learn certain things that were somehow important. Helping with the trotline was one of these duties, and it required of his slight build some strength and coordination to hold the boat by means of the trotline in the river's current while his father checked it for fish and rebaited each hook. Jason appreciated his father's cleverness about catching fish, how time-saving it was to lay a line across the river a few feet from the bottom, tied to willow branches on each side, bait it every day, then just go harvest fish. He knew his life was protected and very different from his father's. His dad lost his own father at eight, and Jason assumed that's what made his dad self-sufficient and sure in ways he didn't think he'd ever know.

"Okay. Gotta pee first." Jason worried that his parents and Sam had begun to notice how often he went to the outhouse. They didn't think it was the most pleasant place to be in July. The heat made it particularly smelly, but the tiny building fascinated Jason, smell and all. It was reachable only by way of the stile, another wonder in itself. The cabin had a fence around its entirety, but instead of a gate in the fence, someone who saw a different world from Jason's had built a staircase the fence's height with four steps on each side and a landing on top the size of two steps put together. Intrigued when he first saw it, he was told it was to keep the cows out of the yard. Jason thought that a gate would do that just as well, but maybe someone was afraid that someone else would leave the gate open. The stile was fun because from it you could see the length of the pasture on the left, and he always stopped to look as he went over. The outhouse was a two-seater, now with twice the odor. But it intrigued him to watch his stream fall the five or six feet into the dark fluid below, to hear the flies buzz as they relocated, and catch sight of the squirming maggots—he had had to ask what they were. But this morning, he didn't linger long.

He saw his dad when he reached the warriors. From the first summer they had come to the cabin, Jason had admired the trees that led from the cabin's front porch down to the river—six water maples and two poplars, in two rows of four on either side of the path to the riverbank. To him, they were the guards, the strong warriors that stood always in attendance, always in waiting, as the members of his family made their way to and from the river. They stood tall, their branches intertwined over his head, making a vault like the dark wood ceiling of a downtown church he had visited once. Often, as he walked by, he nodded his thanks to each of the watchers. His father waited while he turned around to back down the steep wooden steps cut into the fifteen-foot bank.

Jason took his seat at the boat's first bench and remembered how much trouble it had taken to fasten the boat to their Ford station wagon's top, get it off again, and march it through the warriors to the river. Instead of using the motor that had taken up half of the station wagon's storage area, his father began rowing downstream to the trotline visible from the landing's top stair. Even though his father was wearing a yellow cotton work shirt, Jason could still admire his arm muscles. He envied how they moved as if a mouse or a snake was crawling right underneath the skin. He didn't understand exactly what his father had done to have arms like that—though he did do construction work. He had taken them for granted until the night last year of the PTA fundraiser. His father and five other dads were asked to dress in women's clothing as a surprise comic break in a women's fashion show. His father wore a black cocktail dress that had no sleeves and was gleeful when he told Jason that a little boy on the first row had shouted, "He's got muscles!" when he came out on stage. Jason was surprised to feel an electric current flashing through his body to see his daddy like that.

Though he had never heard his father curse, he recognized by his dad's loud "shoot!" that he was somehow disgusted with what he found at the end of the twine link that held the first hook.

Surprised, Jason hesitated, but then asked, "What's the matter?"

"I knew I should've come out here last night to check this line. Look at this carp—we'd never eat it anyway, but it's sure as heck not any good now!" Jason looked at the carp, dead on the line for too long and turned a milky white. Jason knew that some people ate carp, but his dad had always said that they were too bony. Jason could not verify that as a fact, for he had never seen one filleted, but they were always strikingly large fish with big greenish-yellow scales and big mouths. As Jason held the trotline and maneuvered it across the boat's prow, he watched his father toss all the dead fish back on the top of the dark-green water.

As his father rowed back to the landing, he said to Jason, "Remember, you and Sam have to have your baths today before lunch."

"Aw, Daddy, I hate that. Can't we wait till tomorrow?" Jason saw from his father's face that, just like the dead fish, tomorrow would be too late.

As soon as they got back, the ordeal began by carrying the towels, soap, and bucket down to the river through the probably amused warriors who stood in all their glory without clothes. Jason worried that someone would come along the river, motor blasting loudly, as he and Sam sat naked on the boat's benches. After his dad had wet both the boys down, they had to lather up. Jason looked down at his white legs and the sparse hairs above his penis that weren't even the right color, nearly blond, while his head was dark brown. He hoped that would change soon and that somehow he would have muscles like his dad. His little brother's small, squarish body sat in front of him. Sam was intrigued by the unusual occasion of a boat bath. But Jason sat nervously as he lathered up, knowing for sure that some boat would suddenly round the river's bend and its occupants would stare and maybe laugh. All that happened was that his mom came to the top of the stairs. That was embarrassing enough, though she seemed proud of all of her men, two boys ivory with soap tended by a somehow patient father she saw rinsing off the soap with the green river water. In no way nonplussed at the same sight, Jake sat at her feet as dogs do at such times, no more engrossed to see his loved ones naked than if he spotted a black ant crossing in front of his foot. Jason toweled off and couldn't get back into his jeans fast enough.

After lunch he took a walk in the field beyond the stile. The pasture tilted to the left abruptly and rocks jutted out of the grass every so often where a glacier had set them down when it dwindled to nothing before people's memory. The slope down to the river forced the Holsteins to make paths through the luxuriant summer grass. He followed a path close to the river. Soon he stepped around a large rock to see four of the black-and-whites munching the grass as they did endlessly. Spikes of ironweed punched up through the grass. By September the ironweeds would show their antler racks four-feet high of small, intensely dark violet flowers. He made his way with care along the path because it was scattered with cow piles. Unlike the outhouse stink, cows' waste smelled almost sweet. Always intrigued by the piles' sizes and their various composures as they dried in the sun, he stopped to run a stick through a recent deposit on the path and measure how thick it was. He loved the consistency, so rich, it seemed, too good to be thrown on the ground. He noticed places off the path where grass and weeds grew more lush and higher than elsewhere and saw that other living things enjoyed this richness too.

The wind picked up a bit as he rose and discarded his stick, and he turned toward the river to watch the willows in the wind, their tiny slender leaves, sea green on one side and silver underneath, shimmering in the afternoon sun. As if trying to hide something from him that was not intended for him to see, the grass not far away moved furtively. It reminded him of a minnow in a creek he had watched once from above, cutting its path through the water effortlessly, without sound. The water moved out of its way so that it all seemed to be one thing in motion. That's how the grass moved aside as the black ribbon jetted through the grass toward the willows and the water beyond. Jason stood transfixed as if the sight of the black snake had studded him to the ground. He had only seen pictures of snakes before, and for an instant, he couldn't name what he saw, but wondered how the snake and the grass became one thing, the ground alive and moving before his eyes. He wanted to follow it, to see where it was going, to see it do something else as miraculous as this, to see its eyes. But he couldn't move for maybe a minute.

When Jason got back, he told his father of this sighting. As he talked of the snake's wondrous movement through the riverside's lush grass, Jason watched his father: how his eyes got big as Jason's must have done too, how his hands and eyes moved rapidly about—how his dad somehow became a part of this marvel without his even being there with him. But Jason didn't tell his dad that he had stood stuck in the ground like a glacial rock.

In the late afternoon, he and Sam were creating a small road for their cars, three inches wide, through an area of sparse grass in the front yard and planting the tops of grass that had gone to seed and calling them palm trees, which they did in fact resemble. A few minutes after Jason noticed that the sun had left their road, he caught sight of the deep-blue clouds of a summer thunderstorm beyond the pasture field. "Where you going?" Sam asked, but Jason had already run to the stile for a better view of the storm. In town, when storms came, he was immensely excited by the prospect of seeing the strong wind. He would ask his grandmother who lived in front if he could have a limb of a shrub or tree to hold in the wind. He knew all the signs of the coming wind: the increased flights of birds closer to the ground, the warm silence of the waiting, and the scary but beautiful roll of very low clouds, the same beautiful blue gray that meant the wind was less than a minute away. So it was this July day. He stood atop the stile for as long as he dared. He could hear the wind long before he could feel it blowing his clothes tight against his body, and then he saw the rain like a huge wall come rushing over the cow paths making its own sound, like bacon frying in a skillet only louder and deeper. He yelled to Sam, and they just made it to the front porch when the silver wall touched the warriors' right row and the porch roof at the same instant.

Sam went on inside. Though the storm's wind blew rain all over him, he stood with his back to the front wall of the house and became as always the watcher of the rain and the blow, the only one of his family. And as quickly as it had come, it all stopped. As he looked down river, he could see the sun piercing through openings in the clouds and making long blond legs that seemed to buoy the clouds up. The legs glided on the pasture and on the river water, unbothered by the substance they touched, able to stand on anything. As he watched the willows a good distance downriver, sparkling as the sun legs walked over them, an explosion of light made him jump. It came in a long streak, white hot, and he wasn't sure if he saw part of it go back where it came from or not. Then came thunder as devastating a detonation as he had ever heard. The glittering willow tree trembled all over, and as if carefully choreographed by the universe it was a tiny part of, it started ever so slowly slipping downward toward the bank and the water, two things in its flashy beauty it was sublimely unsuited to mingle with.

It floated down and then crashed silently half in the river and half on the bank. He mourned its downfall, its trunk as thick as a grown man, yet at the same time he had never seen such grace and beauty; the air resistance as the tree fell through it was like a gentle breeze, cool after the storm. And its fall could not be heard, as if it had never happened.

With the last of the clouds' passing, the sun returned with a triumphant humidity that made the day seem hotter than before. Jason and Sam were coming out of the back door when they saw the old blue Packard pull up next to the stile. By his auburn hair, all curly, Jason recognized first his cousin Lee, stepping out of the car and smiling from behind its door. The other door released long black hair that belonged to Lee's new wife, Sharon. Jason ran back in to tell his mom and dad about the unexpected visitors, not an unusual event, for his family often dropped in unannounced at friends' and relatives' homes after church or anytime they were out driving and those visited always returned the favor. Jason didn't know them very well and typically saw them only when his family visited his father's relatives along the Big Sandy River. But he remembered also that his dad kept a picture of Lee, taken with the Argus C3, in his wallet. In it Lee was standing on the bank of the Big Sandy, shirtless, tanned, his chest muscles gleaming in the sun. Lee was the new assistant football coach at Van Buren High School.

His father smiled big at the news and immediately stopped filleting the catfish they were to have for dinner. His mom hesitated as she was peeling potatoes and asked her husband, "Amos, do you have any more fish? We've got to ask them for dinner." His father nodded *yes* and hurried out to greet the newcomers. In a few moments the entire group reemerged from the outside into the small kitchen laughing about his father always calling Lee the simple one in the family. "But that's what Sarah always calls you, Amos!" Lee retorted, hoping to gain momentum by mentioning his aunt's gibing.

Jason followed the two men out onto the front porch past Sam who had ensnared Sharon in a game of pick-up sticks. They walked across the porch and on down toward the warriors and the river.

"Go tell your mother we're riding up to the dam and we'll be right back," his dad shouted back to Jason.

"Can I go too?" Jason clamored.

"Just hurry up!" his father conceded.

When he ran through the warriors, he could see his father's black hair and Lee's red as they steadied the boat awaiting his arrival. He almost fell backward off the steep steps as he hurried to get in the boat. His father was manning the motor, and Lee had taken the middle bench to sit near enough to talk to his father over the bawl of the outboard, a Johnson V-35. Before he could sit down squarely on the front bench, his dad was already shoving off from the steps with his arm.

Jason loved going down the river in this direction, past the pasture and around several severe twists to get to the dam where his dad took him to fish for bluegills and pumpkinseeds, with bobbers, of course—he had not yet learned how to fish for bass like his father with artificial bait and a fly rod. The river varied in width from point to point on the way, sometimes creek-like but more often wider in languid-looking pools of dark green, for it would have to rain harder and longer than the afternoon's thunderstorm to muddy it. Jason couldn't hear much of the conversation for the motor's roar, and Lee seemed duly impressed with the seclusion and river's quietness in the evening. He mused about how long it took to build the twenty-foot-high dam with its upper part wood and lower part concrete. The river Lee had spent his whole life near was considerably wider, and as Jason had traced on his West Virginia map and had seen many times in person, it made an impressive border between Kentucky and West Virginia. One of his earliest memories was of his father insisting against his little-boy fear that he stand about fifteen feet from shore to feel the current. Jason couldn't feel the bottom under his feet, but only the swift current between his legs and his father's strong hand in his. He had never understood how with just his one arm his father could hold him suspended in the air and rushing water. He wondered still.

On the ride back when they were about to enter one of the largest pools, Lee shouted for his father to slow down because he wanted to take a swim. Before Jason could wonder much about how that would happen, Lee had removed his shirt straight over his head and had kicked off his sockless loafers, and was pulling down his jeans. Then with nothing on at all he stood straight up on the middle bench before bending to dive in. Before this vision, Jason's eyes, mouth, and face were completely transfigured; his tightened muscles made his skin taut, and he could barely breathe. Lee was perfect as perhaps only his father was perfect, but Lee was younger. In the evening sun, when the shadows seemed to add a border of brilliance to things the sun touched and changed ordinary to magic, his red hair seemed like red flames atop his head. His musculature was amazingly proportional as if someone had measured every part to make sure it was right. His red-freckled arms and legs were strong and poised for movement. The small red flame above his genitals matched the red fire on his head in all ways except size. As that beautiful form doubled, swayed slightly, and then took flight into the dark green, Jason strived heavily to breathe again.

Lee was a strong swimmer and submerged himself several times only to reappear in different places. Jason was jolted out of this dream world abruptly when he heard his father calling toward the bank, "Hey, Missy, come see what Lee's got to show you!" Jason scanned the bank, looking straight into the sun, unable to see any girl or woman there, and he was about to point that out when he caught his dad's face, the flicker in his eyes and the laugh that was forming. Lee's head shot toward the bank also, only to turn around to meet his uncle's amused eyes. Jason was sure Lee uttered a curse word at his father but couldn't tell what it was over the motor's sputtering.

Lee swam up next to the boat and took hold of its rim, and as the motor pulled him along on his back, his body cleaved the water like the boat's blunted front, and spray shot up around his face. The water rushed over the front of him, and his penis and testicles bobbed in the flow like some exotic, bulbous fruit. Again, Jason was transfixed and was exceedingly embarrassed to look and wanted to turn away to stop the redness he could feel suffusing the skin of his face and neck. But he stared helplessly, enraptured as he had never been before in his life. The milky white of Lee's skin and the shadowy greenness of the water rushing over him made him think of one of his favorite pictures in his grandmother's old art book: a male body like Lee's in its perfection barely making it away from the mouth of an enormous shark and his friends reaching for the nude body to pull it into the boat's safety. This reverie only lasted a few seconds, broken by Lee's pushing out into the river away from the boat and his father gunning the outboard motor as if to strand him there. Lee understood immediately what his uncle was doing and with amazing strength soon caught up to the boat and again stabilized himself at its side.

Jason wanted to stay this close to Lee's kind of beauty for as long as he possibly could. Lee, with superhuman strength, it seemed to Jason, pulled himself up on the bench again in one magnificent movement. Jason heard himself gasp audibly. When the boat stopped pitching, Lee stood up on the bench facing his father, and somewhat winded, laughed at his accomplishments. Jason took in the exquisite form of his upper back and buttocks and strong lower legs as water dripped off of him as if he had just been borne suddenly, flawless as he was, out of the river's own flawless green. With this masculine vision before him, Jason knew finally what he was made for.

The naked man emblazoned by the evening sun stood erect and tall between father and son. The moment seemed joyously as if it would not end. Jason could look all he wanted and he did. Jason's face registered only wonderment and a new kind of desire. Then his eyes caught that same wonderment and desire on his own father's face. As before the black snake and the lightning, Jason froze.

JEFF MANN

Jeff Mann has published three poetry chapbooks, five full-length books of poetry, two collections of personal essays, a volume of memoir and poetry, three novellas, six novels, and three collections of short fiction. The winner of two Lambda Literary Awards and four National Leather Association International writing awards, he teaches creative writing at Virginia Tech. His website is www.jeffmannauthor.com.

Not for Long

....

Summer has left before you. A few weeks of drought, a few cold nights, and between one lovemaking and the next the heat has receded, the leaves have started to brown. This morning I notice these deaths as I drive to work. And as I study the mountains, I ask myself why my love for the land—the comfortable earth that outlives and receives us—can be so diffuse, so serene, while my love for men—ephemera of body hair, beard stubble, biceps, and nipple—must be so sharp and maddening.

All about me autumn has arrived: purple tidal pools of ironweed, goldenrod's funeral flowers, the frowsy road-edge foxtail grass. By the New River, golden leaves are congregating along the limbs of sycamore and box elder. Signs of age, like this early silver on my temples. The sunflowers edging garden plots seem exhausted, bending their weary necks to earth. I recognize despair. I recognize resignation before the guillotine.

For adulterers, every touch is furtive, hasty. If only I'd met you first. A few afternoon rendezvous stippled across one summer is what our timing has allowed. And now all the green we shared degenerates. The rain's brief pointillism blurs my windshield, medians of redtop grass rush by. Stratus clouds collect, inside and out.

In the office, I check my voicemail. Nothing. For a week, you have not called. Any day now you and your lover, diplomas in hand, will nail down jobs, load up a U-Haul, and drive off, heading for God knows which city and state. Just when I am convinced that you have finally bolted, that even with you, old patterns and new cowards assert themselves, you appear, grinning reprieve in my office doorway.

My office-mate, teaching southern literature this semester, bends over *A Streetcar Named Desire*. I tap on the office next door, which belongs to my friendly colleague Ethel. "May I borrow your office while you teach?" I ask.

"I have a confused and upset student, and we really need some privacy." She smiles, nods, and heads off to class. I lead you in, turn off the lights, lock the door.

"Romeo and Juliet, Tristan and Isolde, Edward and Gaveston, Jeff and Thomas," I joke, pulling you to me. On this campus there are, for us, no other safe square feet. Any open touch of ours might heap us with scorn, real and metaphoric stones, the swing of pipes, steel edges that would end your beauty in an instant. All summer I have scrabbled together these rare and risky borrowed spaces, these hasty privacies. Outlawed fusions in secret niches, the double stigma of gay adultery. Only here do our bodies exist, our kisses petal into possibility.

Seconds after the lock clicks, I have your T-shirt tugged up around your neck, your jeans jerked down about your knees. My fingers dig into the hard curves of your biceps. My face nuzzles your chest hair, the cleavage-cloud of fur still moist from the gym-shower. I clutch you close as Antaeus did the earth.

Our moustaches mash together, tongues stretched and wrestling to their limits, and still we graze only the shallows, we taste only the surface of each other's darkness and depth. "Priapus," you mutter. "Mephistopheles," I whisper, between mouthfuls of musk and mercy. Soon you will be leaving the room, the town, the state, and I am ravenous in the face of famine, all my frame shaking as you unbutton my pure white professorial dress shirt and touch my chest with what appears to be the silent and studious wonder every inch of you evokes in me. We never know what is mutual, what myths we embody, what myths our lovers stroke.

I want to beg, "Stay, stay!" but instead stifle speech with your cock, with your nipples, with the furry mounds of muscle over your heart. I take as much of your body into mine as I can.

At last we pull back before release. You'll have no chance for another shower before you meet your husband, and he's grown suspicious, having smelt extramarital musk on you before. Seconds after we've buttoned and zipped up, the backwoods janitor, without a knock of warning, unlocks the door and ruckuses in to empty the trash.

I am teaching freshman composition three doors down the hall in half an hour, and you have to head home. In the hallway, just before we part, you say casually, "Oh, I have something you want." Tugging open your backpack, you hand me a package. A quick visit to the men's room to wash my scent from your moustache, a blithe wave at the end of the hall, and then you are gone, dissolving around the corner into memory.

All that denseness of muscle, that softness and ripeness of pubic hair against my cheek, the spill of preseminal sap in my palm like liquid moonstone. One second there, and now suddenly only images stored inside some wrinkle of my brain, the neurons' weak chemical hold on history. How many trysts have we left, I wonder, how many meetings more and more difficult to arrange? When we make love one final time, will we know that touch must be the last?

On my fingers, in my beard, the scent of you still lingers, my lips still sting with stubble-burn. Summoning my usual composed facade, I return to my office, where my office-mate continues to reread *Streetcar*. I borrow the paperback for a moment, and on a whim read the epigraph out loud, my favorite Hart Crane stanza:

> And so it was I entered the broken world
> To trace the visionary company of love, its voice
> An instant in the wind (I know not whither hurled)
> But not for long to hold each desperate choice.

I return the book, then silently behind his back I open the box you left. Amidst gift paper, white jockey shorts. I touch them. Still moist with workout sweat. A few stray hairs. I press the fabric to my face.

It is time for my freshman composition class. While I am teaching, defeated leaves, dry with drought, drop outside my classroom window. As I discuss the fine points of comma splices, the lurking dangers of mixed metaphors, I lift my left hand to my face, ostensibly to smooth my beard, and breathe you in, the vestige of your musk.

Not long after the seed-tops of redtop grass comes first frost. You can stay no more than summer could. Back in my desk drawer, from your jockey shorts the sweat evaporates. From my fingers, your aroma fades. *Collect what relics you can,* derides autumn. *You retain nothing.*

Training the Enemy

....

Well, Appalachia, you've done it.
You've made a man of me. I'm no longer that
shy, bespectacled boy who aroused contempt
in the sternest of you, the boy who lived for
Tolkien's Middle Earth and Mary Renault's Greece,
The X-Men, *The Avengers*, *Bonanza*, and other
alternatives more appealing and heroic than
Hinton, West Virginia. Oh, I was timid, I was
polite, the sort of little gentleman my mother
wanted me to be, fit for dinner parties or idle
chat in candlelit antebellum drawing rooms.
Elderly ladies doted on me; I flattered their
twinkling arabesque brooches, their rose bushes'
hot pink. Not effeminate really, just unsure,
awkward, amorphous, sexless, another pudgy
adolescent who learned early he was no good,
nothing special at sports, and so pumped out
A's for want of more manly achievements.

Your mockery, Appalachia, made me
change. One fist upside my mouth made me
cut off high school's long hippie hair, wear
lumberjack boots and leather jackets, lift
weights. My hometown would not know me
now, my shaved head and silvered beard, furry
hard pecs, cowboy hats, tattoos, boots, rage.
Watch me shoot the redneck shit as well

as any local, puffing stogies and sipping bourbon
straight. What I read's martial, new translations
of *The Iliad*, *Beowulf*, *The Saga of the Volsungs*.
What I collect's dirks, scimitars, swords.
How's that for manly? Now do you approve?
Hell, nothing's changed except how much I hate.
Yesterday a slim queer kid told me how
half his dorm floor turned on him, how he had
to move out or bleed. America, Appalachia, my sweet
small mountain towns, I'm native here, I'm going
nowhere. It's a damn fool who makes a youth suffer,
makes a child feel wrong, then teaches that new-
honed foe how to grow tough, how to grow strong.

Yellow-Eye Beans

....

I sort them as I was taught
(is this the way the Norns
allot destinies?) picking out
gravel, bits of dirt,
the shriveled, discolored ones
not fit to eat, fated for
the trash. Sort, rinse, soak
overnight, season with
onion, hog jowl, bacon grease.
Some more objective
observer might see in
my kitchen gestures—sorting
these yellow-eye beans, or
stringing half runners, or
rolling out pie crust or biscuits—
my father's, and, behind those,
his mother's, yours. Hillfolk
head for beans and cornbread
when the world turns surly—
pinto, yellow-eye, October.
These were your favorite.
Simmering them, I remember you.

Nanny, what would you think
of me now, twenty years after
your death, with my bushy
grizzly-bear beard, my myriad

tattoos, my lust for chest hair,
the man I live with? My guess
would be, after a short lecture
on the Bible, a book I never
much cared about to begin with,
you'd settle down to table
with us, admiring how
handsome this home is
John's made for me. I've
learned a lot in twenty years,
and at last it would be my turn
to cook for you. I promise
you'd be proud
of how well the beans
and cornbread came out
(and if you like this meal,
y'ought to taste
my buttermilk biscuits). But
before we ate, I'd invite
you to say what grace
you wanted in this queer
and pagan home, and so you
would, words brief and deep,
Pass the chowchow
following closely on *Amen*.

The Gay Redneck Devours Draper Mercantile

He wakes late, aching for the throb and pound
of a man inside him. Paul Bunyan, perhaps,
striding the snowy cover of the latest Duluth
Trading Company catalog, smiling giant
with a full brown beard, chest bulging
beneath a forester's flannel shirt, yule tree
hoisted over one huge shoulder.

Hungry, the drive up over Draper Mountain,
past soft siennas of foxtail grass, past breezy
Blow Job Knob where the furtive marrieds
hope and skulk, too horned-up to savor
sprawling vistas of the Alleghenies
and the Blue Ridge. His rusty pickup's blaring
Jason Aldean's new CD of redneck
rock, and what a liner cover, what
a plump and pretty set of lips, the ways

they might be used. Down to Draper, set
among its Valley pastures, where welcome
outside money has saved the Mercantile.
In he lopes, our ridge-runner rump-ranger,
in rural manhood's signifiers: camo pants,
Everlast sweatshirt, Western duster,
cowboy boots, the gray felt hat
bought at a rainy Civil War battle
reenactment, cavalier touch

he likes to think Jeb Stuart would
have worn. Southern small talk with ladies
behind the counter, though the hot lean cook
he's so often admired is nowhere to be seen.

Grilled pimiento cheese, that lunchtime treat
his mother used to make, followed by
blueberry pie and a batch of barbeque
to go. Modal and melancholy, just
the way a weary mountain romantic likes it,
the banjo and the bluegrass. He chews slowly,

trying to savor all—cheese, mayonnaise,
the rich and peppery taste of childhood,
the memoried crust of homemade country sweets
before love fled or bled or was proven
insufficient. What he tries to forget—
how friends and family would feel about how
deeply he longs for a bigger, stronger man
to master him. What he tries to believe,
humming through rapt mouthfuls of Dixie's
caloric comforts—*here in the hills*
I still belong. Here, I'm safe. Here, I'm home.
Here, one day, may all I am be welcome.

Three Crosses

....

(for Cynthia Burack)

Isn't the ironweed enough?
And the hemlock needles edged with frost,
as if a castle's crenellations were carved from crystal?

To remind us of God's glory,
he said, and squandered a fortune on crosses,
trios blue and gold, making calvary common as the next pasture,

the next interstate curve.
Isn't the Storm Moon enough, white pine boughs
shaking off snow? Crocus resurrection, purple and gold?

——

This is what you do,
with your fat book of black and gold,
your love of mirrors, your stained-glass abattoirs.

He sagged on that prairie
fence for hours. She ran away from home.
His body was found in a toilet. She hanged herself in the barn.

This is what you do,
your prayers muttered in the voter's booth,
your certainty that a soiled world is soon due to end with you.

——

Evil sees evil
everywhere. And so the streams run
orange, mountaintops peel off like scabs, red spruce needles

dissolve beneath sulfuric drizzle.
Evil only loves its own reflection, in broken
glass, in slurry puddles. Evil only loves what is eternal.

———

What I want's a savior
in my sheets, brief as that bliss might be.
Brown eyes, brown goatee, thunderheads of body hair.

Some scruffy Christ
roped down, ball gagged and melodic, eager as any sacrifice
to be eaten. What I want's a mountain landscape without a wound.

What I want's the skill
to break the jaw of vicious piety, the strength
to rescue what I love. What I want's a chainsaw on Easter Sunday,

and a heap of broken crosses
for the Beltane bonfire. My new world's the ring-dance,
the blaze, wine scented with woodruff, benediction of maple leaves.

Homecoming

....

Today, mid-November, my lover, my sister, and I,
we're carrying box after box of Ball jars to the basement,
riches my father has grown and canned. Lime pickles,
spaghetti sauce, green beans, tomatoes, strawberry jam.

Hinton, West Virginia, is much the same, that Appalachia
my teenaged years so wanted to escape. There's a storefront
preacher shouting about perversity, a bookish boy with a split lip.
There's a gang outside a Madam's Creek farmhouse shouting
"Come out here, you queers. We'll change you."

Now I know only five hours away, amidst DC traffic,
crowded sidewalks, men are holding hands along Seventeenth Street,
buying gay novels in Lambda Rising, sipping Scotch
and flirting in the leather bars. But I want to be here,

in West Virginia,
where my ancestors worked their farms, where, today,
we form this assembly line from kitchen to basement.
John hands me a box of bread and butter pickles,
I lug it down the cellar stairs. There, amidst cobwebs,

Amy's lining up the jars, greens and reds,
with their masking-tape dates, joining other summers
packed away. I want to be here,
where first ice collects along the creeks,

where the mountains' fur turns pewter gray,
and my father mulches quiescent gardens with fallen leaves.

Early evening's hard rain, hill-coves filling with mist.
After pinto beans, turnip greens, and cornbread,
John's drowsing on the couch, I'm finger-picking
a little guitar by the fire. There on the coffee table,
gifts Amy's left for us: a jar of spaghetti sauce, a jar of jam.
There on the mantelpiece, my mother's urn.

The boy who fled Hinton twenty-five years ago,
he's here too, the boy who dreamed
of packed disco bars, summers on Fire Island,
fascinating city men, the boy who did not yet know
what family meant. His hair is thick and black,
his beard is sparse, still dark. He shakes his head,
amazed that I've come back willingly, even for
a weekend. An ember flares up, fingernails of freezing
rain tick the windows. The boy, bemused, studies
the lines on my brow, shyly strokes the silver in my beard.

MESHA MAREN

Mesha Maren's debut novel *Sugar Run* was published by Algonquin Books in January 2019. Her short stories and essays have appeared in *Tin House, Oxford American, Hobart,* the *Barcelona Review, Forty Stories: New Writing from Harper Perennial,* and other literary journals. She was chosen by Lee Smith as winner of the 2015 Thomas Wolfe Fiction Prize and is the recipient of a 2014 Elizabeth George Foundation grant, a Jean Ritchie Fellowship from Lincoln Memorial University, and residency fellowships from the MacDowell Colony and the Ucross Foundation. She currently teaches fiction at the MFA program at West Virginia Wesleyan College and serves as a National Endowment for the Arts writer-in-residence at the Beckley Federal Correctional Institution.

Among

....

Among \ə-ˈməŋg\ *preposition*—**a:** in the presence or company of < *Hail Mary full of grace, blessed art thou among women.* I grip the sleeve of Lindsay's sweatshirt so tight my knuckles turn white. *What are you mumbling?* she says and I shake my head. Even if I had continued to believe in her, I know Mary would not intercede on my behalf now. Lindsay offers me her arms but I turn away and walk up the steps onto the Greyhound bus. From my seat I can see her standing just where I left her, waving wildly. She looks ridiculous, I think. Sometimes I hate my girlfriend. I wish she would hate me too, but she just stands there waving like a mom sending her kid off to school. She won't even be angry that I didn't kiss her goodbye. And if she is, soon she will get over it. Her gray sweatshirt is puckered up tight around her face and her little white cheeks are turning pink from the cold > **b:** in shares to each of < My mom always told me the rich are stingy. *It's how they keep the wealth among themselves, they know how to hold on.* For the first six months that Lindsay and I dated I did not even know she owned a car. She was always asking and I was always giving her rides. Me, in my '88 Cutlass with old license plates welded over the rust holes. The night I saw the sleek European machine waiting for her in the basement garage, I felt hollowed out, breathless with confusion. *I don't like to drive it too much,* she explained. And now she needs me to tell them. To tell my people about her. *Three years,* she says, *we've been dating for three years.* As if that amount is some sort of tipping point. She has lain waiting in my basement all those years like some slick black car and now I am supposed to pull her out. I am supposed to *explain* and *pave the way* so that she can see where it is I come from. She wants to meet them face to face > **c:** in or through the midst of: surrounded by < In the third grade I asked

Tina Weinshotzer why she hated me. *Catholic*, she said, pointing out
the school bus window to the five-foot statue of the Virgin Mary that
my mom had roped to the roof of our house among the weathervanes
and cable antennas. When I asked her what the difference was she told
me *you all pray to Mary but we talk to Jesus face to face* > **d:** through the
joint action of < The Greyhound driver leans out the door of the bus
and yells across the parking lot at a group of women in puffy jackets and
tight jeans, laughing and gossiping beside brightly painted low riders.
When they speak their breath comes out in frosty vaporous clouds that
hang among their faces. What Lindsay doesn't understand is that in my
town the women will kill you slowly with words and with lack of words.
Deprivation mostly, no more standing in the aisle of the Super K and
trading gossip anymore, you are the gossip, no more getting tipsy and
singing old love songs together after the kids are in bed and the men are
who-the-hell-knows-where. If you tell them something like *that*, you're
on your own. They already think I'm a stranger. Ever since I moved
to Chicago they tell me my accent has changed and my words sound
funny > **e:** in the presence or company of < The bus jerks and jumps
and rolls out of the parking lot. I twist the strap of my backpack in my
hands and stare up at the rooftops, neon signs and pillars of brightly lit
windows. I asked my mom once about what Tina Weinshotzer said and
my mom just smiled. She pulled me close and led me outside into the
purpling evening air and pointed up to Mary statue, spot lit above our
heads. *Hail Mary, full of grace*, she said, squeezing my hand excitedly,
blessed art thou among women and blessed is the fruit of thy womb, Jesus >

KELLY MCQUAIN

Kelly McQuain grew up surrounded by the mountains of West Virginia's Monongahela National Forest. His poetry collection *Velvet Rodeo* won the Bloom Prize, and his writing has also been featured in such anthologies as *The Queer South, Drawn to Marvel: Poems from the Comic Books, Best American Erotica,* and *Men on Men.* He has twice received fellowships from the Pennsylvania Council on the Arts and has been a Lambda Literary Fellow as well as a Tennessee Williams Scholar at the Sewanee Writers' Conference. As an artist, his series of poet portraits can be found in *Fjords Review* and his comix-based critical essays online at *Cleaver Magazine.*

Scrape the Velvet from Your Antlers

....

As you take the hill, the hill takes you—
raking you and your siblings into
a grassy sway of beetles and spiders moving,
and the day's hot ricochet of blue bottle flies
and bees gone crazy in their looping.
Your brother and sister run to catch the horizon.
You wade slowly through the lashing,
alive with combustion, eager for bursting.
This hill, once a forest, has long been cut low,
untilled, rock-strewn, stubbled
with stubborn flowers. Soapwort,
Queen Anne's lace, whorled loosestrife
seeded scattershot, while—downhill—

laundry bows a slender line and inside a house
men tune fiddles, a banjo strums—
melody in the making. But you have no time
for the old-timiness of old men, won't be quaintly
clothespinned. You are joe-pye weed and yarrow root,
resolute with purpose, pinioned for sky.
Why then is your skin nothing but cockleburs?
Who fiddled with you—rewired *deference*
into *difference*? What if you never meet
the person you are meant to be? The future
is a cocked gun—pretty, but peacock mean—

and you are devil's paintbrush,
a blister of orange-red and velvet need.
You've yet to steady into friends
who will ride life's curves with you,
yet to meet men come to wreck you.
There is only the splintered heart of now:
this house, this hill—a horizon spurned
as you cast your gaze down-road, past trailers,
to a line of pines
gloating their evergreen promise of shade.
What kneels to drink in that dark?
What hooved thing—some player
of panpipes moving? A preacher
might call this moment choosing.
Only nine

and already you've packed up your belonging
—every out-of-bound path
boyhood's sweet undoing.
This hill beneath your feet is cracked,
as aching as an insect's rasp. When a tune
ignites from the house you feel its lull,
its *not-quite-yet*. Imagine a table
where comfort food lies spread.
But what if you'd rather be the hunger
than a child spoon-fed?

A lick of wind on nape of neck,
a secret transmission that coils and threads
as grasshoppers leap away like longing.
Someday soon you'll understand

how music marks a mating move,
how forewing against notched leg strums
the same tune teenage boys knead
into the pockets of fraying jeans
as they bum for smokes and try their luck
among trucks purring in parking lots.
Their plea? *Unravel me,*
snap me free of all ties. Show me answers
apart from lies. But where to learn
of this authentic self?
Not on this hill, not in that house.
Something calls you somewhere else.

Brave

....

From rough burlap we cut loincloths, fringed the ends,
strung cheap plastic beads into wampum belts,
sucking our thumbs when our needles drew blood
—done not so much for merit badges as for
the Kool-Aid crazed shenanigans got up to that day
in our frazzled den mother's cluttered house:
ersatz Indian finery pulled over blue uniforms
as we danced and whooped and bounced like hooligans
from La-Z-Boy recliner to afghan-covered couch.
A turkey feather fell from my paper headband
on the long walk home through kickable leaves.
Part of a pack, but where was my true tribe?
Those Cubs in their happy savagery? Boys whose hands
I sometimes longed to hold, hard like a toy tomahawk.
I needed stealth, a new way to hide in the world:
patient as stone, elusive as water. I wanted to become
a stranger to myself, someone stronger in different skin.
I knew my bedroom slippers were not Indian moccasins
that night as I stood naked before my closet mirror—
lipstick war paint striping my cheeks, a welcome scratch
of burlap on my hairless balls (it was always
so *involved* being me). No uniform. No fear. No one to see.
I was alone and for once loving my aloneness. My body
an arrow shooting somewhere far off, its bow and quiver
triggered in this act of making the invisible visible at last.

Fringe on my loincloth tickled my thighs and knees
as I wound my wampum belt around my waist
and wondered what my new Indian name should be:
Feathered Dream-Catcher? (we had one in the kitchen)
Or *He Who Sees Shapes in the Random Patternicity of Things?*
But I was only a kid too quiet in his room;
at the sound of someone's feet on the stairs, I hid.
A turn of the doorknob and my father leaned in to ask
what the hell was I doing crawling under the bed?
He laughed as I rose, my hands hiding my bare chest,
my pale skin reddening as I stammered to explain.
I couldn't explain. What was I in his eyes? A silly boy,
his little wild thing. So I laughed, too—what else could I do
as I stood before him revealed:

being scared

being brave.

Vampirella

....

It wasn't her boobs that appealed to this gay fellow
or the fact that she wore a red bikini thong.
She was a superhero with fangs, my gal Vampirella

—no tangled-up Rapunzel, no ashen Cinderella.
An ass-kicker in knee boots ready to get it on
with any handsome, hot-blooded earthly fellow.

I fell under her spell too, I have to tell you,
though her curves didn't appeal to my ten-year-old dong.
Still I was bewitched and bedeviled by Vampirella

and her pulp-mag adventures, their pages long yellowed
along with old comics left in boxes too long.
In back of the Book Mart, past the fat owner fella,

is where I found her, a slick cover by Frazetta
peeking out past *Creepy* and *Eerie*, one shelf-rung
below forbidden *Playboy*: my wild bitch, *Vampirella!*

She fought werewolves, demons, witches, night terrors;
she seduced handsome men with her succubus song.
Though I followed her stories, I never could tell

a soul that I wanted what every straight fellow shouldn't:
to be a hot vampire chick and super strong—
my high-heeled, raven-haired, bikini-clad Vampirella.

At ten, I was a good kid, no holy terror,
though I suspect my parents feared I was turning out wrong.
Maybe that's why they let their queer little fellow

spend his allowance on soft-core mags that might quell
a desire already starting to steer him along.
Blame me. Don't you dare blame double-D Vampirella.

Monkey Orchid

....

Orchis simia

Found throughout southern Europe as well as the Mediterranean, Orchis simia, the Monkey Orchid, is remarkable at under twenty-four inches for its speckled clusters of purple-pink blooms. Each flower is simian-shaped and complete with what can best be described as an engorged monkey "phallus"— thus necessitating this orchid be kept far from the bouquets of impressionable young ladies of genteel upbringing.

> —Lord Basil Attenborough, *A Field Guide to the Flowers and Grasses of Western Europe*, London, 1899

Trust me.

> —Circuit party. New York City, 1999

Tonight I'll wear my joy
    erect, conspicuous and speckled,
        opening a turnstile
to a tumble of tribal brothers
    clanging cymbals, clinging arms,
while what dazzles
           dangles
                for all to see—
so let's dance!
    Shoulder the weight
           of our bodies' burdens,
    fling our funny crap,   laughing

as a mirror ball sequins our skin:
        We are locked in a roving sea
of sweaty chests and clamoring hands

     each of us waving our Day-Glo glans
                    ornamentally, raving
   to a techno-beat.   You, me?
We blend into one   ecstasy,
    an orgy of blossoms,
             of bottoms and tops
living as if we will always be
     a party to the circuit party
           —a parable of pleasure
almost parody.

       Tonight   I am scared
and electrified by everything I could become:
    pure monkey desire,
           my cock a loaded gun
    blossoming on this shared stamen
of desire
     —don't think of disease—

We are   a monkey orchid
seeking release
                         from mostly awkward
        daytime moments
                         that drive us half-insane,
surrounded now by similar selves,
        drugs dreaming in our veins.

        Tonight   I am sacred:
watch me unfold:
        a wallflower at the orgy growing bold.
Are these spots on our skin
        the blotchy purple-pink of sexual flush?
Amyl nitrate on our breath,
                 a popper-bottle head rush.
        Each lick
                is like a whisper
                              not quite confessional
as our bold stamens keep unloading
        in this strobe-light processional
of desire aping love,
        of young men exploding,   all the while

our secret saner selves
            haunted, wondering:

                        Will we survive
this ravenous age of plague
            when blood wants to become
                              one river running
            through many bodies?
      Oh, we playful, foolish monkeys.
Oh, this petal cage of desire and death.
      Kiss me quick—first you, then you—
as I bare my teeth
            and keep barreling through.

Alien Boy

....

In San Miguel, two iced tequilas in, my friend
tells me her infant brother died only days after birth.

The announcements were mailed out
despite complications, *It's a boy* trumping fear,

as if hope could ward off an incubator stay
or the vast array of tubes and devices all working

to manage an ailing boy's
breath and blood. My friend's parents rarely spoke

of her brother. Years later, she searched
old medical records to find out what happened.

She sketches me a worry of days:
endless tests proctored, sad looks from nurses,

hushed words of doctors who finally explained
to her parents that among their boy's many problems,

a genital deformity: micropenis.
Should he live, a choice: flood him with hormones

and raise him a girl, or . . . ?
Or let nature take him as nature nearly had. Should he live?

Their choice? The dice? A nudge?
My friend couldn't say for sure. Who among us could

tell which fear finally exhausts us?
My friend's brother starved from a tube taken out

or perhaps his lungs failed first. Exactitude
is no more recorded than our parents' private words,

choices that might savage an alien boy's
flesh and blood. Any wonder the marriage failed?

Each time a cell divides is a new chance
for the world to go wrong. I'm lucky not to have had to draw

such large lines between loves.
The sun is going down in our Mexican town.

Our drinks are a watery, diluted gold.
I reach to take my friend's hand, think better, and lift my glass instead.

Mercy

....

The Hells Angel claimed to have died
                              in Death Valley, aptly enough,
when his motorcycle slid out from under him:
          loose rocks on hot highway asphalt,
                    a sudden swerve and a sideways skid
that nearly undid him.
                              Lying then
                                        in the hot desert sun
where shadow birds would soon come
          to make new feathers from the pluck and pull
of his meat.   Instead:
                              a miracle of paramedics
to stanch his blood, to brace his neck
          —red sirens screaming for miles—
and a swelling in his head.   A heart that flatlined
for six minutes on an operating table
                              —but man,
what that Hells Angel learned in that eternity of time
—and now
                    here to share it with our high-school class,
thanks to a hippie English teacher and a visitor's pass,
the Good News there was a Heaven
                              even for Hells Angels.

I listened to him tell us

    in his beer-breath-and-cigarette way

       how we lived in a universe

            of infinite grief and loss

      —and grace—

where earthly ignorance equaled fear,

           where fear

equaled hate. But after death, that transitive equation

    no longer held sway.   Imagine:

no lost souls, no loners anywhere

    —only a place   outside of time,

      where those who did wrong

realized the wrong they had done

          and were absolved,

released from the damnation

           I'd always been taught

—locked in that blast furnace of church and youth—

    was fitting retribution

for all the evil

    mankind had done   or would ever do.

My heart fumbled over itself,

        a football I couldn't catch.

      A force of grace freed from wrath?

I couldn't fathom it, had to ask: *"Even Hitler?"*
"Even Hitler,"
                    smiled our leather-jacketed guest lecturer
through a stubbly face still scarred by stitches.
At fifteen,
          I had a hundred Hitlers
                                        sinning inside me
          and needed angels with fiery swords
                                        to do my dividing.

Tonight, as I write this,
                    Reverend Fred Phelps lies on his deathbed,
the Westboro Baptist preacher
          who dared mock a boy   crucified
and left for dead.
                    Can you picture Matthew Shephard
          tied to that cold Wyoming fence?
          I'm sure Phelps raised his sign,
                    GOD HATES FAGS,
far more over the years
                    than I raised SILENCE = DEATH.
The plague stole friends
          —Charles, Peter, Harvey—
left me body-shaped outlines
                    chalked on asphalt at die-ins.

Forgiveness is a virtue, yes
                    —but it's a shiv that comes in slant.
Reverend Phelps, as he dies, had better pray
     hell's angels show him grace.   I can't.

Ritual

....

My mother and I find a bat
reeling above our heads the evening we arrive
    with light bulbs
to screw into the ceiling sockets of the half-
    finished home
my father began building before he died:
    the bat startled
by our flung door and blithe conversation,
    my mother and I frozen
among dusty paint rollers and push brooms,
    equally shaken
at the veering path of such sudden
    unexpected flight—like a black scarf
let loose in a stiff, chill wind.
    Hearts calming,
we follow the bat. We formulate a plan:
    a plastic bowl and a small piece
of cardboard to use as a makeshift lid
    so I can trap the tiny body
when, exhausted, it finally alights
    against the ceiling
in the recess of another lightless
    light. A stepladder,
a careful climb. The bat no longer nimble
    but trembling

and looking not so terrible: dustbin fur;
    a faint twitch
among his folded wings' leathery creases—
    strange architecture
I bury beneath my white plastic bowl.
    I slip in
my cardboard lid, press it tight,
    carry the bones and skin
I could break so easily apart
    to the open door my mother holds
and release him. Our bat disappears
    into a sky embroidered
with the first faint stitches
    of the coming night.
My bag's already packed
    and in the car; my mother
will have to finish building
    this house herself.
In these ways, we rescue ourselves.

RAHUL MEHTA

A West Virginia native, Rahul Mehta is the author of a novel, *No Other World* (2017), and a short story collection, *Quarantine* (2011), which won a Lambda Literary Award and the Asian American Literary Award in fiction. He teaches creative writing at the University of the Arts in Philadelphia.

A Better Life

....

When, by the end of the summer of 1990, the summer they graduated from high school, Sylvie had not only *not* lost the ten pounds the modeling agency had wanted her to lose, but she had, instead, *gained* fifteen pounds, she was told she shouldn't bother coming to New York, the agency couldn't represent her, they couldn't find her work. She was told this over the phone by a woman she had met in New York in the spring, an "ugly" woman, Sylvie now said, whom no one could ever find pretty, so who was she to judge?

Sanj saw Sylvie that Sunday night, two nights after she'd received the news, and just three days before he himself was leaving for the University of Southern California—as far from West Virginia as he could manage. Sanj reminded Sylvie that the local community college had rolling, open admission.

"*Community* college," she said snidely.

"You can transfer somewhere better next year."

"I'm not going to college."

"Then lose the weight," Sanj said. "I don't understand why you didn't lose it in the first place. Ten pounds. That's nothing."

"It's easier for boys," she said.

They were in the wood-paneled rec room at Sylvie's, watching MTV's *120 Minutes*: two full hours devoted to alternative music videos—Cocteau Twins, The Cure, Siouxsie and the Banshees—musicians never played on the pop-rock station in their small town.

Sylvie's twin brother, Chris, had wandered through twice already, on his way to and from the kitchen. He was a football player. He was on the starting lineup, even though he wasn't very good. Chris wasn't very good at anything. His grades were appalling, one year so low he was disqualified from sports. He wasn't even particularly good-looking. But for some reason Sanj had secretly fallen for him. Maybe it was the way he padded around the house, always in sweatpants, always shirtless, regardless of the temperature outside, his muscles taut and toned. Maybe it was his curly hair, ringlets framing his face, and the rattail he grew in the back, unfashionable even then. To Sanj, part of what was seductive about Chris was the thought that this was the best time of his life. It wouldn't get any better. He wouldn't get better looking. He wasn't skilled enough to go further in football. He wasn't going to college. This was it for him. For Sanj, being around someone who was living the best years of his life, while Sanj was living perhaps the worst of his, was seductive.

Sylvie's was a sweatpants household. That's all Sanj had ever seen any of them wearing, at least at home. Sylvie was the exception. Even when she didn't need to be, she was stylish. Tonight she was wearing designer jeans and chandelier earrings.

Sylvie and Sanj had been outcasts in high school, each the other's only friend. They were proud of their status. As far as they were concerned, no one in the high school was worthy of their friendship.

In spring, they'd attended the senior prom together. ("Just as friends," Sylvie had said. Sanj hadn't told anyone he was gay, but he wondered if Sylvie had guessed.) Neither had particularly wanted to go, but Sylvie, at the last minute, had said, "What if we don't go and regret it for the rest of our lives?" Sanj instantly recognized that she was quoting the nerdy character from a teen soap that had been their Thursday night guilty pleasure. He shot back, "What if we *do* go and regret it for the rest of our lives?" but in the end he relented. He was glad. At the prom, he was proud to have Sylvie on his arm. While the other girls wore tacky pastel confections, Sylvie wore couture. Well, not quite couture, but close: an emerald green Yves Saint Laurent cocktail dress she'd picked up on sale at Bergdorf's, where she'd stopped after her interview at the modeling agency. It was an unbelievably extravagant expenditure for her, and she'd had to use all the money she'd saved over two years working part-time at the mall; even then, she'd had to charge the rest to her parents' credit card. But she'd thought of it as a reward, and reasoned that she would need such clothes for her new life in New York.

During an R.E.M. video—"It's the End of the World as We Know It (and I Feel Fine)"—Sylvie reached for Sanj's hand and said, "I can't believe you're leaving me here."

Sanj squeezed her hand and said, "I'll always be here for you."

Three days later, the day Sanj left for college, Sylvie came to say goodbye. He and his father were almost finished packing his new Jeep Cherokee—a graduation gift—which they would be driving together cross-country to L.A. They had a circular driveway, with a large fountain in the middle. Sanj's mother was perched on the front porch of the house supervising when Sylvie pulled up in her dented Toyota Tercel.

Sanj saw his mother's face before he saw Sylvie; he saw her jaw drop, her eyes widen, her arms fold tightly. She'd never liked Sylvie. She didn't like where Sylvie lived, or what she knew of Sylvie's brother and parents, not that she'd ever met them. She'd said as much to Sanj, as gently and tactfully as she could manage, coming to his room one evening as he was preparing to meet Sylvie. "Most people around here won't amount to much. We are not like them." She'd taken his chin in one hand. "Sanju, beta, find better friends."

Looking at Sylvie on their driveway, Sanj saw why his mother was clicking her tongue and shaking her head. The last time Sanj had seen Sylvie, her hair was long, luxurious, honey-blond, falling halfway down her back. Now she was completely bald.

Sanj didn't need to ask her why she'd done it. A few months ago, they'd watched an interview with O'Connor on *120 Minutes*. She'd said that before she shaved her head, no one took her seriously; she was too pretty. Her decision, she said, had changed everything.

Sylvie walked up to Sanj and threw her arms around him. He pulled her close, stroking her bald head. "Your hair."

"We're both starting new lives," she said bravely, and for a moment he believed her. Then he noticed she was trembling.

"You'll get out of here, too. One day, soon. I'll help you. I promise."

He didn't see Sylvie again for four years. During that time, he barely even spoke to her on the phone. When he first moved away, she called fairly often, leaving messages on the answering machine in his dorm room. He was always out. He rarely returned her calls. They had drifted, it was natural. He didn't understand why they should pretend to be friends forever just because they had clung to each other during a few miserable years of high school.

So he wasn't quite prepared for what he saw when he ran into her in the pharmacy. It must have registered on his face. She had gained a little more weight, but that wasn't what threw him. Her whole being seemed to have changed. Whatever bright light had shone from her in high school was gone. She resembled neither the siren in the emerald-green cocktail dress, nor the beautiful bald young woman Sanj had last seen. Now she wore gray sweatpants and a bulky, navy hooded sweatshirt emblazoned with the Mountaineers football logo. Her hair, long again, was pulled back in a ponytail. Sanj wouldn't have recognized her, wouldn't have thought to say hello, had she not approached him, saying his name timidly, tentatively . . . *Sanj?*

"Sylvie?"

"It's great to see you."

"You, too," he said.

"Are you here long?"

"Just a couple weeks," he said. "I'm taking care of my grandfather while my parents are in India." He held up the white paper bag from the pharmacy: "Heart medication."

"How's California?"

"I live in New York now. I work for *Vogue*." Sanj struck a pose from the Madonna "Vogue" video. He saw pain flitter across her face. He'd forgotten she'd once dreamed of being photographed for such a magazine.

"I've only been here a few days. I'd been planning to call you," he said, though the truth was that he'd had no intention of getting in touch.

"I'm at the same number."

He said, "I'll call."

Sanj had only been living in New York for four months when his parents
summoned him back to West Virginia to stay with his grandfather. At first
he'd said *no*. "I can't take off just like that. I have a job."

"Internship," his mother corrected. "Unpaid. *Vogue* isn't paying you.
Your parents are paying for you."

"Even so, I've made a commitment."

"He doesn't need to be taken care of," Sanj's mother said. "You won't
have to do anything. I wouldn't even ask you, except I don't feel comfortable
leaving him alone for so long." After a minute she said, "Don't make me
beg."

Later, Sanj called her back. "Fine. Three weeks. That's it."

His parents were going to India to close up his grandmother's house
in Rajkot, to sort through and sell her possessions, and to bring her to live
in America for good. This was his mother's mother. The grandfather they
wanted him to look after was his father's father, who had been living with
them since Sanj was a child. His mother's mother didn't want to come. She
didn't want to leave Rajkot to live—for the first time in her life at the age
of seventy-eight—in America, in West Virginia, but Sanj's parents insisted
she was too old to live alone.

Sanj wasn't exactly living in New York, not in the city anyway. He was
living in Long Island with family friends. Chandu had been Sanj's father's
childhood friend growing up in Gujarat in a village near Ahmedabad.
They were like brothers. Chandu and Sanj's father, Bipin, had immigrated
together to America at age seventeen. Literally *together*. Together, they had
taken a bus from their village to Ahmedabad, a train from Ahmedabad
to Bombay, a ship from Bombay to Spain, a train from Spain to London,
a ship from London to New York, and finally, a Greyhound bus from
New York to Oklahoma, where they were both enrolled, pre-med, at the
university in Norman. (Later, Bipin told Sanj that his only ideas about
Oklahoma, before arriving, were from the movie version of the musical.)
Their journey took close to two months. Eventually, he and Chandu would
attend different medical schools, do their residencies in different hospitals,
settle in different regions, but they always kept in touch and saw each other

as often as they could. Over the years, a surprising number of young men from their village ended up immigrating. Now, every four or five years, they'd have a big reunion, in rotating cities where one or the other lived, and everyone would bring their families. Sanj remembered one, years ago. He remembered in particular watching the men—soft in middle-age—playing volleyball. They seemed so happy, like they were in the village again, like they were twelve.

Chandu's wife, Lala, didn't speak English, which made it difficult for Sanj to communicate with her, since he himself didn't speak any Indian languages. Almost thirty years she had been living in the United States, and she'd learned barely a handful of words and phrases. Sanj was shocked by this. True, Long Island had a vibrant Indian community, and Lala had plenty of people to talk to in her native languages. And true, Lala had never worked outside the house, and so she didn't need English for those purposes. But still, how had she passed her driver's exam? How did she manage while shopping?

Chandu and Lala had three daughters, all a few years older than Sanj. They all still lived at home. They were beautiful, with thick black hair. They were good Indian daughters: practical, responsible, accomplished. One was in med school; one was in law school; and one had just finished business school. Chandu seized every chance to brag about them.

The Princess Jasmine association wouldn't have occurred to Sanj, except that someone from Gita's MBA program told her she looked like her, from the Disney movie *Aladdin*. "Isn't that a little culturally insensitive?" Sanj had said at dinner. "Princess Jasmine isn't even Indian." But no one else thought so, and Gita liked the comparison. She thought it was flattering. Princess Jasmine was beautiful, even if she was just a cartoon. The more Sanj thought about it, the more he agreed: she did look like Princess Jasmine. In fact, all three sisters looked like Princess Jasmine. So privately that's what he started calling them: The Princess Jasmines, or sometimes just The Jasmines.

The Jasmines had the entire third floor of the house all to themselves. Each had her own bedroom and her own en suite bathroom. It smelled like hair products up there.

The parents' room was on the second floor, as was Sanj's. He stayed in what was usually the family's pooja room, where they did their morning and evening prayers. There was a small mandir with statues and framed pictures of various gods. Sanj slept on a foldout futon.

He liked to sleep late. Mornings, the family members came in, one by one, whether or not Sanj was awake. If he woke up during their prayers, he would shuffle off to the bedroom of whichever Jasmine was already awake and climb into her empty bed to catch a few more minutes of sleep. The parents didn't like this, Sanj could tell. The father seemed particularly bothered. It was inappropriate, borderline scandalous. After all, Sanj was a young man, and these were young, unmarried women. The Jasmines didn't like it either. But no one was going to say anything. Sanj was the son of their father's dear childhood friend. They had traveled together in search of new lives in a new country, and together had weathered difficulties others could only imagine. A few transgressions from Bipin's only son could be overlooked.

The Jasmines hated New York. They thought it was dirty and crowded and expensive. They wanted to move to L.A. Sanj said L.A. was superficial. The Jasmines said New York was overrated. They narrowed their eyes. "You'll hate it here. You'll see."

Sylvie asked, "Do you still have that huge screen, with the projection television and the sprawling sectional?"

Three days after running into her at the pharmacy, Sanj had called and invited her over to watch a movie. She said she would bring the video.

When she arrived at the house, she rang the doorbell at the front door instead of the side door, where anyone who knew the family would have rung, and where Sylvie herself would have rung back in high school. Back then, Sylvie didn't even need to, she could just walk right in.

Sanj greeted her at the door, and, glimpsing the same dented Toyota Tercel, he remembered their goodbye in the driveway more than four years ago. Sanj invited Sylvie in.

The house's foyer was designed to impress. The ceilings were almost thirty feet high, and there was a five-foot-tall bronze statue of Nataraja

Shiva, dancing his dance of destruction and re-creation. Sanj's parents had had it shipped from Chicago, along with other decorative items, including several large tapestries and an ornate indoor swing. They patterned their house after the fancy havelis in Bollywood films. The verandas in the back had floors of imported marble (as did the foyer) and ornate columns with gold-toned scrolls.

Bipin had been the first Indian to move to the small town. The job at the local hospital was the first one he'd been offered after his residency, and, eager to find a place where he could settle so he could bring his new bride from India, he'd taken it. Not long after, he decided to open his own oncology practice. When it was time for him to expand, he recruited an Indian. Then another. Other Indian doctors followed: family members, friends of friends. Word spread that there were opportunities in the area, and those who had nowhere else to go, who had Indian degrees and few options, began arriving. Most were doctors. Some were engineers, working in the chemical plants that dotted the river valley. Many of them lived with Bipin's family for a time—two, three weeks, sometimes longer—until they could find their own places and send for their wives and, in some cases, children. Bipin's family lived in a smaller house then, and the young men would sleep on a foldout in a room that doubled as Bipin's study. Now, thirty years later, there were more than twenty-five families. They were some of the wealthiest residents in what was otherwise a poor stretch of Appalachia.

Not only was Bipin the first Indian in town, he was also the first to buy land in Mulberry Hills, the first to build a house, custom designed with a basement large enough to accommodate most, if not all, of the Indian community. This was useful, since Diwali celebrations could no longer be held in the recreation hall of the Episcopal church, not since a janitor had told the deacon about the statue of the elephant-headed god, the chanting and dancing and burning of incense. Other Indian families followed, building several houses in a row. At Diwali and Holi and Navrarti and at the monthly dandiya parties, the guests could easily hop from one house to the next. The Indians referred to Mulberry Hills as Malabar Hill, after the tony Bombay neighborhood.

The circular driveway and the accompanying fountain were added a few years after the house itself. Bipin had bought them for his wife as a surprise for their twentieth anniversary. Meenakshi had gone alone for a short trip to India, and when she returned—only half-awake after the long journey—the driveway she pulled into was this one. The driveway itself was fairly simple; it was the fountain that was the real gift. It was exquisite. What made it so extraordinary, aside from its sheer size, were the handcrafted tiles encircling its base. Most had standard decorative motifs Bipin had selected from a showroom: curlicues or geometric patterns or sunflowers. But scattered among them were a few very special tiles Bipin had commissioned to document his and Meenakshi's lives together—a tile with a mangalsutra exactly like the one Meenakshi had worn at their wedding; a tile depicting the Taj Mahal, where they had gone on their honeymoon; one with a baby's crib and the birth date of their only child; one with a palm tree to represent the trip to Hawaii they had taken on their second anniversary, staying at an expensive resort, long before they had yet made the kind of money to afford such a vacation or resort, telling themselves the trip was an act of faith, a message to the universe that this was the kind of life they expected and that they would settle for nothing less.

Three years later, when the driveway needed to be repaired (long before it should have), Bipin, unable to secure the contractor who had originally built it, hired a local man. After the work was done, the two men argued, the local man demanding much more money than his original quote. The man got angry, shouting, "You foreigners don't know how hard it is. You all live in mansions. One day, come see where I live. Then you'll understand." Bipin ended up paying the man the extra money, though he continued to complain about it even years later.

Shortly after the driveway and fountain were built, Sanj's grandfather, getting into the car one day, said, "Life is a circle. One way or another we return to the beginning." The comment had irritated Sanj; it seemed to him both sentimental and false. In fact, it had become an inside joke amongst him and his parents. Bipin would imitate Sanj's grandfather in an exaggerated Indian accent, stabbing the air with his finger, "Life is a circle," and Sanj and his mother would laugh. Though now, standing in the grand foyer with Sylvie, Sanj wondered if his grandfather hadn't had a point. After all, here Sanj was, four years after leaving, back where he started. But it was temporary. What Sanj hadn't mentioned to his grandfather, when his grandfather first made the observation, was that the driveway, though circular, did have an entrance, and, importantly, an exit, and Sanj had full intention of using it.

The first thing Sanj noticed about Sylvie when she stepped into the foyer was that she was wearing sweatpants again. She looked out of place, her sneakers ratty against the marble floor. She'd brought Krzysztof Kieślowski's *La double vie de Véronique*. Sanj had already seen it, but he didn't mind seeing it again. A professor had screened it in a film class in college. In the movie, Irene Jacobs plays a double role: a Polish singer and a young French woman. The women never meet, yet for a time their lives seem to parallel one another's before eventually going off in different directions. Sanj remembered the professor having said something about the film being a moody exploration of identity, of freewill versus destiny, but Sanj couldn't remember exactly. He'd earned a *C* in the course.

Sanj liked the soundtrack. Sylvie liked the styling: the clothes, the hair, the makeup. She was enthralled by Irene Jacobs. "Fuck Julia Roberts," she said, "*this* is a star." The comment sounded just like something Sylvie might have said four years ago, and for a moment Sanj felt like they were back in high school. But then he glanced over at her—her shapeless sweats, her greasy hair—and remembered neither of them was the same.

The basement had a wet bar, and after the movie, Sanj made margaritas, and the two sat on the sectional, talking, watching MTV on mute. Sylvie asked if he'd ever seen Anna Wintour.

"Of course. I've seen her several times in the halls and the lobby."

"I heard she had a skylight installed in her office so she can wear sunglasses even while she's at work."

"I've never been in her office. But once, in the elevator, she told me she loved my watch. 'It's Lucite,' I said. 'I have it in three colors.'"

A few minutes later Sanj said, "I love working at *Vogue*, but it's a little superficial."

Sanj noticed Sylvie's eyes welling up with tears. Her body crumpled, curling in on itself like a worm.

"Four years," Sylvie said. "Why didn't you call me? Why didn't you stop by? I thought we were best friends."

After a minute, she said, "These years have been really hard for me."

"I know," Sanj said.

"If you knew, you would have called."

Sanj remembered a night their senior year in high school. It was February, and they had driven to Cleveland to see a Nine Inch Nails concert. In honor of the show, they were clad head to toe in black. It was midnight by the time the concert was finished and they started driving home. They'd gone in Sylvie's Tercel, and somehow they'd taken a wrong turn and ended up on a back road driving through farmland. Something Sanj said, he wasn't sure what—was it about the concert? about Nietzsche, whom they were both reading, and whom they had been discussing on and off during their drive?—upset Sylvie so much, she stopped the car, and stepped out into the cold night without her coat, slamming the door behind her. Sanj waited several minutes, wondering what to do, before finally getting out himself. Sylvie's back was turned to him. She was facing the field, her hands tightly gripping the fence. In the silence of the frigid night, Sanj could still hear the concert ringing in his ears. A cow was mooing somewhere in the distance. Sanj put his hand on Sylvie's shoulder and said, "I'm sorry," although he was unsure what he was apologizing for. He felt her shoulder beneath his hand soften and relax. They got back in the car and drove home without discussing it further.

Sanj tipped his margarita glass back, trying to get the last few sips. The ice cubes were cold against his lips. He set the glass down on the table and reached to put his hand on Sylvie's shoulder, to tell her he was sorry, as he had that night on the side of the road. But as he reached, he saw Sylvie's shoulder slightly, though perceptibly, pull away.

"I'll make it up to you," Sanj said. "Somehow. I promise."

Sanj was lying to everyone about what he was doing in New York. He didn't have an internship at *Vogue*. He didn't have an internship anywhere, not anymore. When he first arrived, he'd worked at a trade publication which served the prescription drug industry, and which he'd seen advertised on a flyer in the journalism office at USC. But he didn't last long.

In college, when Sanj had fantasized about his first job in New York, he'd pictured a spacious, light-filled office, with an open floor plan—no walls or cubicle barriers. He pictured himself wearing tight charcoal gray pants (wool, with a little bit of Lycra for stretch), a white shirt, and a skinny tie. He would share—with an equally stylish young woman, in a blue blouse, with short, ruffled sleeves—a large, antique table, and they would sit facing each other, gold-rimmed tea cups carefully positioned on coasters within easy reach. Occasionally, they'd look away from their work to exchange a clever comment about an art exhibit or a new dance club.

His real job, of course, was nothing like this. The office had drop ceilings and fluorescent lights. The job itself was tedious and uninspiring. Sanj was assigned to an editor and was responsible for sorting through his mail, screening his phone calls, and typing and sending his handwritten correspondences to freelance writers.

His boss had a ridiculous name—Jeep—made all the more ridiculous by how poorly it suited him. Far from rugged or virile, Jeep was stout and fey. "I had a Jeep," Sanj said, the first day, "but I totaled it on the way back from Burning Man." He thought Jeep would find this anecdote funny and that it would break the ice; instead, Jeep just shrugged.

Jeep had only been at the trade publication for six months. Before that, he'd been a senior culture editor at *Newsday*, but he'd been pushed out during a restructuring. For Jeep, the job at the trade magazine was a huge step down, something Sanj understood almost immediately. Jeep mentioned *Newsday* at least twenty times Sanj's first day. In his previous position, Jeep had also had his own assistant. Here, he'd have to settle for an intern.

Among Sanj's duties was fetching Jeep's lunch—a different place every day—so Sanj, still trying to learn the lay of the neighborhood, often found himself lost. Jeep always paid Sanj after Sanj returned, not before. Sanj wondered if Jeep didn't trust him with the money. One afternoon, during Sanj's second week, Jeep sent him out for a turkey sandwich. When the man behind the counter asked if he wanted mustard, Sanj didn't know. He couldn't remember. Had Jeep said anything about mustard? To be safe, Sanj ordered two sandwiches—one with mustard, one without—deciding that he would allow Jeep to select the one he wanted and that Sanj would eat the other himself. Back at the office, after Jeep selected the sandwich without mustard, he forgot to pay Sanj, and Sanj couldn't think of a polite way to ask. Later, sitting alone in the break room, Sanj couldn't stop thinking about the money. His internship wasn't even paid, and now he had to buy his boss' lunches? On top of everything, the sandwich left a bad taste in his mouth. He hated mustard.

The next day, Jeep sent Sanj to a sushi restaurant on Twenty-Eighth, again without any money. Sanj ordered the sashimi lunch his boss had requested. At the last minute, he amended the order—"To stay, not to go"— and, sitting on a stool at a long table facing the street, he ate the sashimi himself, savoring the delicate fish, relishing it even more knowing that Jeep would go hungry this afternoon. After finishing, instead of returning to the office, Sanj walked across town to Penn Station to catch a train back to Long Island. He never went back to work, never even called to explain his absence, and Jeep, to Sanj's surprise, never called Sanj in Long Island to find out why he'd disappeared.

Sanj knew his parents wouldn't pay for him to live in New York unless they thought he was working, so he didn't tell anyone he'd quit. To explain to his parents why they could no longer reach him at the work number he had originally given them, he told them he'd found a better internship at *Vogue*. When they asked for the new number, he explained that the editors there were very hierarchical. "I don't even have my own desk, let alone a phone."

Every day, Sanj would take the Long Island Rail Road to Penn Station, and then he'd kill time in the city until it was a respectable hour to return home. Some days he'd walk over to the Mid-Manhattan Library, and he'd read the papers, looking for possible employment. Other days, he would take the subway to various neighborhoods and walk around, trying to orient himself to New York.

Sometimes he'd wander around with a handheld tape recorder, and he would approach random people, claiming he was working on an article about this or that for *GQ* or the *New York Post* or *Paper Magazine*. He was having a tough time in New York. If he could better understand the minds of New Yorkers, he reasoned, maybe he could figure out how to live in this city. Besides, he had no friends and was starving for conversation. On Forty-Second Street, he asked pedestrians what they thought of the haikus an artist had installed on the marquees of the derelict porn theaters. Another time, on a particularly bleak stretch in the Meatpacking District, he asked people what they thought the city should do to beautify the neighborhood. "How about a park?" he'd suggested. "Don't you ever wish you had more green in your lives?" Part of what amazed Sanj was how quick people were to believe he was who he said he was. No one ever seemed to doubt him.

One day, wandering around Times Square, Sanj noticed, next to a Howard Johnson, a steep stairway with an awning that read GAIETY THEATRE. Sanj remembered seeing a small ad in the back of the *Village Voice*. It featured a naked male torso—slender and smooth—with the words, *Male Burlesk*.

He climbed the stairs and paid the cover admission. Inside was a large room with small tables and a stage where the striptease took place. Most of the customers, at least this weekday afternoon, were businessmen dressed in suits, taking a long lunch or an afternoon break from the office. Or so Sanj assumed. Maybe they weren't businessmen. Maybe they were like Sanj: pretending. Pretending to be businessmen, pretending to have jobs they went to every day.

The strippers were pretending, too, though, of course this was their job: to pretend to be soldiers or airline pilots or gang-banging thugs or firefighters. They were all different. Some were thick with gym-won muscles. Others were wiry. Some were out-of-work models and actors and dancers. Sanj thought he recognized one of the dancers from Madonna's Blond Ambition World Tour, which he'd seen when it aired live on HBO. Some were strung-out junkies. This particular afternoon, there was also a guest headliner, a porn star. Sanj had seen one of his videos in college and already knew what the man looked like naked, somewhat spoiling the tease part of the striptease. But it was more than made up for by the excitement Sanj felt being near someone he'd seen onscreen having sex.

The end of each striptease was always the same. When the performer got down to his G-string, he would disappear backstage, music still playing, and then reemerge completely naked, with an erection. Sometimes he emerged quickly. Sometimes he was backstage for a very long time, trying to get hard.

When he returned to stage, his penis erect, he wouldn't dance; his erection was an encumbrance. Instead, he'd sort of saunter, and then he would pick a customer and walk right up to him, standing inches from him, hands on his hips, pelvis thrust forward, like Superman, his dick right in the customer's face. The customers knew they weren't supposed to touch. The stripper just stood like this: motionless, smiling, the customer staring at his crotch. If there was time, the stripper would go around to two or three or four customers and stand in front of them one at a time. Sanj could tell he was choosing men he thought might be interested in hiring him out later, men who seemed old or closeted. The stripper could only stay onstage as long as his erection lasted. Once his dick reached four o'clock, he would disappear behind the curtain.

Sanj liked imagining what went on backstage, what the performers had to do to get aroused. Was someone helping them? A boyfriend? A girlfriend? Another stripper? Or was there a special employee whose whole job was to aid them with their erections? Hadn't Sanj heard of that? Wasn't it called a fluffer? What images did the men rely upon? What fantasies, what private desires? Sanj wished he could crack their heads open and see. Oddly, his favorite part of the whole show wasn't when the men were visible, but when they had disappeared backstage, and the crowd was waiting for them to reemerge. He loved the anticipation.

Sanj returned to the Gaiety many times. Once, he even tried to interview one of the performers: a British guy, who, during his act, had worn a G-string with a Union Jack on the crotch. Sanj found him in the small, adjoining lounge where the strippers would sometimes loiter afterward, hoping to pick up tricks. Claiming to be from *Genre* magazine, Sanj had thrust his tape recorder into the man's face. "What were you thinking about backstage to get hard?" Pushing the tape recorder aside, the man winked and said, "You."

Lala, Chandu's wife, had her suspicions about Sanj. There were days he didn't wake until noon, didn't leave for the train until two. She didn't know much about internships, about the working world of Manhattan, but she knew enough to recognize that there wasn't a job on earth that would let you show up whenever you happened to feel like it, not a job this boy could get anyway.

And then there were days he didn't take the train into the city at all. He'd claim he was going to work, but instead he'd put on his Walkman and embark on long walks, returning sometimes two or three hours later. She knew because once she saw him from her car while running errands. He was just standing in front of a Carvel, less than a mile from their house, headphones on, gazing in the shop window.

Lala remembered when she first arrived in America—when her husband was working long hours at the hospital and before her daughters were born or she learned to drive—she, too, would go for long walks. Her mind would often drift back to Ahmedabad, back to some typical scene from childhood, like the view of the Sabarmati River from her bedroom window, or the dosa shop her family would visit on Saturdays, or the crowded, narrow streets of the Old City, the jumble of scooters and camels and cows. Then she'd look at her watch and suddenly realize three hours had passed, and she was in a public park she didn't recognize, sitting on a bench, watching a blond couple playing with a puppy in the grass under a grove of oaks, and she'd wonder, "How have I ended up here?" Sometimes she saw in the boy's eyes, when he'd returned from his walks, that same lost look.

Yes, there was something she liked about Sanj. These days, her daughters were all busy with school or their first jobs. She saw them only in the evenings, and even then they seemed to come home later and later. She was grateful for Sanj's company.

One morning when she was vacuuming and her back, which caused her chronic pain, was particularly achy, the boy—at the table pouring a bowl of cereal—noticed. Without either of them saying a word, he gently took the vacuum handle from her and finished the work. Since then, twice a week he ran the vacuum without being asked.

There were smaller things, too. On nights when he came home very late—which happened often—entering the house long after everyone was asleep, he tiptoed so quietly, no one ever woke up. Lala would leave a plate of leftovers for him, whatever the family had eaten for dinner that night. She'd set the plate and a glass of milk on the kitchen table under a small tabletop mosquito net she'd bought in India on one of her annual visits. Each morning, she'd find the dishes, the glass, the cutlery all carefully washed and dried and put away in the cupboards. Such a small thing, yet she loved this about him. This back and forth—her leaving the food out each night, his washing and putting away the dishes for her to find the next morning—felt like a private communication between them, their only communication, since they shared no languages.

Once, when Lala had invited three ladies over to the house to prepare sweets for an upcoming holy function, the boy sat down with them at the kitchen table and sliced almonds into paper thin slivers, thinner than any of the women could slice. When Neela looked at him sideways, and said, "Lala, three daughters on their way out of the house, but no matter: you have found a fourth daughter," and the other ladies giggled, Lala was glad the boy didn't understand Gujarati.

One morning, when Sanj was toasting bread in his parents' kitchen in West Virginia, he noticed his grandfather hovering. Several times, he seemed to start to speak to Sanj, but he couldn't quite form the words, and Sanj did nothing to make it easier. Sanj had never felt close to his grandfather. He was, at best, a vague and ghostly presence in Sanj's life.

After several false starts, his grandfather said, "Sanju, beta, tell me about your life in New York."

Why was his grandfather asking? Sanj wondered. Besides, what was there to tell? What could his grandfather possibly understand about his life?

"I'm working," Sanj said. When his grandfather seemed to want more, Sanj added, "At a magazine."

"What kind of magazine?"

"Fashion."

Again his grandfather struggled to find words, before asking, "Are you happy?"

Sanj didn't know how to answer. "Were you happy? When you were young and just starting out? Were you happy?"

His grandfather thought for a minute, then said, "It was a different time. I had different responsibilities."

Sanj remembered, when he was ten, visiting the house in India where his grandfather lived and where his father was born. It was his one and only trip to India. He and his parents had taken a local bus forty minutes from Ahmedabad to the village. Children had followed them from the bus station, through the dusty lanes, all the way to the house. The structure itself was dilapidated, with a badly cracked facade and a trash-strewn entryway. Several families shared it. Sanj's grandfather's flat consisted of just two small rooms upstairs. But no one from the family had lived there for twenty years, and no one knew who lived there now. Pointing to the dark window upstairs, Sanj's mother said, "Can you believe your father is from there?" and, in fact, Sanj could not.

Speaking with his grandfather now, Sanj realized that when his father was born his grandfather must not have been much older than Sanj currently was. He considered the sacrifices his grandparents must have made to get his father out of that village, to send their son to America. The fare alone must have required months, if not years, of careful saving.

"I know fashion may sound frivolous," Sanj said, "but it's a very famous magazine. Anyone would want this job. My friends can't believe how lucky I am."

After that first night, watching *La double vie de Véronique* in Sanj's basement, Sylvie and Sanj saw each other every day, sometimes twice a day. Mostly they watched movies at Sanj's, downing margaritas or daiquiris or vodka tonics. From the stories Sylvie told, Sanj pieced together that she had taken classes at the community college, but had only lasted one semester. He learned she had spent much of the last year doing what his parents were doing in India now: helping to clean out the apartment of her mother's mother, who had been terminally ill, and who had died just two months earlier.

One evening, Sylvie asked Sanj to meet her at her house. He arrived around seven. Sanj hadn't been to Sylvie's since high school. It was only a couple miles from where he lived, just down the hill in the jumble of small houses crowded in the narrow valley close to the riverbank, in the part of town that flooded when it rained too much. Sylvie's house was a compact, two-story structure that looked neglected, with peeling blue paint and a sagging front porch. A stone goose stood sentry in the front lawn; Sylvie's mom liked to dress it according to the weather and the season—a yellow slicker when it rained, earmuffs in the winter, a red Santa hat around Christmas. Today had been beautiful, and the goose was wearing sunglasses.

Sanj knocked on the door that entered into the kitchen. Sylvie's father swung the door open and shook Sanj's hand. The kitchen was small, with a linoleum floor that needed replacing, and a floral curtain rod ruffle over the window above the sink. The kitchen radio was set to an oldies station. Sylvie's mother was standing at the counter, chopping carrots. She turned to Sanj. "We haven't seen you in forever! Look at you!" Sanj noticed right away that they were both wearing sweatpants, just as he'd remembered them. They looked older, though, more so than the four years that had elapsed. Sylvie's mother came toward him, her arms open, and hugged him.

Sanj saw Sylvie, who had been lurking in the doorway. She came over to him, grasped his hand, and pulled him away from her mother, whom he was still embracing. At first, her mother looked hurt, but then she resumed her work at the kitchen counter. As Sylvie dragged him into the hallway, Sanj thought he saw someone sitting on the couch in the other room watching television.

Upstairs, Sylvie's door was shut and locked. It was a heavy bolt lock, the kind you would find on the front door of a house, not an inside bedroom. Sylvie fished a key out of her sweatpants' pocket.

Her bedroom looked nothing like Sanj remembered. In high school, the room had been decorated with dingy wallpaper, some country theme, cornflowers perhaps, Sanj couldn't remember exactly. Not that you could see the wallpaper. Almost every inch was covered with posters or pictures clipped from magazines: bands Sylvie liked, models she admired, fashions she hoped to one day wear. He remembered, in particular, above her bed, a poster of Morrissey looking both sullen and seductive.

Now her room was stripped of all that, stripped, it seemed, of Sylvie, or at least the Sylvie that Sanj had known. The room was austere. The matted, beige wall-to-wall carpeting had been ripped up, leaving roughly finished hardwood floors. The walls and the door were painted blue, and the trim around the windows was green. Pushed against one of the walls was a narrow wooden bed made up with a scarlet blanket of rough wool. There were two straight-backed wooden chairs with straw seats. Arranged on a small wooden table in the corner of the room were a blue pitcher and a blue washbasin and a drinking glass. Three blue shirts—men's shirts, from what Sanj could tell—hung on pegs along the back wall, and next to them, a straw hat. Everything about the room seemed odd to Sanj—unlikely, yet somehow familiar. It evoked another time and place.

Sylvie gestured for Sanj to sit on one of the chairs, which proved uncomfortable, while she took a seat on the other.

"You've redecorated your room," Sanj said.

"It's Van Gogh's."

It took Sanj a moment to understand. Then he remembered the painting—Van Gogh's *Bedroom in Arles*—which was famous, and which he'd seen at the Art Institute of Chicago one summer when he was visiting his cousins.

"Why?" Sanj said.

"I don't know. I guess I felt a connection."

"A connection to the monastic atmosphere, or to the desperate guy who sliced off his ear?"

"Both."

He wondered, too, about the locks—what was it she was trying to keep out? or was it something she was trying to keep *in*?—but he didn't ask.

"Was that Chris I saw downstairs?"

"Probably," she said. "He's back again."

"What's he been up to?" Sanj asked, trying to sound casual, though he was eager to know.

"He had a baby with Trisha Meyers, but they're not together anymore. He installs car stereos. Ironic, since he lost his driver's license. DUI. He'd been smoking pot that night, but believe me, when it comes to drugs, that's the least of what he does. *Did? Does?* I don't even know anymore. I asked recently, and he said he was clean, but I don't believe him. There was a time when we could never lie to each other. We were so close: we're twins, after all. But that time is long gone."

The room was very quiet. They could hear beneath them, through the thin floors, the faint sounds from the kitchen: the oldies station ("All the leaves are brown . . ."), kitchen cabinets slamming, dishes being stacked. Sylvie said. "Let's not talk about Chris anymore. It makes me tired." In fact, the story was all too familiar, echoed in the lives of countless other young men they'd known in high school.

Sanj said, "I got a call from one of the *Vogue* editors today. I might get to write a piece. Well, really just a blurb, maybe three or four hundred words. But it's exciting, partly because the story was my idea. See, I know this guy in L.A., a graffiti artist, a friend of a friend. He recently sold his novel. It won't be out until next year, but I pitched the article as a 'next big thing' piece. No one knows about him now, but this time next year everyone will be talking about him."

Sylvie smiled. "I'm happy for you," she said, though her eyes said otherwise. Sanj heard a tightness in her voice as she continued. "It seems like things have come easily for you since high school. First USC, now New York. Not that you haven't worked for it, or that you don't deserve it. It just seems to have been easy for you. Not for me." She leaned forward. "Why do you think that is?"

At first, Sanj wasn't sure if it was a rhetorical question, or if Sylvie expected a response.

After a minute, he said, "I've been lucky."

Sylvie sighed. "Lucky."

The sun was setting. The light in the room was fading; they were almost sitting in the dark.

She stood up. "Let's go downstairs. Maybe Chris will be gone."

Sanj's parents called every two or three days to check on him and his grandfather. When they'd call, it was morning in India, but evening in America, and Sanj would often be out. His grandfather would leave scribbled messages.

On the days Sanj did talk to his parents, he reassured them about his grandfather. "He's fine. You know him. He spends all day shut up in his bedroom doing pooja." Sanj's mother would want to know about food. "Is it lasting?" Before leaving for India, she'd cooked nonstop for days, and filled the freezer. "If you run out, you can always call any of the aunties to bring something."

Sanj was on his way out the door to meet Sylvie when his father rang. "How's it going?" Bipin asked. "How's your grandfather?"

"Fine," Sanj said. "What about over there?"

"It's been tough for everyone, especially for your grandmother. She knows she'll probably never return here, not to this house anyway. Sorting through all her belongings has dredged up years' worth of memories, which hasn't made it any easier."

After a minute, Sanj's father said, "Do you remember that card you made for Dada when he was in the hospital? You must have been ten. You drew a carnival, remember, with a Ferris wheel, bumper cars, a shooting game with cartoon ducks? You raided the photo album, cutting out the heads of all your cousins, aunts, and uncles to paste on all the bodies you drew, even on the ducks. Your mom was so mad; they were the only copies of the photos. Dada was so proud, he showed it to all the nurses and doctors at the hospital. Your grandmother kept that card all these years."

Sanj had forgotten about the card, though he had a vivid memory of the trip to India a few weeks later, after his grandfather died. It was the same trip when he'd visited his father's village.

"I remember seeing the house where you were born," Sanj said.

"I went there over the weekend," Bipin said. "Just for the day. Just to look around again."

Visiting the village, Bipin had had his own flood of memories. He had thought about the day he left for America, meeting up with his friend Chandu that morning. Chandu's mother had made them hot parathas and potato vegetable, and even though Bipin had eaten breakfast at his own house just half an hour earlier, he ate again.

The journey had been exhausting. He remembered in particular an incident during their stopover in Paris. Chandu and the two other Indian men with whom they'd been traveling wanted to go to a burlesque show. "Paris is famous for them," they'd said. Bipin said he had a stomachache. In truth, he felt awkward about going. It seemed somehow wrong, although, even after the men left, there was a small part of Bipin that wished he'd gone, not just for the titillation, but also because he wished he were the type of man who would go: adventuresome, fearless. Instead, he stayed in the hotel and wrote his father a long letter thanking him for the sacrifices he'd made to send him to America, ensuring him that they wouldn't be for nothing. "I'll make you proud," he'd written. When he went to the post office, he got flummoxed, struggling to understand the French system, and ended up never mailing the letter, pocketing it instead and carrying it with him to America. Months later, he ran across it while sorting through some things. It was the end of his first year in college. Reading the letter, he was struck with homesickness, and he wanted so desperately to go back to India, if not for good, at least for a long summer visit. But he had no money. In fact, it would be another six years before he'd set foot in India, before he'd see any of his family. Bipin spent days moping in his room, refusing to come out.

It was Chandu who had rescued him. He organized a summer sublet, a large Victorian house in disrepair, which he and Bipin would share with four other foreign students who also had nowhere to go. In exchange for free rent, the men would fix up the house so the owner could sell it at the end of the summer.

That first night in the house, Chandu prepared a Gujarati feast. Well, not quite a feast, but Chandu had done the best he could with what ingredients he could find locally and with what limited cooking skills he possessed. Still, Bipin was impressed. He wondered where Chandu had learned to cook. Eating the food, Bipin swelled with memories of home, understanding, too, that as long as Chandu was there with him, he wasn't alone.

Bipin had never told his son this story. There was so much he'd never said. He'd never told him how many days he'd cried in Oklahoma; or how scared he was, when he brought Meenakshi to America, that he would disappoint her or fail her somehow; or how much he'd struggled. What Bipin *did* tell his son about his early life in America is what he thought he needed to know: that he had come with nothing and that it hadn't been easy, but he had worked hard and now here they all were. When Sanj asked his father *why* he came to America, Bipin answered, "For a better life," which was, in Bipin's estimation, what they now had. As for the details of what he'd been through, why would his son want to know? Bipin barely wanted to know himself.

Toward the end of their phone conversation, Sanj mentioned he'd been seeing quite a bit of his old friend Sylvie. "You remember Sylvie Pearson, right?"

"Of course," Bipin said. "You two were best friends."

When Sanj said he was eager to return to New York, Bipin said, "I'm glad Chandu Uncle is looking after you. I can't imagine how I would have survived in America without him. I don't know how either one of us could have survived."

The next time Sylvie came over, they watched *Sid and Nancy*. It had been one of their favorite movies when they were in high school. They were watching a scene in which Sid and Nancy are lying in a bed in the Hotel Chelsea, barely functional after shooting heroin. As Sid passes out, his lit cigarette accidentally singes Nancy, and she flicks it into a pile of rubbish on the ground—discarded clothes, empty fast-food containers, the crumpled wrapper of a Burger King Whopper—which catches fire. Instead of extinguishing it, Nancy merely watches the blaze, her eyes half-closed, as she curls her body against Sid's. Sid awakens, lights another cigarette, flicks the match into the growing fire. Neither of them does anything to save themselves.

Sanj paused the movie.

"What's wrong?" Sylvie asked.

He wanted to tell her the truth. He wanted to tell her he didn't work at *Vogue* and that his grades at USC had been dismal. He wanted to tell her he wasn't lucky, as he'd claimed in her bedroom (as he'd claimed to his grandfather, too), at least not lucky in the way she thought. He looked at her. The light of the television was blue on her face, though the fire on the screen was yellow and red.

He couldn't say it.

"Would you like more vodka?"

"Sure," Sylvie said. He got up to fix two more drinks. When he returned, handing Sylvie hers, he tried again to tell her, but said instead, "Let's toast."

"To what?" she asked.

He held up his glass. "To the future."

"To the future," Sylvie repeated, though her voice sounded more hesitant than Sanj's. Her eyes looked away as they clinked glasses.

He pushed play. The scene resumed. The firefighters break down the door, dragging Sid and Nancy, against their will, to safety. In the doorway, Nancy looks back at the inferno with longing.

Sanj had heard rumors about a gay bar: a place called Diff'rent Strokes. It was located in the deserted downtown, under a highway overpass. It was next door to a biker bar, about which he'd also heard rumors: a woman could get a free drink if she gave the bartender her bra to hang on the wall, two drinks if she gave up her panties. The biker bar and the gay bar had abutting parking lots and back-door entrances.

He had to show his ID and pay a dollar and sign a registry. The bar was technically "members only" ever since there was a stabbing a few months earlier. Sanj looked at the names above his to see if he recognized anyone, perhaps someone he had heard whispers about growing up: the newspaper editor, the math teacher, the chef at the French restaurant. Sanj was nervous about signing his name. What if someone he knew saw it afterward?

Inside, the space was dark and narrow, dominated by a long bar with stools. The floors and walls and ceilings were painted black. There was a tiny dance floor and two pool tables that seemed smaller than regulation size. Besides Sanj, there were only six or seven other people, mostly middle-aged men, no one Sanj would be interested in. They didn't seem particularly interested in him, either. Sanj knew they wanted rednecks in pickup trucks, not skinny little Indians. Sanj knew it, because that's who he wanted, too. He stayed almost two hours. The crowd didn't improve much, though at one point it peaked at about twenty. He shot one game of pool, though mostly he just sat at the bar.

Toward the end of the night, Sanj found himself talking to a guy who had come late and had sat next to him, a man in his late twenties or perhaps early thirties. He was cute, and he wore a red baseball cap pulled low on his head. He introduced himself as Chad. Sanj thought he recognized him, but wasn't sure. Sanj flirted with him. He took his baseball cap and put it on his own head. When Chad leaned in to retrieve it, Sanj kissed him long and hard. He whispered, "Take me home." Chad said, "I can't."

Driving home afterward, Sanj remembered him: Chad *Webster*. His house was near Sylvie's. He was a few years older than they were; in fact, Sanj remembered Sylvie saying he'd been her babysitter when she was a kid. Sanj remembered seeing him once, a few years ago, washing his car in the driveway—a sleekly beautiful, sixty-nine Dodge Charger, plum

186 / RAHUL MEHTA

colored. At the time, Sanj had fantasized about riding in the passenger seat, driving into the horizon with Chad's arm around him.

The next time Sanj talked to Sylvie, he asked about Chad.

"He went off to DC right after high school. He lived there several years, but then he got sick. He's been sick for a while. 'He's come home to rest.' That's what his mom told my mom. Why are you asking?"

"No reason," Sanj said. "I saw him in line at Foodland. He looked familiar, then I remembered he was your neighbor. I was just curious."

At home that night, Sanj couldn't stop thinking about Chad. *Sick?*

A few days before Sanj had left New York, he'd gone out to a bar in Chelsea. Soon after arriving, he downed three vodka tonics. Much of the night was a haze. A man groped him by the pay phones outside the bathroom. He'd introduced himself as Paul. He was accompanied by a young Indian man named Asher, who lived with his parents in Queens and was a med-school student, though apparently he was on the verge of failing out. Paul kept telling Sanj he and Asher were "just friends."

When Paul was getting them drinks, Asher took Sanj aside and said, "Paul and I used to be a couple. We're going through a rough patch, but he still loves me and I still love him. As a fellow Indian, you would never want to come between us. I'm trusting you. You are my brother."

Outside, Paul put Asher in a cab headed for Queens, and he put his arm around Sanj and said, "Let's go." His place was nearby. It was a large, loft-style apartment, beautifully decorated. Sanj recognized the black chaise longue as a Le Corbusier. In bed, when Paul started to enter Sanj, Sanj asked, "Where's the condom?" Paul said, "We don't need it. I'm clean." When Sanj tried to push Paul away, Paul said, "C'mon." He kissed Sanj on the mouth then said, "It doesn't feel as good with one of those things on. It kills all the sensation." Sanj said, "Fine, but if you cum inside me, I'll kill *you*."

Afterward, it was too late to catch a train back to Long Island. Lying next to Paul, Sanj couldn't sleep. He felt guilty for betraying Asher, not that he'd actually promised him anything. But more than that, Sanj couldn't believe, knowing all that he knew, that he'd let Paul fuck him without a condom. Sanj lay awake the next few hours, imagining Paul's fluids, *infected* fluids, Sanj imagined—a few drops of cum or precum—invading his body. He imagined he could actually feel it: tiny cells of Paul—a complete stranger Sanj wouldn't even recognize were he to see him again—coursing through Sanj's body, up his torso, down through his arms and hands, up through his neck, the liquid pooling in his head in the hollows just behind his eyes. It was like Paul was a part of him now.

At five, Sanj got out of bed and left, Paul still asleep. He slogged onto the A train to Penn Station, waited half an hour for the next train, changed at Jamaica, walked the twenty minutes from his stop in Long Island to his uncle and auntie's house. The shops along the main street were just beginning to pull up their metal shutters. When he arrived at the house, Lala Auntie was in the kitchen in her nightgown and dressing coat, scraping into the garbage the food from the plate she had left out for Sanj the night before. She barely looked at him as he walked past her.

Sylvie's words about Chad echoed in Sanj's head: *He's come home to rest.* Sanj realized he needed to leave. Now. His parents were due back in just a few more days, but Sanj couldn't wait. He had to get out while he still could. He thought of the visit to Sylvie's a few days earlier: the sagging porch, the buckling linoleum floor, everyone in sweatpants. He remembered the promise he'd made to her four years ago, when he'd said, "You'll get out of here, too. I'll help you." He thought, too, of what his father had said on the phone about Chandu Uncle and their early years in America, how neither of them could have made it without the other. He decided that, this time, he wouldn't leave Sylvie behind.

Sylvie didn't need much convincing. She told her parents she was going on a week's vacation with Sanj, though she and Sanj—in words whispered to one another, as though saying them too loudly might jeopardize or jinx them— both hoped it would turn into something more. Aside from occasional trips across the river to Ohio, she hadn't set foot outside West Virginia since high school. She was ready for an adventure.

They took a cab to the bus station, a bus to Charleston, and a train from there to New York. The train would take twelve hours overnight.

In the row in front of them were a large woman and her young daughter, who must have been about eight and who was clutching a Bart Simpson doll. Across from them was an out-of-work coal miner—muscular and compact, with dirty fingernails. He was planning to show up, without forewarning, at the New Jersey house of his half brother, with whom the man had never been particularly close. But he had nowhere else to go, or so he explained, over the course of a couple hours, to the large woman across the aisle. "I tried calling, Lord knows I tried. But I could never finish dialing. Partly because I was worried he'd say no, and then where would I go? But mostly because I'm just so embarrassed for screwing everything up." Later, he said to the woman, "You're so easy to talk to. Why can't everyone be like you?"

Sitting behind Sanj and Sylvie were preteen boys on their way back home to the Bronx (reluctant to be returning—"The Bronx is *tough*"— after having spent the summer with their aunt in South Carolina). As Sanj passed their seat on his way back from the toilet, he thought he'd heard one of them mutter "faggot," but wasn't sure. Later, the same boy popped his head over the seat, and asked Sanj if he could borrow the batteries from Sanj's Walkman to use in his own Walkman, and Sanj, for reasons he couldn't understand—given what he'd thought he'd heard the boy say earlier—complied. The boy blasted Tupac, sharing the earphones with his brother, listening through one speaker while his brother listened through the other.

It was night. Most of the lights in the train car were off, but many passengers hadn't pulled their curtains shut, and Sanj could see the lights from the street lamps outside roll across Sylvie's face. The half light gave everything in the compartment a dreamlike quality.

Sanj heard giggling, then moaning from the seat in front of him. When he ventured a peek, he saw that the man and the little girl had switched places. The man was now in the seat with the large woman, the woman's daughter sitting by herself across the aisle. Sanj saw the man on top of the woman, one hand over her breast, the other under her skirt. Sanj thought about the man's dirty fingernails.

Sanj and Sylvie slumped down in their chairs, theirs knees pressing against the seat in front of them. Sylvie whispered, "I want this to work. I want a new start." Sanj took her hand. She rested her head on his shoulder. In the dark car, cocooned among these people all coupled off—the man and the woman in the seat ahead, the boys sharing the earphones behind them, the little girl across the aisle hugging her Bart Simpson doll—Sanj felt the train tracks rumbling below him, the train car hurtling forward, and he felt hopeful, like they were heading toward something.

Early the next morning, groggy eyed, they switched trains at Penn Station, and hopped on the LIRR to Long Island. Chandu was waiting for them at the stop.

Sanj hadn't told him he'd be bringing a friend, much less a *female* friend. Chandu Uncle looked surprised then disappointed, shaking his head, but he didn't protest. At the house, The Jasmines gave Sylvie the once-over, their lips curling in disapproval as they tossed their perfumey hair. Only Lala showed any sympathy. Speaking to Meghana in a firm tone Sanj hadn't heard before, she arranged for Sylvie to share Meghana's bedroom. She also managed to teach Sylvie, through a series of gestures, how to eat Indian food properly, how to tear the roti with only one hand and to use it to scoop up the vegetables.

Still, Sanj could tell, almost immediately, it was a bad idea to have brought Sylvie. Whatever courage or resolve she had managed to muster in the dark on the train had quickly vanished. Instead, she retreated into herself. She didn't want to leave the house. When she did venture out—Sanj dragging her through Soho ("This is the newsstand where I saw Naomi Campbell buying three copies of a magazine with her face on the cover; doesn't her manager provide her with copies?")—she lagged behind, barely looking up from the sidewalk.

By the third night, Sylvie had given Meghana the emerald green Yves Saint Laurent cocktail dress which she had bought at Bergdorf's four years ago, and which she had packed for the trip, not out of any rational belief that she would be able to wear it again, that she would be able to fit into it or have the life that would warrant it, but out of a hope she was too frightened to even fully imagine or name. When Meghana, cooing over the dress, asked with disbelief, "This was *yours*?" Sylvie replied, "No, it belonged to someone else."

By then, Sanj's parents had returned from India with his grandmother. He spoke to them on the phone. His father told him about his briefcase, which had been stolen at JFK ("I only set it down for a minute in the restroom") and about his grandmother, who had pouted the whole way and had barely spoken a word since arriving. "She's miserable," Bipin admitted. "But that's to be expected. It takes time."

Toward the end of the conversation, Bipin said, "You shouldn't have left your grandfather alone."

"He didn't need me."

"How do you know?"

Sanj had resumed his charade of pretending to go to work at *Vogue*, leaving Sylvie, most afternoons, alone with Lala. One day, he said, "Great news! They're letting me write the preview after all, the one about the emerging writer."

"I know," Sylvie said.

"How could you know? I just found out myself."

"No," Sylvie said. "I *know*."

"Know what?"

"The truth."

"About what?"

"Everything." She was looking directly at him, something, Sanj now realized, she rarely did. He noticed, too, for the first time, her eyes: emerald, like the dress, and glowing.

Sanj said, "You'll have to be more specific."

"I know why you were asking about Chad Webster."

Sanj didn't respond.

"I know you're gay."

"No shit, Sherlock."

"I know you don't work at *Vogue*." She looked to Sanj for a response, but he was quiet. It was he, now, who was averting his eyes. She said, "You're not fooling anyone."

"My parents. . . ."

"Your parents," she said, interrupting, "don't *want* to know the truth."

He wondered how she knew about *Vogue*, and for how long she'd known. Had she known sitting on the sectional in his basement, watching *La double vie de Véronique*, when he told her about Anna Wintour and the Lucite watches? Or when they sat together in the Van Gogh room? Had she listened to him rattle on and on about the article he'd pitched, knowing he was making it all up? When he'd said he was lucky, was she secretly laughing at him? *Lucky, my ass.*

"You're jealous," Sanj said.

"Of what?"

"My life has possibilities. I may have had a rocky start here in New York, but I guarantee, I have a bright future. What does your future hold? Getting fat in your parents' house in West Virginia? Another failed attempt at fucking community college? Sitting on the couch with your brother, smoking pot? You'll never be anything other than a loser."

Sanj took a step back, looked her up and down—the way The Jasmines had when she first arrived, the way so many had over the past four years—and said with disgust, "Look at you."

He stormed out of the house and toward the station to catch a train into the city. The LIRR was empty, as it usually was this time of day. No one was taking the train into the city; rush hour was long over. Sanj had a whole row to himself; in fact, he practically had the whole car to himself. He lay down across the seats, on his side, curling his body into the smallest ball he could manage. He wanted to disappear. Was it true, what Sylvie had said? Did everyone know? Had everyone always known?

When he arrived at Penn Station, he pulled on his headphones, and started walking. The city still seemed so strange to him. He tried to imagine what it had been like for his father arriving in Oklahoma at age seventeen. How many times must his father have stopped in the middle of the sidewalk, seeing the houses and the lawns and the trees and the cars in the driveways, and, remembering his village, wondered, "Why am I here?"

Sanj looked around. Without realizing it, he'd wandered over to Bryant Park, where he'd often spent time when he was pretending to be at work. Over the summer, several days in a row, Sanj had noticed a South Asian homeless man, which shocked and surprised him. He was more accustomed to the Indians in their mansions in Mulberry Hill. Several times Sanj tried approaching the homeless man, often with his handheld tape recorder, but the man always retreated. Sanj wanted to ask him what it was like for him. "How do you survive?" Now the man was nowhere to be found. Summer was over. It was fall, the first in seventeen years when Sanj wasn't preparing to go back to school.

He sat down by the statue of Gertrude Stein. He'd admired her work when he'd read it in college in a twentieth-century literature class. The statue's artist had rendered Stein round and sage as a Buddha, her eyes cast downward. Sanj remembered a quote, which he now imagined Stein leaning over and whispering to him: "A real failure does not need an excuse. It is an end in itself." When he'd read the quote in class, he'd instantly felt a connection, and had scribbled it on the cover of his lit notebook; it seemed appropriate, since, though he wasn't quite failing the class, he wasn't doing particularly well, either. Still, Sanj wasn't quite sure what the quote meant.

First L.A., now New York: Sanj's attempts at carving out a life for himself had been failures. He thought of his father. He had come to a new world and built a life in the unlikeliest of places. He'd constructed a mansion, erected a fountain, encircled it with scenes from his life. Sanj couldn't even manage to keep an unpaid internship.

"A better life" his father had said. When Sanj pressed him about what that meant, Bipin said, "More opportunities for myself and for your mother. But mostly for you, my darling son." He had held out his hands, as if offering a gift, "It's all for you."

It was eight by the time Sanj returned to Long Island. The house seemed particularly quiet. He could hear clattering dishes from the dining room. He found the family there—Lala, Chandu, The Jasmines—along with Sylvie, eating dinner. Sanj sat down. Lala had already set his place, even piling the plate with food. Little was said at dinner, but Sanj couldn't help feeling that he was being stared at. The Jasmines shot him harsh glances, narrowing their eyes. Had Sylvie told them? Had they told Chandu Uncle? Lala Auntie?

After dinner, Sanj found Sylvie in Meghana's bedroom. She was sitting alone on the large, queen-sized bed, curled up on top of the pink duvet, reading. She looked up from her book for a moment, but then went back to reading.

"I'm so, *so* sorry," Sanj said. He realized how insincere it must have sounded. It seemed to have become a mantra in their relationship, Sanj saying over and over to Sylvie *sorry, sorry, sorry.*

He noticed that she had packed her suitcase. "Are you leaving?"

Sylvie didn't answer. He couldn't believe the horrible things he'd said to her. He wondered if his father and Chandu Uncle had ever fought those first years in America. Surely, they must have. Had they hurt one another? How had they mended it?

"Please stay," Sanj said. As he formed the words, he realized how desperately he meant it—not for Sylvie's sake, but for his own. "Please don't leave me here alone."

He said, "Or maybe, if you're going back to West Virginia, I'll come with you."

Sylvie put down her book. "No," she said. "You can't."

Sanj stood in the doorway, blinking. He understood.

Downstairs, Lala was sitting in the living room, reading a Gujarati-language newspaper. Sanj sat down next to her. They were silent. They had nothing to say to each other, no common language to speak.

At first, Lala didn't look at him. Sanj sat quietly for a minute or two, and then found himself, almost without knowing it, scooting a little closer to her. Sanj felt his eyes well up with tears. Lala put her newspaper down, and looked at him. Her eyes were soft. She lowered her lids slightly. She opened up her right arm, and Sanj slid in, eventually resting his head on her shoulder. She held him.

He knew he would have to call his father and tell him everything. Safe in Lala's arms, he imagined it now. He would say, "Dad, I need to talk to you." His father would be in the enormous living room, which was a sunken room, two steps down from the rest of the level, making the already high ceilings even higher. He and Sanj's mother would be sitting on the sofa—a divan, really, with red brocade. They'd be watching a Bollywood movie, as they often did in the evenings, the videocassettes shipped to them from the Indian grocery store in Columbus. So many of the Bollywood films Sanj had seen had the same plot—a boy falls in love with a girl, but his parents have already fixed up an engagement to someone else, have already planned out another life for him—and this one would be no different. Bipin would pause the movie and say, "Tell us. We're listening." Sanj would be on speaker phone, and he would try his best to make his voice heard, to not let the cavernous house swallow him.

ANN PANCAKE

A native of West Virginia, Ann Pancake is the author of two story collections and a novel, *Strange As This Weather Has Been*. She has received a Whiting Award, a National Endowment for the Arts grant, the Bakeless Prize, a Pushcart Prize, the Weatherford Award, and the Barry Lopez Visiting Writer in Ethics and the Community Fellowship.

Ricochet

....

(from *Strange As This Weather Has Been*)

All Sunday morning and into early afternoon Corey and Tommy work on Corey's bike in the road. Dane pretends to watch the races with his dad, Jimmy Make, but every once in a while, he goes to the window to check on them. Jimmy tells him to settle his butt down. Finally, on one of his trips to peek out the drapes which Jimmy has drawn to make the races more vivid, Dane sees that his younger brothers are gone. He grabs a piece of bread while Jimmy's not looking and heads out to see what they're into now.

As he walks down the road, he squishes the soft bread into little packed balls that he sticks in his mouth and sucks. No threat of rain in the sky, but the road, the yards, too, are empty, and Dane wonders if that is because of the races or the heat. Then he spots two figures trotting up the road toward him, but he knows they aren't Tommy and Corey because they're exactly the same height. It's the twins, David and B-bo. Even though they're identical—each blond mallet head shaved uneven, near bald in spots, brushy in others—you can easily tell them apart. David acts normal, while B-bo acts like a car with bad brakes.

"You know where Tommy and Corey's at?" Dane asks them when they get close enough. B-bo had come up with his head lowered and his right hand jerking his gear shift. Now he jogs in place, his motor idling in his mouth.

"They're up in the Big Drain," David says. "Corey and Seth are having a bike contest."

"Idiot!" B-bo shrieks. "We wadn't supposed to tell nobody."

"Oh, idiot yourself," says David. "It's just Dane."

B-bo squeals his heels in the gravel and speeds off, David following, both moving in the direction of the Big Drain. Dane watches. He weighs whether seeing the contest, being there with the others, is worth the dangers of the Big Drain. He sucks on his bread, the nuggets lodged between teeth and tongue a comfort in his mouth. Doesn't look like rain. Even if it does rain, the water probably won't come out of the Big Drain because the water always comes from where it shouldn't, and the Big Drain is where it should. Dane leans over, ties his shoe, and jogs after the twins.

The Big Drain sticks out of Yellowroot Mountain about a third of the way up its side. It is hidden, deeply buried in woods and in brush, it's a secret place, despite how big it is, and the only people who even know about it are those who other people have shown. Exactly why it's there, Dane does not know. It's twice as tall or more than he is, and where it disappears into the mountain, about forty steps from its mouth, it's capped with a grate. Many people have tried to get through this grate, but the grate is a thick, rusted crisscrossed steel and nobody has ever managed to get past it. On its other side, the grate is hung up with shale and slate and rocks and coal, mountain guts, and the guts wash onto the floor of the culvert now and then, the water behind them coming from who knows where. Beyond the grate and the dirt, the drain disappears in a narrowing dark, and Dane, when he goes to the Big Drain at all, keeps well away from the grate.

He hauls himself up to the Drain's mouth, huffing and stumbling, passing the NO TRESPASSING signs. He pauses at the opening, taking in the scent, a heavy odor of cool dirt and old concrete and get-in-the-ground. He rolls his bread in his mouth, peering into the Drain. It is hard to see from light into dark, and although Dane squints and strains, he still makes out only the boys' drain-distorted voices and their shapes, darker darks that move against a lighter dark that doesn't. A mucky ankle-deep spit crawls out of the Drain and dribbles from its mouth.

The temperature drops as soon as he enters the tunnel. He walks the culvert spread legged, straddling the gooey water, his tennis shoes slanting awkward down the concrete walls. His eyes slot open to the dark like a cat's, and he sees it is Corey and Tommy and B-bo and David, and also Clyde

McCaffey, Seth not here yet. They have to know Dane has come in, but they act like they don't. This is what they always do, even Tommy, only six, ignores his older brother, here where he can afford to, when he doesn't need Dane to listen. B-bo is trying to climb the drain wall by reversing up one side the tunnel as far as his tennis shoes will take him, then barreling down through the bottom and sprinting up the other side until he crashes to his knees. The drain rocks and booms with the muffler noises from his mouth. Clyde, a boy about fourteen, but ignorant acting, catches on and starts shouting his own voice through the drain. His voice is changing, he can holler from low, moany *hoooo*s all the way up into whistle-pitched shrieks, the concrete rolling and largening his voice, and that sets off David, who sings a commercial at the top of his lungs, and Tommy, who makes like a fire whistle, and B-bo, who simply screams. Dane shrinks. He feels the crotch of his pants stretch from the pressure of the straddle, and he wills it not to split. The noise sluices back and forth along the drain walls, deafening and crazy. He wants to slap his hands over his ears, but he'll lose his bread.

Only Corey doesn't holler. Corey, ten, two years younger than Dane, stands near the grate to the side of the water, up the wall a little, his arms crossed over his chest, his bike leaning against his hip. His heavy bangs shield the top part of his face like a visor. Corey wears his camouflage pants and an army-green T-shirt, its sleeves pushed up to his shoulder nubs to show off the chamois rag he has tied around his bicep. Dane knows it's Corey's favorite outfit. At the sides of his body, he feels his own arms flabby and frail.

Suddenly, they all shut up. They're watching something behind Dane. Dane turns. Although he couldn't see from the light into the dark, from dark to light he can easily, and he sees Seth pushing his bike to the drain mouth. What has shut up the others is not so much Seth's approach as it is Seth's clothes. He wears some sort of racing getup, maybe motocross, and, true, he has outgrown it, the waxy groundhog blubber popping through so the shirt can't stay tucked, but, still, it is a racing uniform, neon colors and a big black *44*. For a moment, it strikes everybody silent.

Tommy is the first to crack it. "Coor-*ee*! Coor-*ee*! Coor-*ee*!" He chants his loyalty, which triggers Clyde again, and then David and B-bo, and Dane, caught off guard, claps his hands over his ears. And loses the last of the bread slice to the poison water trickle.

"What's the winner get?" Clyde asks.

"Ten bucks," Seth says. Something Dane knows Corey doesn't have.

"That's if he wins," says Corey. "I win, I get to ride his four-wheeler."

B-bo revs the engine in his mouth.

"Clyde'll mark it," Corey tells Seth. "Three tries." Seth nods. Everyone knows Clyde is impartial and has shown up only to see somebody get hurt.

Corey pulls his bike as high as he can up one side of the culvert. Their mom bought the bike last summer at the IGA lot off some man from McDowell County, a mock mountain bike with no gears, and it was rusted, so Corey and Tommy have sanded it down and repainted it with some old paint they found that didn't stick good to metal, which turned the bike into a kind of mess that Corey has convinced himself and Tommy looks tough. Dane watches Corey climb the wall.

Corey pauses once he gets the bike as high as he can—he seems to focus and then gauge where he is headed on the other side of the tunnel—and he pounces on the bike. Then he's pedaling as hard as he can down the face of the wall, Corey so close to the bike it's like he's melted to it. He sprays through the slime in the drain bottom, still pedaling, B-bo shrieking when he gets splashed, and Corey sails up the opposite wall, pedaling still, as high as he can until he has to spring off the bike to keep from wrecking. The bike crashes back down to the floor of the drain—but Corey lands like a fly on his hands and feet on the curve of the wall. Clyde jumps up with a piece of coal and scratches a black scrape to mark how high Corey has gone. Corey slides back down, brushes off his hands and knees, and picks up his bike. He saunters to a spectating position.

Seth's bike matches the motocross outfit, a neonish grasshopper green with jet-black piping, and Seth claims the bike has twenty-one gears. He clambers up the culvert wall, trying for the offhandedness Corey carried. He doesn't start quite as high as Corey did, and although he begins pedaling, by the time he hits the bottom the pedals get ahead of his feet so he has to throw his legs out and away from the bike, the pedals spinning free, and he has barely mounted the opposite wall before the bike, not moving fast enough to keep its balance on the incline, starts to sway. Seth slams a shoe to the ground and catches himself before he tips.

"Coor-*ee*! Coor-*ee*! Coor-*ee*!" hollers Tommy.

"I didn't get a decent start on that one," Seth says. It's a mutter, but the culvert swells it to where they all hear.

"You can't be worried about hurting your bike," says David.

B-bo and Tommy scream, "Coor-*ee*! Coor-*ee*! Coor-*ee*! Coor-*ee*!"

Corey sidles back into view. In the poor light of the drain, Dane can't see Corey's face very clearly, and the absence of detail throws into even greater relief Corey's bearing, his stride, his body-shape, Dane sees how all of Corey matches. Dane feels himself shrinking, and then there comes to Dane a picture of Corey as a toddler in Pampers, half Dane's size, Dane holding Corey's hand. Dane looks at Corey climbing up the Big Drain wall. He can't unsort the feelings that he carries.

Corey leaps on his bike. This time he rises a good five inches higher than the last time because this time he lets himself wreck harder. He splits from the bike at the last second, tumbling into a deliberate roll like a stuntman, his arms wrapped around his head as a helmet, and just before he strikes the water, he springs to his feet. The bike, in the meantime, has slammed to the drain floor with more force than earlier.

When Corey pulls it up, they see the fender is so badly bent Corey has to twist it back with both hands to get the tire to turn free. Tommy and B-bo and David and now Cyde drop the name Corey altogether, chanting instead a massive animal grunt—"*huh! huh! huh! huh!*"—and the *huh*s spiral the drain walls, ricochet and loop, until they overlap with one another. Dane hunches his shoulders up around his ears.

This time it looks for a little while like Seth might actually forget the bike and try. He manages to drag it to a starting point even farther up than Corey has reached either time, and he pounces onto the bike after it's already in motion, and he keeps up with his pedals. But, then, again, the hesitation. The second thought. And Seth, in the process of trying not to wreck the bike, turns it over anyway, gently, without damage, far, far short of Corey's marks.

"Corey won!" screams B-bo.

"*Coooreeee!*" shrieks Tommy.

"He did not," says Seth. "We get three turns."

"That's two outta three," says David. "Ain't no way you can win."

Then they hear Corey's voice, cool, from down the tunnel. "Let's just erase the two earlier and do 'er sudden death. Don't matter to me."

The confidence in Corey's voice, the offhand charity he grants Seth—all of this moves in Dane. A mixed-up moving. Dane sees Seth nod at Corey's offer. Corey snatches his bike back up the concrete wall, the wheel under the just-bashed fender making a peculiar click. He climbs so high he has to tip his head to keep it from grazing the drain ceiling, it seems he's too high to even mount the bike without overturning the moment he does, and Dane flares up in his chest, a hot-chill panic.

But Corey does mount the bike, and he does not turn over, and, again, molded against the frame like a movie Indian on a war pony, he swoops down the wall, hits the water so hard it parts more than splashes, and then catapults up the other side, by some miracle still managing to pedal. Too awed to feel fear anymore, Dane watches with his neck craned back from his squat, his mouth gaping open, as Corey shoots up the other side, passing both his old marks, and then, Dane sees, Corey is flying. He is not pedaling anymore, but the bike's still going, it's like the bike is coasting, but up, not down, and all five boys realize that Corey's going for a 360, a complete circuit of the tunnel, marble in a tube, Corey has busted gravity, and every face is upturned, every mouth sprawled wide, while Corey flies.

He's maybe ten feet short of where he began the circuit, so upside down his hair streams straight down off the top of his head, when gravity remembers. Dane's breath makes a quick moan-suck. Corey is coming down first, because by this point, Corey is underneath the bike, and Dane springs to his feet in time to see Corey slam into the bad water, the bike close after him, landing partly on top of his legs. Corey cringes into a crumple, his

202 / ANN PANCAKE

knees pulled to his chest, his hands cupping his face, and the other boys
rush to huddle around him, Tommy dropping on his knees, David pulling
at the bike. But Dane cannot move. Rigid leaning, forward straining, but
he cannot move, his stomach chock-full with the horror of a dead Corey.
When he sees Seth sneaking out.

Not blatantly sneaking, he's too proud for that, he's making it look like
he's just quietly waddling home, but Dane knows what he's doing. And he
knows, too, that he has to stop Seth, no one else sees, he can make up for not
being able to run to Corey by stopping Seth, and as Seth passes him, Dane
tries. He reaches out and takes Seth's thick soft arm without really clamping
down on it, without a real grab, and he is surprised at how taut the skin is
stretched over the flesh. Seth snatches the arm away, the fat popping out of
Dane's fingers, and snarls, "Get your goddamn hands offa me."

Corey is not dead. From his heap in the putrid water, Corey has already
sensed what Seth will try. He tosses the bike off his legs, it clattering against
the wall, the four-boy huddle scattering in surprise, and Corey vaults up
on his one good leg, half of his body soaked in that who-knows-what-all's-
in-it water, and he screams after Seth, "You damn well better get me that
four-wheeler ride!"

Seth stops right there in the entrance to the Big Drain. He casually
turns around. So backlit by daylight he is, Dane can't see any particulars of
him, can't see the look on his face. He sees only his sloppy silhouette, a box
with bulges. Seth, so smug he doesn't even bother to raise his voice, speaks
into the amplifier of the Big Drain: "Soor-ee. My dad says can't no kids ride
that four-wheeler but me." He pauses. "Liability."

Dane swings his face back toward Corey in time to see Corey's mouth
drop, the first nondeliberate emotion he has let slip. Then it snaps shut,
and his loose hands seize into fists. The mouth bawls back open, and Corey
is yelling, "You sonofabitch! You promised, you sonofabitch! You lyin'
sackashit!"

Seth has stepped clear down out of the drain so Dane sees him only
from his thighs up, but he turns, and in the light like Seth is now, Dane
can see his face lifted in a sneer, again, casual. And then Seth tosses back,

like it really doesn't matter, but he'd just like to throw them a last bone to worry: "At least I ain't got a faggot for a brother."

He sinks away down the bank, until Dane's seeing only the back of his pinkish head, and then nothing at all.

Corey has started after him, forgetting his hurt leg, and when he comes down on it with his second step, he screams, "Fuck!" and falls again. At the *faggot*, Dane's face shot full of warmth and he shut his eyes to hide himself. But he's been called *faggot* more than once, and coming from the defeated Seth, it doesn't mean as much as it might have. It means mostly the embarrassment that the others heard, and the faggot humiliation is dampened by Dane's worry over what he should do now that Corey is hurt. The others have pulled in around Corey again, stunned by his sudden vulnerability, and finally Dane is moving toward Corey (funny how sometimes in his dreams, Dane makes them all little, and when he prays, he sees Corey little, too), Corey is his little brother and he is hurt. Dane is moving to check on Corey, see how bad it is, then run down and fetch Jimmy Make, and he creeps in and leans down to get a better look. Dane can see the bright water in Corey's eyes from the anger and the pain, what little light the drain holds reflecting in that water, and Dane knows Corey has his mind jammed down on keeping those tears tight in their sockets. Corey stares Dane right back, hard.

"You," Corey hisses. "You goddamn homo."

For several seconds, they are all quiet in a new way.

Then David steps away from Dane, a delayed flinch. And B-bo states, at a normal volume, like he's just trying it on for the fit in his mouth: "Homo." Then he decides he likes it. A candy fireball on his tongue. "Homo! Homo!"

"Homo!" Clyde echoes with a crooked snicker. He cackles. "Homo! Homo!"

And then it's all five of them at the same time, Corey included, it is even Tommy who has only the vaguest notion what the word means. "Homo! Homo! Homo!" Homo-hollering and homo-hooting and homo-squealing, they slosh the tunnel to its brim with the word, they ricochet it side to side. At first they shout at cross-purposes, one voice's word overlapping the end of another voice's and canceling part of both out, the *homo*s knocking against each other, but soon they hit it in unison, a harmonized cheer, the *homo* sluicing from concrete wall to concrete wall, the drain doubling the word's volume and size, tripling it, quadrupling *homo*, and Dane turns and runs.

He jumps out of the Big Drain and tears off in the opposite direction from where Seth has gone. Smashes through third-growth trees and scrub and vines, angling the steep thick-weeded bank, slipping and picking himself up before he full hits ground, his hands and arms beating a way in front of him. Then, before he sees it, he's crashed into an immense thicket of blackberries.

He's snared deep before he even knows where he is, their canes whipping at him, thorns ripping, they snag in his oversized pants, Dane swims and wheels. Writhing and twisting, Dane thrashes through the confusion of bloody bushes, but on the inside of his eyes, he's fighting the boys. He's already kicked Tommy, B-bo, David, and Clyde into weepy balls curled at the end of the Drain like wadded hamburger wrappers, he hears the Drain echo swirling with their groans and sobs, and now he's turned to take on Corey. Dane turns to Corey and slams the heel of his hand into Corey's chin. Dane fights Corey with fingernails and fists, feet and teeth, he punches, pinches, bites. He kicks, slaps, trips, rolls, the blackberry patch continuing far past where he thought it would end, canes pricking and tearing, Corey coming at him, Dane hammering back.

Suddenly, he finds himself at the brink of the four-foot drop to the road fifty yards from his house. His momentum carries him right over it, and he hits the road so hard his shins ring, but he does not fall. He hears his tennis shoes smack through the broken asphalt, the chunky gravel, and as he sprints past home, Chancey surges out from under the porch to follow him. Dane tries to jump the creek, but lands not just inches, but feet, shy of the far side, and, wet to his shins, he scrambles up the eroded bank, Chancey right with him, both of them on all fours, and then Dane is loping up the old road toward the Ricker Place.

His breath's worn thin, tearing in his throat. The bones in his legs wobbly as grass stalks. When he's far enough up the draw to lose sight of their house, he drops from a lope to a trot, and, finally, Dane walks.

He stiff-walks. His legs trembling, his hands on his hips now. Him shuddering for breath. Greasy with sweat, it's running down the middle of his chest, the small of his back. The strange new smell that sweat carries these days. His face is downturned, and the old road under his feet has gone to grass. He passes the old pigpen, wooden slats atumble, empty now even of pig odor. The old chicken house, an exhausted slump. Finally, he drops down into the fine humped grass. And he sits with his head on his knees, heaving after his breath, but he doesn't cry. Dane never cries. Corey does, Dane whispers. And although his belly grates chock-full of hard stuff, grinding, he almost never throws up. Almost never, Dane whispers out loud.

Once Dane sits down, Chancey turns back. He pads over and noses Dane's ear, then he notices the blood on his arms and starts licking it. Dane lets him. "Dogs got stuff in their mouths can heal cuts," Jimmy Make will say. Chancey licks the blood back to where Dane can see the exact holes the thorns have made, each hole with a little blood bead hard on it. Lined pricks of blood beads Chancey leaves all over his arms. Then he realizes the front of his T-shirt, too, has been ripped, and he lifts it to get a look at the cut on his stomach.

The *homo* ringing in his ears, once he's lifted the shirt, he has to see more, so he pulls it over his head. He stands up to where he can see himself better. *Homo.* The blocky ill-fitting yard-sale pants, soggy with sweat over his thick lower parts. Hips and thighs, womanish, mismatched. The stomach and the chest still a little boy's, a softness to both. The slack fatness in the belly drooping down, the slight droop around his nipples, them peaking out, just barely, and Dane wonders if this is how a homo looks, and he feels pretty sure, yes, he thinks.

Quick, he slips the shirt back over his head to hide himself even with nobody but Chancey to see. He looks up the road to the old house.

He never enters the old house, rarely even approaches it. Too much chance of running into the ghosts of Grandma and Pap. But now, Dane still pumped full of the Corey-hate, the homo-shame, something draws Dane to the house. No room left in him for fear, and he's drawn to it. Dane finds himself walking right up and stepping into the ruin of the porch. Standing stands on the slant of boards in the stale odor of abandoned house, kudzu snarling up the insulite walls on either side of him, and he stares at the front doorknob. He knows it is not locked.

Chancey snuffles the porch rubble. Thunder rumbles, distant, even though it hasn't looked like rain all day. Dane takes a step backward, off the boards, but then he hears Corey's voice, a twisted-steel: *Goddam homo.* Dane reaches out, touches the knob, turns it. He pushes open the door.

At first his eyes won't focus, and it has nothing to do with dark. It's how what he expected to find just isn't, and there's too much other and in the wrong places. All that's left from his grandma's day is the stern coal stove, the Naugahyde couch foaming with burst stuffing, the wallpaper dangling in tongues, but Dane just barely sees that. He mostly sees nothing but metal.

Rusted metal, mud-crusted metal, broken metal, Dane cannot right away even separate it into things, and less than the metal, but still everywhere, plastic and wiring and cable and rope lengths and tires. Dane steps up onto the floor, his anger gone for the moment, it's pushed out by surprise. But then he understands, and the anger rushes hot right back and punches him full. This is Corey's doing. It's where he's been storing his parts. The trash he and Tommy have been pulling out of the creek and along the road for their plan, Dane has many times come up on them when they're talking of the plan, they bait him to eavesdrop, then shut up fast in an obvious way when he gets close and stare knowingly at each other. It's sheer meanness is all it is, and here now they've turned his grandma's house into a genuine dump with their mean secret mess, and the anger doubles in him, thickens, heats.

His arms and hands tingling, he weaves through the junk to the kitchen, completely crammed with metal parts and the old metal smell so strong Dane can taste rust in his mouth. A rusted sorrel-colored barrel, looking crunchy to the touch, wire screens off kerosene heaters and the heaters themselves, aluminum poles, a car battery, a car hood, there is junk piled on the floor and stacked on the old knock-kneed table, junk even wedged on top of the refrigerator, screws and bolts lined up in the windowsills.

Then, like a gift, Dane spies what he's been wanting, although he doesn't know he wanted it until he sees. A metal bar leaning against the refrigerator. Maybe part of an axle, it's hard to tell, but it looks hand-fitting, the heft looks right, and suddenly, Dane's mouth actually waters.

He picks it up. It feels unnatural in his hands. He lifts the bar over his head and brings it down, a practice stroke, and it jerks his arm down faster and harder than he expected, the swing unnatural, too. Ignoring that, Dane scans the junk and picks a tin bucket, mucked inside with dried tar. He raises the bar with both hands and heaves down on the bucket, following through with all his weight, but somehow he mis-aims. The bar glances off the bucket, the bucket topples and rolls rattly away, and Dane almost loses his balance and falls, but catches himself with the ball of his foot.

He steadies his legs and inhales. He hefts the bar again, swings it into an iron pulley-looking thing with dirt-clogged teeth, and again, the bar just bangs and bounces off, leaving no mark on the pulley. Now his breath comes quicker and lighter. Dane hears it at a distance from himself. He whams at a hubcap on the table, the hubcap ricochets off the wall and wobbles to rest on the floor without so much as a dent, and then Dane is just swinging. Wildman blind, both fists around the metal, he is hammering, he is whaling, he is slamming everything the bar can reach. Metal, tires, empty milk jugs, even Grandma's old refrigerator, the noise in his ears at first a crashing but soon narrowing to a high hurt whine, until he bashes the sorrel-colored barrel, and this time something happens, the bar does go through the crunchy rotted shell. But then it gets stuck. It somehow gets wedged in the barrel's side, and Dane jerks and twists and wrenches, but no matter what he does, he cannot pull it out.

Panting, sore in his arms, he looks around himself. As far as he can see, besides the barrel, he hasn't damaged one single thing.

He climbs outside through a hole in the wall. He hears fresh the machinery working overhead. And suddenly Dane understands, in a wave that washes all his anger away, just how pathetic the junk is. How it's not even worth destroying. For the first time, he sees the childishness of the scheme. And after that, he understands that the house is entirely unhaunted. That the old house contains nothing but gone.

Once more, he hears a far-off thunder. "I'm twelve years old," Dane says out loud. "I'm twelve years old, and I'm going to see the end of the world." But this time it comes without panic. This time it comes with grief.

He stands in the old yard and "Dane," he says to himself. "Dane. Dane. Dane." He bows his head. "Dane. Dane. Dane, Dane, Dane, Dane Dane Dane DaneDaneDaneDaneDaneDanedanedanedane." Until the word loses all its meaning, snaps off, and careens into the dark. Where, still, it keeps ringing. Ringing.

CARTER SICKELS

Carter Sickels is the author of the novel *The Evening Hour*, and the editor of *Untangling the Knot: Queer Voices on Marriage, Relationships and Identity*. He is the recipient of the 2013 Lambda Literary Judith A. Markowitz Award for Emerging LGBTQ Writers. His essays and fiction have appeared in various literary journals and anthologies, including *Guernica* and *BuzzFeed*. Sickels is assistant professor of English at Eastern Kentucky University, where he teaches in the Bluegrass Writers Studio low-residency MFA program.

Saving

....

"Dean, you okay?"

I realize the engine is still running and turn the key. "Yeah."

Jillian still looks a little woozy. I had to pull over for her a couple of times after we left the highway. This is her first time in Kentucky.

"Finally." She opens the door. "Fresh air."

We left Brooklyn early this morning and now the mountains throw long shadows. I hesitate, then get out, as Jillian strides across the overgrown lawn, marveling at the trees, commenting on the loud cacophony of crickets and spring peepers, carrying herself like she's never wanted to be in any other body. Her skirt rides up, revealing long muscular legs. Her hair is thick and red. She looks beautiful, and out of place.

My grandmother's house is a little one-story clapboard hidden in the hills behind a fortress of maples and oaks. The paint is dingy gray, sloughing away like old skin. A dented GE washer sits on the front porch. Before I go in, I take my time walking around the yard. Jillian does the same, framing her hands around her face like she's looking through a camera. A dense web of kudzu has swallowed the henhouse. At the edge of the woods rests a heap of aluminum cans, old tires, and discarded appliances. From here I can hear Sugar Creek, which cuts through the lower woods. When I was a kid, my grandmother and I fished for catfish and trout, but after the coal company started stripping above us, the water turned the color of Tang and most of the fish died. A pillowcase still droops from the clothesline, as if my grandmother had been hanging clothes one day and then vanished into air. I feel like I've come back to bury her, but she's not dead; she is in a nursing home, where I put her.

I push open the door, step into the musty, warm, familiar smell. It is eerily quiet. My grandmother usually had the TV and radio going at the same time. The house is dark and gloomy except for a few drizzles of sunlight. I flip the overhead switch and look at what I'm faced with. Boxes of old medical bills and Sunday circulars, tin cans with the labels scrubbed off, piles of clothes and fabric. Empty mayonnaise jars, plastic ketchup and dish-soap bottles. Stacks of newspapers, yellowed church bulletins.

"You were right, she was a hoarder." Jillian picks up a framed picture of me. I'm seven or eight, wearing a ruffled dress, a yellow bow in my hair. "I can't wait to start filming."

When I first asked Jillian to come with me, she didn't want to leave the city, then she started seeing it as a filming opportunity. "Back to your roots," she said. "Transguy in Appalachia."

Now I feel embarrassed, her seeing where I grew up. I light a cigarette, she looks at me with disappointment. Smoking on testosterone increases the risk of high blood pressure. I've been smoking since I was fourteen. When I started injections last year I recorded the changes in a notebook— weight gain, body hair, muscle mass—and Jillian took pictures. But after awhile, the changes became too subtle, or maybe we both stopped noticing. Everyday I look at myself in the mirror, wonder if this is the real me.

"God, it's stuffy in here. I need a shower." Jillian lifts her wild mane off her neck, puts one hand on her hip. "You grow up without running water?"

"Funny."

When she smiles the lines around her mouth pop out. Jillian is almost forty, six years older than me. She's got a horsey face and a yoga-trained body, and she's flirtatious and loud; when she walks into a room, people look at her, draw close. Only I get to see her in the mornings, her eyes puffy, her brow grainy with creases and lines.

While she showers, I walk through the house. Last year when I moved Grandma into a nursing home, I felt too overwhelmed to deal with the house, so I just left it stuffed with all her crap and hoped no one would break in. The coal company wants to buy the land. I told them it's not for sale. Back in Brooklyn, I started dreaming about fixing the place up. It will be Jillian's and my vacation house. She'll work on films, I'll plant a garden, our New Yorker friends will visit for long weekends. We'll have barbeques, sun ourselves at the swimming hole, read under the shade trees.

My grandmother's room looks exactly the way I remember: chenille bedspread, wallpaper printed with tiny roses, a dresser cluttered with ceramic animals and miniature teapots, and framed pictures of family, including her husband. My grandfather died before I was born. He was a deep miner and a drinker, and one day he was discovered by the creek, his skull cracked. He'd gotten drunk, fell on a pile of rocks. My grandmother never remarried or even showed interest in another man, at least as far as I know. I moved in with her after my mother died. I was eight years old. My grandmother wasn't affectionate, but she raised me and she always thought I'd come back one day to take care of her.

In the walk-in closet her faded dresses drape from the wire hangers like the skins of animals, the coats and blouses moth-eaten and old as the bones of this house. Bulging boxes of scrapbooks, photo albums, and loose pictures are stacked next to my grandmother's thick-soled brogans and a pair of navy-blue church shoes. I take out a handful of snapshots, shuffle until I find one of my parents. My dad in fatigues, slim and handsome in a weaselly way. My mother in a blue cutout dress, her thick hair falling below her shoulders. She's leaning against him, her face open and smiling. I don't remember them ever looking this happy.

"Find something?"

Jillian is standing naked in the doorway. Her ropey wet hair is a tangled nest, her skin pale and freckled and smooth. A Japanese-style tattoo of a pink budded tree stretches across her ribs. Her heavy breasts hang downward, the large pale nipples like a pair of closed eyes.

For the first time in weeks, she reaches for me.

"Not here," I say, stepping out of my grandmother's closet.

Back in the front room, Jillian slips into a T-shirt and underwear. I've missed my chance. She is thinking about her film again, studying the room. Jillian's work is experimental, and I usually don't understand it. She has shot me hundreds of times, but there is still so much she doesn't know.

She asks about the history of the house, about my grandmother's collections of junk. I don't know where to start. Grandma was always a pack rat, but it wasn't until after I moved away that she started to save so much. I push open the window by the sofa, blow a line of dead flies off the sill that scatter like ashes.

I tell her it's my turn to shower. "We can talk about all that stuff later," I say.

In the steamy bathroom, I strip and wipe a clean circle on the mirror. My eyes are milky brown, like my father's. My face is squarer now, also like his. My hair is short and spiky, and stubble peppers my chin. It is strange to think that I am here and that my grandmother is not. It is strange to think that my lover is on the other side of the wall. I hear her moving things around. I flex my muscles, clench my jaw, admiring the angles. This is what I used to dream about, years before I had language for any of this. My chest is flat and scarred, the nipples numb. After the surgery, nasty blue and yellow bruises made it look as if I'd taken a beating. I remember how it felt the first time I could run my hands down my chest without feeling the rise and knots of soft flesh, how that nothingness, that hardness, thrilled me.

We're exhausted, collapse on my bed. Grandma never took down the posters from my youth—Madonna, Depeche Mode, and INXS now yellowed, curling at the edges. I turn off the light, and when I reach for Jillian, she doesn't move. It's been like this for awhile.

"Dean," she says sleepily.

"Yeah?"

"Tomorrow you promise to talk about your parents? For the film?"

I haven't told Jillian much about my family, about my childhood. This has always been a sore point. Jillian wants to know everything. Transparency, she says. Trust. I was an only child, didn't have many friends. Grandma and I did not need to talk about what was in our hearts, we weren't that kind.

"Okay."

Soon, she is sleeping. She breathes openmouthed like a child. I lie here for a long time, wide awake, trying to make myself little. Jillian takes up most of the twin bed. I finally get up and fish a couple of blankets out of the cedar chest and make up the couch. But I still can't sleep. Can't stop thinking about what I'll say to my grandmother. Can't stop thinking of my parents, their fuzzy faces materializing like Polaroids behind my eyes. It's all the stuff in here, I think, suffocating me.

I slip on shorts and sneakers, and head out to the creek, breathing in the country air. The silver moon leads the way. This was who I used to be, a country kid who loved the woods. Not boy nor girl, just a kid. People think that the decision to transition is something you've always known, or that one day you experience a single earth-shattering epiphany. Maybe for some it's like that, but for me, for so long, I've both known and not known; I've had experiences that led me here, took me away, and brought me back, a tide I can't predict. Something rustles in the brush, probably a coon. The warm air smells clean and woody. "This is my home," I say, but the words, spoken aloud, sound empty.

In the bright daylight everything about Perry looks worse. Burned out storefronts, rows of old coal camp houses pressed close to the road. I start to drive through quickly, but Jillian asks me to slow down. Jillian grew up in the rich suburbs of Long Island, a train ride away from the city. We met at a mutual friend's birthday party in Williamsburg. She pulled me onto the dance floor, pushed her hips against mine. She told me I was handsome, her voice low in my ear.

"What did you do for fun around here?" She's wearing big sunglasses, and her hair is piled on top of her head like a stack of flower petals.

"I don't know," I say. "What did you do?"

"Hung out in the East Village, went to clubs."

"No clubs here. People had parties in the woods."

"You're such a country boy." She says, "It's sexy."

I glance over to see if she's kidding; the glasses make it hard to see her expression. "I just mean, you know, it's so different from how I grew up." She adds, "More real."

What I see are poor people and falling-apart homes and hardscrabble lives and junker cars on blocks. Families that go back for generations, and keep going, sprawling with cousins, half-siblings, step-kids. But not my family, whittled down to just me and my grandmother. A tight, closed-off circle; we will die out. I drive by a duplex where a girl I used to have a crush on lived, and then to where my parents' house once stood, now rubble.

"Do you miss your parents?" she asks.

"I try not to think about them."

We pass the diner where my grandmother used to work. Jillian wants to eat breakfast there, but it would be too complicated. "I might see people I know."

I continue on Route 12, taking us out of Perry and toward Murphy, where my grandmother now lives. It's a bigger town, feels safer—I don't know anyone here. On the way Jillian asks me questions about my parents, trying to open me up. The digging makes her happy. She's won awards for her films, shown them in art galleries.

I exhale a stream of smoke, remembering how my mother's hair fell out after the chemo. "My dad was only nice to my mom after she got sick," I say.

"He felt guilty." Jillian clears her throat and hesitates like she's just thought of this question but I know she's been wondering. "Did he hit you, too?"

Earlier, when I admitted that my father sometimes hit my mom, Jillian's face cracked with interest, and I quickly backpedaled, downplaying it. She wanted to know why I'd hid something that big from her. "I wasn't hiding anything, I just don't like to talk about it," I said.

Now I say, "He never paid much attention to me. After she died, he spent even more time on the road." My father was a long-haul truck driver. Whenever he'd first get back from a trip, things were good, but they never stayed that way for long.

"My parents would sit in the kitchen and eat doughnuts, listen to the radio. He'd tell stories about what he saw on the road, sometimes he played checkers with me," I tell Jillian, remembering how when he laughed, which was rare, his eyes crinkled, his thin mustache jumped.

"He didn't know what to do with me, so he gave me to my grandma," I explain.

"You were twenty, twenty-one when he died?"

"Twenty." Willowy and athletic, with shoulder-length hair and slender hips. "I was away at college when my grandmother called with the news," I say. "He'd had a heart attack on the road. A few days before, I had just had sex with a girl for the first time." At the funeral I couldn't stop thinking about her, her hot breath on my face, the way she'd bucked against my hands. "I don't think I could have ever come out to him . . . as anything," I add.

"You came out to your grandma though. As a lesbian."

"A long time ago. She was cooking soup beans. She stopped what she was doing and said, To each his own. Then she kept right on stirring. We never talked about it again."

I pull into the nursing-home parking lot.

"What do you think she'll say when she sees you now?"

"I don't know."

Last year the sheriff called to tell me that my grandmother had taken to wandering. She'd stolen the neighbor's mail and his pickup, which she'd driven across the county line. I had sensed from our phone conversations that she'd grown forgetful and nervous, but I didn't know how bad it was. I'd just started hormones and there was nothing noticeably different about me; some saw me as male, others as female. I booked a round-trip flight, didn't stay long. After several doctor appointments and meetings with nursing home staffs, I signed the papers. She didn't fight me. Half the time, she didn't know who I was.

Before we get out of the car, Jillian takes off her glasses and looks at me with clear blue eyes. "I'm glad you brought me here."

"For your film," I say.

"Not just that." She reaches for my hand. "It means something, you sharing so much. I know it's not easy." Her long fingers curve over mine like ribs of a small animal. "Telling me all this, it's good for you, too. Don't you think?"

"Yeah, maybe." I add, "I'm glad you're here."

Her smile is big and loose, and gives me the extra encouragement I need to go inside. Jillian asks if I'm sure I'm okay with her filming, and I tell her it's fine. She carries the camera under her arm like a pocketbook, and I suddenly wish I'd brought something to give to my grandmother, flowers or a cake. I try not to look at the old people parked in wheelchairs, slobbering, sleeping, staring, and I walk up empty-handed to the woman at the desk and tell her that I'm Gertrude Pearson's grandson. She doesn't bat an eye. Jillian and I pass as a straight couple, no problem, a thin, delicate boy and his sexy girlfriend. Sometimes I still feel nervous inside my skin, wondering how people see me, what they think. Jillian says I worry too much: "Just be yourself."

Outside room twelve, I take a deep breath. I've played this scene in my head over and over, but I don't know how I'm going to explain to my grandmother who I am. It's not like I've radically changed. My clothes, hair, all of that is the same. For years I've been presenting as male. But my voice is deeper and the hair on my arms and legs is dark and thick. I debated whether to shave my sideburns, but left them, the faint soul patch too.

There are two beds, two beat-up TVs. The roommate is not here. My grandmother sits in a pale-green armchair staring at her palms as if she's reading her fortune.

"Hi," I say.

She looks up, thinner than I've ever seen her, an emaciated elf with long ears and a nose two sizes too big for her face. Gigantic glasses slide down the bridge. She wears a pink terry-cloth robe and fuzzy slippers, clown shoes.

I go to her, kiss her forehead. "How are you?'

She looks at Jillian, then back at me. "Is that the new nurse?"

Jillian's lost her big smile and she seems nervous now, like she's afraid to get too close. I wonder if all this is too much. The junk in Grandma's

house, the dilapidated town, the stink of the nursing home. All this decay.
But then she recovers and steps toward my grandmother with her hand
outstretched, and I think about the way she used to smother my hands
and face in kisses when we first started dating. Jillian's face is tender and
kind. My grandmother doesn't take her hand though, and Jillian drops it
to her side.

"I'm Jillian," she says loudly. "Dean has told me so much about you."

The blank expression on my grandmother's face doesn't change.

"Grandma," I say, moving closer to her.

As I do that, Jillian quietly lifts her camera. "Pretend I'm not here,"
she instructs.

I put my face in front of my grandmother's. "Do you know who I am?"

Her eyes narrow. She purses her thin lips, then opens her mouth. "Last
night a man come in here through the window and tried to rape me," she
says.

Everything inside me locks together and then explodes into pieces in
a matter of seconds. "Grandma, that's not true."

She smacks her lips. She's wearing new-looking false teeth that are
straight and white. "Yesterday they strangled that girl."

"Grandma."

She shakes her head, impatient. "You don't know what goes on around
here."

"What are you talking about?"

She's quiet, then mumbles under her breath, "My Jell-O."

"Wait, what you said about that man."

"I'm hungry."

I take a deep breath. "Grandma, do you know who I am?"

She lifts her gnarled hand, brushes my face. The skin of her hand is
shiny like bone, the wrinkles like the ridges on a shell. I wait, my heart
pounding.

"I'm your granddaughter," I say because I don't know how else to do
this. "I'm Anne."

She spots Jillian's camera. "What's that thing she's got?" She looks alarmed. "What is she trying to do?"

Jillian lowers the camera, nervous again, like a kid caught stealing candy. My grandmother glares at her, then orders Jillian to bring her a bowl of Jell-O. She says to me, "These people, they don't know what real work is."

I sit behind the wheel, shaky and sick. "I shouldn't have put her in there."

"You did all you could. The place isn't that bad."

"I could have come out to stay with her. I'm all she has."

"You can't live here, and she wouldn't want to move to New York."

I swallow hard and close my eyes, feel Jillian's hand on the back of my neck.

"What if there's some guy really hurting her?"

"That window doesn't even open, didn't you notice?" Jillian softens her tone. "Dean, she's confused. Maybe she's getting mixed up with things that happened in the past."

I open my eyes and start to ask what she means, but stop as her hand falls away. I turn the key, the engine rattles, starts.

"You look so sad," Jillian says.

"I'm fine."

"Don't think I'm fucked-up." She stops. "I'd really like to film you."

"Doing what?"

"Nothing, just be yourself."

I'm quiet and can feel her waiting, worried about what I'm thinking of her. Then I tell her to go ahead. I drive back to my grandmother's, the wheel pulsing in my hands, the camera on me, a weird monster eye. Everything rushes past. I don't see any of it.

The next several days go by quickly. I put in few hours of work—I design boring websites and brochures for a living—but without internet service, I can't do much. Our cell phones don't work either. New York is far away. Jillian spends the days behind her camera, filming me, filming the house.

I spend the days organizing and cleaning, still thinking about how I can fix it up. Wondering if I should move my grandmother back here where she belongs. She wouldn't recognize the place now. I'm only throwing out what's clearly junk, but still, that's a lot. The rooms are beginning to open up, to feel brighter.

The closest neighbor, Paul, lives on the other side of the hill. He comes by each day to complain about something, and he offers to haul my grandmother's junk to the landfill for free. He's some relation to the old guy that used to live there and has no idea about me: he assumes that Jillian is the granddaughter, that I'm her husband.

"New York," he says with disgust. "Why in the hell would you want to live there?" Paul is in his late fifties and can't talk for too long without breaking into a heavy smoker's cough.

We stand by his pickup. When Jillian walks by, waving, he winks at her. Then he says to me, "Watch out for that one." He hasn't said much to Jillian, but he's always polite. She says he leers.

"I don't like him," she says. "He thinks we're this heteronormative couple. That's not us."

"We've got to be safe," I tell her. "We can't be raging queers out here."

Jillian has dated transguys and cisguys and women, and she told me early on, "All of my relationships are queer, doesn't matter if I'm with a guy or not."

Now she says, "It's fucked-up."

But we fall into a kind of routine and move easily around each other like the married couple Paul imagines us to be. I tell myself this is who I am—no hiding anymore. I pretend this is where we live, that we are happy.

Jillian volunteers to make dinner. I'm on the front porch, looking through my old sketchbooks that I found in the back of the hall closet. The pages are soft, velvety. I used to draw all the time when I was a kid. I flip the page to a leggy princess with rhinestones in her hair, then a boy pirate with quick fists and the power to turn invisible. Strange animals fill the pages, mythological deer and horses and owls.

I can see Jillian through the window at the kitchen counter, her back to me. She moves quickly, with purpose. Chopping, tossing. My grandmother used to can green beans and tomatoes in the summers, steaming up the kitchen. She'd warn me to stay away from the hot mason jars. She always seemed old to me, her hands bent and gnarled, her back hunched.

She still doesn't know who I am, although she seems to be getting more used to me. One of the nurses thought I was Anne's brother, and I let her believe it; another called me by my old name, and I didn't deny it. Jillian comes with me in the mornings to film. She and my grandmother have grown more at ease around each other, even though my grandmother still thinks that Jillian is a nurse and orders her around. Sometimes in the afternoons I go back alone, and we just sit and look at each other. Grandma always has a horror story, someone hitting her or trying to shoot her. I asked the nurses about it and they looked at me with pity. "Oh, you poor thing. Nobody's hurting her. She's delusional."

We eat outside, swatting at mosquitoes. Lightning bugs hover, and the bushes look like they've been sprinkled with glitter.

Jillian needs more material. "What are your most vivid memories of your parents?" she asks.

When I think of my mother, I see her crying or cowering from my father. Nothing was ever right—the food she cooked for him, the house she cleaned for him. I know this is what Jillian means when she says *material*. Jillian's parents give us tickets for the opera, and over dinner, they discuss the Whitney Biennial. Everyone in the family goes to therapy.

"What about good memories? Did you ever go on vacations or anything?" she presses.

I start to say no, then remember. "Once we went camping in the Smoky Mountains." Jillian presses, how did the trip make me feel? "My mom fried bacon over the fire and sang country songs, and my dad, he seemed at peace, for once," I say. "We all slept in a tent together. I never wanted to leave."

"What was it like when he was on the road, when it was just you and your mom?"

222 / CARTER SICKELS

I remember her looking out windows, staring at the phone, always waiting for him, always sad. "She missed him," I say. "How fucked-up is that?"

"Do you think your grandma knew about how he treated her?"

"I think so. At church she used to ask the congregation to pray for her lost son."

"Is she scary religious?"

"Everyone down here is religious. Grandma is a good Christian lady, but she's also superstitious. She's spiritual. Everything counts. Animals, trees. Everything's connected, the dead and living."

"So she's Buddhist. In a way."

"In a way."

I don't want to talk anymore. I set down my bowl of pasta salad and lean toward her, and push my lips against hers, force her mouth open with my tongue. I move my hand under her T-shirt, but she does not soften to my touch. The noise of the crickets is a hum inside of me, my heart trying to get out.

Jillian pulls back; we untangle.

"Maybe we should go out. What do people do? Honky-tonking?"

"You want to?"

"Maybe tomorrow." She picks up a sketchbook, thumbs the pages. "You had a wild imagination."

"Grandma used to tell me stories."

At first, after my dad left me with her, my grandmother didn't know what to do with me. I stayed out of her way, the way I was used to doing with adults. Then one night after supper she called me out to the front porch. She was sipping homemade wine that she got from old man Ruffy up at the head of the holler. After a couple of jelly glasses, she started telling me about ghosts, about the creatures that walked the hills. "I know you sense them out there," she said, "just like I do."

"I want to use these sketches in the film."

"I don't know."

"Come on. These will be great. They tell a story."

"What story?"

"Your story." She pauses dramatically. "Dean." The way she says my name scares me.

"What?"

The pause again, but then she shakes her head. "Oh, nothing. I'm just tired." She stands and stretches. "I'm going in, I'm beat."

I crack another beer and wonder if she misses the city. Jillian's friends are artists and queers, and she's always taking me to openings and parties and films. I don't have many of my own friends. I moved to the city to escape the isolation of my childhood, but it followed me, a disease in my bones. Grandma encouraged me to go off to college. "Live your life," she ordered. I just kept going and going, a wind blowing me north, rarely came back to see her.

I've been spending the nights on the couch. We haven't said much about this. Jillian asked if anything was wrong and I said *no*, and she said, "The bed really is too small for two people," and I agreed. Now I lay here staring up at the ceiling and thinking of my mother on the couch. Whenever my dad was on the road, she would just lay there, forget to make supper. She didn't put on makeup, didn't do her hair. I would comb it out for her, and she'd absently pat my hand. She'd tell me stories about how they met, how he swept her off her feet, saved her: I never learned from what. When she got sick, her hair falling out, her breasts cut off, my father became desperate, hugging and kissing her, and finally, she was happy. Happy and light, rising to heaven.

I can't sleep. I go in the kitchen and watch moths flutter wildly against the screens trying to get to the light. After another beer, I walk past the couch and go into my childhood room. I can't tell if Jillian's sleeping or not. I put my hand on her hip, waiting, my heart beating fast. Jillian sighs, shifts away. I start to get up, but then she changes direction and moves against me, her ass pushed against my hips. When I move my hand between her legs I feel her wetness and she moans. I want her to feel all of me. I hold down her wrists with my hands and press my flat chest against her, and we stare at each other in the dark, and I am waiting. I am waiting for her to tell me what is wrong. She gives me a sad little smile; I loosen my grip.

"He tried to kill me last night."

Rain pelts the only window, which looks out onto a parking lot. The light from the lamp next to the bed is a sickly yellow.

"He's after me."

"Who?"

"There are things," my grandmother says. "Things you wouldn't understand."

I hold her hand until the anger in her face subsides. I've shaved off my sideburns and soul patch. I've shown her photographs of my parents, herself, me, her parents, her dead brother, her dead husband; I've played the music she used to listen to, like Patsy Cline, Hank Williams. Nothing works, nothing pulls her back into herself.

"Remember that time you caught a snapping turtle when we were fishing? Remember?" I try again. "Grandma, I'm your son's kid. You remember your son? Do you remember Charlie?"

"You're going to be late for school," she says, suddenly perking up. Then, nothing more.

Before leaving, I ask to see the director. The receptionist picks up the phone and in about fifteen minutes, he's next to me, a chubby, balding man in khakis and a baby-blue golf shirt.

"I'm Gertrude Pearson's grandkid. From New York."

"Right, um, Anne," he stumbles.

"It's Dean."

"Dean." He is still smiling but his nose crinkles.

I tell him what she's been saying, that I'm thinking of moving her out of here, maybe someone is hurting her. He rests his hand on my arm, then looks nervous and removes it.

"It's the dementia. People hallucinate."

"Why would she say those things?"

"She's getting it from the TV, probably. The nightly news, TV shows. Could also be her medication. We'll talk to her doctor about it." He pauses, thinking. "Or maybe she's remembering something from her past and mixing it up."

"No," I say. "I don't think—"

"I promise you, she gets the best possible care." He lowers his voice like he's telling me something nobody else should know. "We're taking good care of your grandma."

When I wake up, I don't know where I am. I sit up, my heart racing. Then I see all the boxes, the mantle cluttered with pictures and figurines. I reach for my cigarettes, and the dream slowly comes back, my mother standing over me, clumps of hair falling out. Jesus. Everything is stirred up. I stretch, look down at my naked body. Touch the scars on my chest. After my mother had the mastectomy, she refused to wear the falsies that my father bought for her. Her chest was flat like mine.

In the kitchen I find a note from Jillian: *Went to town, be back soon.*

After I shower, I swab my skin with alcohol, draw in the testosterone. I do this once every two weeks. There is not this single moment that you transition, like Clark Kent ducking into the phone booth. It's not a magic pill, you don't go instantly from girl to boy. There is not a clear start or end. It's ongoing. The way you dress, the name you choose. If you have surgeries or not. Hormones or not. There is no easy path, no before or after. You're the same, and yet more yourself. More the person you imagine yourself to be.

When I met Jillian, only a few people knew me as Dean. But Jillian introduced me to everyone by my chosen name. When she talked about me, she used male pronouns, like there was nothing strange about it. I remember how right the *he* sounded, how everything else melted away, and this part of me, so hidden and protected, was finally seen. She's been with me every twist and turn of my transition, but now that I'm here, at last growing comfortable with who I am, I'm scared she's not.

The needle sinks into my flesh, a shot of sweetened pain. I am a project, I think, that will never be finished.

Someone is knocking at the front door. I pull up my underwear, zip my jeans, grab a shirt to hide the scars.

Through the window, I see a fraction of a person. I open the door, and Paul greets me. "Hey, how you doing?"

"Good. You?"

"Alrighty." He pulls at the bill of his hat, which says *Sit Down and Shut Up*. Paul is a big guy, over six feet. His belly hangs over his jeans. He's got a craggy face, a head of thick dark hair.

"I just come by to see if you needed me to haul anything."

"Uh, not today. Maybe tomorrow."

He stands there lingering at the door, so I ask him if he wants any coffee.

"I could use a cup. Thank you." He follows me into the kitchen. "Where's the little lady?"

"Oh, she went into town."

"You better keep an eye on that one."

I laugh uneasily, wait for the coffee to brew. Paul coughs for a long time, his face turning red and sweaty. Then he catches his breath, looks at me.

"I'm heading to town too. Got to take care of some paperwork." He shakes out a cigarette. "Care if I smoke?"

I tell him I don't mind and he offers me a cigarette. He mentions the paperwork again, like he's waiting for me to ask. So I do.

"The ex-wife." He makes a sour face. "Goddamn trying to clean me out. This house that Thomas left me, it's about all I got left."

He tells me that they got divorced a year ago. "Women." He shakes his head. "*Women.*"

Paul blows on his coffee, drinks it black. I don't say anything, and he keeps talking. "She was messing with one of my buddies. I wanted to kill the both of them, but then he got throwed in jail for drunk driving. She moved out, served me with papers." He looks at my hand. "Thought you said you was married, I don't see no ring."

"Oh, well, we're not really married yet. We're engaged."

I sip my coffee, trying to act like this is normal, the two of us hanging out.

"You best think twice before you get married," he says. "Best think twice."

If Jillian wasn't with me, Paul probably wouldn't be such a friendly neighbor. He would peg me as a queer, an effeminate New Yorker. Jillian is what he recognizes: she gives me hetero credibility. Paul goes on about his ex-wife and women in general, and I just sit there, feeling ashamed, listening to his rant. Jillian would be disappointed. I'm a coward.

He takes a long drag on his cigarette. "For a goddamn year she was running around on me. I was too damn pussy-whipped to see it."

He shifts his long legs. He has no idea who I am. For so many years I tried to ignore my feelings. I was scared for a lot of reasons. But one of the biggest ones was that I would turn out to be like my father, the one who taught me what it meant to be a man.

"I better get back to work," I say. "I'm trying to get a lot of stuff packed up."

"You think y'all are going to stay?"

"I don't know."

"You thinking of selling?"

"Thinking about it," I admit.

"Well, I wouldn't blame you none."

Then he reaches out, catching me off guard, and we shake hands. Something crosses his face, just a subtle twitch.

"Catch you later," he says.

I drag boxes out of the back room. One is as light as a carton of eggs. Inside I find folded clothes in plastic, like evidence from a crime scene. Little clothes. My clothes. Tiny T-shirts and shorts and dresses, ruffled socks and shoes the size of my hands. I hold them up in front of the mirror and wonder how I ever fit into them. My grandmother was glad I'd been born a girl. "The female's got a harder lot than the man, but we're better for the earth." She didn't say much about the men in her life. Her husband, father, son. They only caused pain.

When I hear Jillian come in, I set the clothes aside, thinking she'll want to use them for the film. She's in the kitchen, putting away groceries.

"What's all this?"

"Stuff to grill, liquor. I thought we could make margaritas." She's wearing short-shorts and a T-shirt that dips into a *V* at her breasts. "I got some good shots of the place where your parents used to live. I'll show you later, if you want."

I tell her about Paul coming by.

"He was ranting about his ex-wife."

"I'm glad I wasn't here." Jillian takes peppers and onions and mushrooms out of a bag. "I think it'll feel good getting back to New York. Don't you?"

I nod, but I'm afraid of returning, what will happen to us. Jillian was the first person to see me for who I was. Now I don't know what she sees.

"I need to go see my grandma," I say.

"Now? I was thinking we could have a few drinks. Talk."

I've told her too much. She's stripping me down, turning everything inside out.

"More recording?" I ask.

"No, just talking." Her smile is small, forced. "About us."

She looks tired, crow's feet around her eyes, a few new lines hugging her lips. The light coming from the windows shines on her face and glints on a single silver strand of hair. Her face is open and sad, and wanting too much.

"Later," I tell her, "when I get back."

Her face clouds as I give her a peck on the mouth, taste her waxy lipstick.

Instead of going to the nursing home, I turn on a back road that leads to the cemetery. My grandmother used to take me to visit my mother's grave, but I never knew what I was supposed to do or say. I take a few wrong turns, then find the headstones planted at the bottom of a hill. There are no flowers. The day is bright, hurts my eyes. Many of the headstones are flanked by little American flags, framed pictures, plastic flowers. My chest feels heavy, like it's sprouted phantom breasts. After I first got my surgery, there were nights I'd wake up panicked, swearing that I could feel my breasts growing back, and I'd have to touch my chest over and over.

I sit down in front of my parents' graves, but just like when I was a kid, I don't know what to do or say. The cemetery is butted up against a forest. A crow caws. My grandmother used to say that some spirits never rest. Her husband was one of them. My father, too. Now I know what she means. He's still out there, stumbling through the forest, tripping over tree roots. But not my mother, her soul is at peace. She's not here in the ground but in a big nest somewhere, high in a tree, protecting a clutch of tiny blue eggs. Hidden from my father. Hidden from me. Before I go, I pull up the weeds, revealing my parents' names, the dates that they lived and died.

Jillian has started the grill, and she stabs the vegetables through the skewers. By the time I finish my first drink, she is on her third. Her cheeks are red, her laugh too loud. She puts her hand on my crotch, and a hotness shoots up my chest. Then she pulls back. Studies me.

"What?"

Her eyes flick past me. "Have you decided what you're going to do about this place?"

The junk pile is still there at the edge of the yard, the washer sits on the porch. The paint peeling away, the roof caving in. Fixing it up is not going to bring Jillian back, and none of our friends will visit, I know that. It will always be a separate part of my life, the part that is the deepest and oldest.

"I don't know," I say.

The blackened vegetable bits on my plate look like pieces of bone. My mouth tastes charred. I start to ask what she thinks I should do, but a loud rumbling blasts from the driveway; both of us jump.

Paul climbs out of his pickup. "How y'all doing?"

He asks me if I want him to take a load of junk to the landfill.

"I thought you were coming by tomorrow."

"Shit, you're right, I forgot." He rubs his face, leaning in. "I didn't sign those damn papers," he talks low. "She ain't gonna get another cent from me."

Jillian grabs our plates. "I'm going to wash up, honey," she says in a fake polite voice, but her face is hateful.

Paul doubles over in a coughing fit, then sits in Jillian's chair. He takes a deep breath, wipes his eyes.

"I kind of gotta go, Paul. We're, you know, talking."

He grins, thinking we're on the same page at last. "Don't let her boss you."

I start to laugh, but then I don't. I wonder if Jillian can hear us from the house. "It's not like that," I say. "We've just got things to figure out."

Paul's eyes crinkle, like he's going to cry. His face is splotchy from too many years of drink, his hands tremble. He's just a lonely old man, heartsick. "Things are gonna be all right," he says. "You go in there. Everything's going to be all right."

Jillian's at the table, resting her forehead against her fist, her hair falling around her. I can't see her face.

I slowly pull out a chair, careful with my movements, as if I'm carrying loose eggs. She finally looks up, tears in her eyes.

"I don't know how much you want to know."

I don't know either: I want to know all of it and none of it.

"Someone I know?" I finally ask.

"No."

"Tell me."

She says he's an artist who has a studio in the same building as her.

"How long?"

"A few months," she says quietly.

I'm staring at the scratched table, my hands clasped together so hard that the knuckles whiten. Everything feels speedy and wild, my heart beating too fast, my mind racing. My face throbs with heat like I'm standing too close to a fire. I squeeze my hands tighter, trying to stop this thing that's growing inside me, this rage that fills my throat like bile, that spreads through my body burning me.

"Is he trans?" My voice sounds too loud, strange, an echo.

"Dean," she says. "You know that doesn't matter."

"It matters," I say, but I don't know if it does. I just want something that will make me understand, a clear answer, a reason.

"I knew you would think that, that's why I couldn't tell you, I knew you wouldn't understand. Would you look at me? Listen. It's not like he's some straight dude. We're still queer."

The *we* slices through me, and I don't want to look at her but I do. She is weepy, but when she talks about him there is a light in her eyes. I let go of my hands. Words are thick in my throat; I force them out like I'm spitting teeth.

"You love him?"

She doesn't answer, and I want to hit her, I want to hit her the way my father hit my mother. All this rage that's been inside me all my life, waiting. I force myself to flatten my hand against the table. She rests her hand on top of mine. I clench my other hand into a fist, dig it into my leg.

"I wanted to give this another chance," she says. "I thought coming here would do that."

"You just wanted to make a goddamn film."

"That's not true. I wanted to feel closer to you, to fix things." She shakes her head. "It's not working, Dean."

Her hand on mine is warm and beating like a heart. Finally, something snaps, movement returns. I get up and go outside, leave Jillian crying at the table. The air is stagnant, covers the yard like a sheet of plastic.

At the creek a school of tadpoles dart behind a rock. The gnats are thick; sweat rolls down my neck. My father stood over my mother when she was on her deathbed, cried like a baby, but it was too late. I crouch down like I'm going to be sick, but nothing will come out. My hands press into the damp dirt. All these months have been a lie. This trip, a lie. A dull thumping rises from my chest to my skull. She doesn't love me—she didn't say that, but she doesn't have to. I've known for months now, just couldn't admit it. Maybe I don't love her anymore either. I loved her because she knew me, but maybe that's not enough.

I take a deep breath, walk back. Early evening light slants across the house.

"Where are you going?" she asks.

"Town," I say.

"I'm coming with."

I don't tell her *yes* or *no*. She gets in, and I shift into gear, the tires grinding dirt and gravel. I've never spent much time on the road, but my father trucked thousands of miles, all of it blurring by like the years, gone. I punch in the lighter on the dash, hold the red circle to my cigarette.

Jillian tells me she didn't mean for it to happen. Sometimes things just happen, she says. "I felt terrible, all this time. He did too." She explains that they have a lot in common. He makes paintings. Goes to therapy. They talk. She feeds me details that I don't want. The sun descends, turning the sky a dusky, depressing blue. I drive faster, and as soon as I get cell service, I make the call to the coal company.

"What was that about?" Jillian asks.

"Nothing." When I look over at her the rage returns. I feel sick with it. I look at Jillian and I see her with a cock in her mouth, I see her waking up in the mornings with her soft puffy eyes, I see her laughing in his arms.

I speed up. Something shifts in the road and I don't swerve fast enough. There is a loud, sickening thud.

"Stop," Jillian yells.

I pull over and look in the rearview and see a dark lump. Jillian scrambles out, and I chase after her and pull up short. It's a puppy, a mutt. Chocolate brown with floppy ears. Positioned weirdly on its side, shuddering. Blood seeps from underneath it, and its hind legs look tangled, like the roots of a gnarled plant.

"Oh, God," Jillian kneels next to it. "Dean."

I touch the dog's velvety head and it bares its teeth, whimpers, and then it goes limp. I can't tell if it's alive or dead. It's not much bigger than the length of my forearm.

"We have to find its owners," Jillian says.

There are no houses, only an empty field, a patch of dying woods. A burlap bag is tangled in the high weeds. "Someone dumped it," I say.

Jillian is on her knees, like she's going to give the dog mouth-to-mouth, and I run back to the car and get a blanket out of the trunk, drape it over the dog, leaving its head exposed. I'm crouched next to Jillian. I can smell my own sweat, the blood of the dog, the expensive product that Jillian uses to tame her curls. No other cars drive past. Swallows sweep across the field. I reach out and touch the dog through the blanket. Its body is still.

I stand and take a deep breath, and Jillian stays crouched, her shoulders hunched like an old woman's. "Come on, it's dead," I say, reaching for her.

She knocks my hand away, then suddenly jumps up and rushes at me, punching my chest, smacking me.

"Look what you did," she says.

I grab her wrists. She tries to break free, but I won't let go. Her breath is ragged, cheeks flushed, the way she looks when we fuck. Her face crumples and there are tears in her eyes. "I'm sorry," she says. "It's not your fault, I'm sorry." I tell her I'm sorry, too. I let go and she wraps her arms around me and we stand there in the fading daylight, our hearts pounding against each other, until a truck rumbles by blaring its horn.

When I pick the dog up, still wrapped in the blanket, blood drips through onto my hands. It's heavier than I expected, like a sack of oranges. I carry the body into the field and set it under a tree. Jillian watches from the side of the road, arms crossed over her chest, hair lit up by the setting sun. I feel like I should say something, a prayer, or a goodbye, but I don't have any more words.

My grandmother sits near the window. It feels as if I've been treading water for hours, gulping air. I'm signing over my grandmother's property to the company she despises. The coal company will mine the land, bulldoze the house, and she'll never know.

There are specks of blood on my palms. I shove my hands in my pockets. "Hi Grandma."

But she is looking at Jillian, sunglasses perched on her head, T-shirt clinging to her breasts. Grandma says, "Sara." My mother. "I'm so glad you're here."

Jillian doesn't look at all surprised. It's the first time she's come in here without her camera and she walks over to my grandmother and cups her face in her hands and pretends to be my mother. "So am I," she says.

"Tell her who you really are. Jillian, tell her. Grandma, this isn't Sara."

My grandmother touches the hand on her face, then holds it in hers. Jillian and my grandmother holding hands. "Honey, are you okay?"

"I'm fine," Jillian says. "I'm okay."

My grandmother looks at me. "Charlie."

"No, no. I'm not Charlie," I say. "And this is not Sara."

My grandmother just smiles. At my father's funeral she did not shed a tear, but she said, as we left the cemetery, "I tried to raise him right." She knew there was something in him that was wrong, just like something was wrong in her husband. But wasn't something also wrong in my mother? One time my father was punching her, and when I ran over to put myself between them, my mother pushed me away. I always told myself that she was protecting me. But she didn't even look at me. She rubbed her jaw and gathered herself, and then she followed him into the bedroom and locked the door behind her. The violence haunts me, just like it does my grandmother. My father's blood is in me, so is my mother's.

"Charlie?"

"Grandma, no. It's me. Your grandchild. Sara and Charlie's kid. I go by Dean now. I used to be Anne."

"Anne's gone," she says. "Who's Anne?"

My grandmother blinks wildly like she's woken up from a long dream. She can't stop talking. She's not saying anything about anyone hurting her—she's just repeating names and dates and little bits of memories. She calls me Charlie, her son, she calls me John, her husband. Him, a man she rarely spoke of, but I know that he is the one who is after her now. Like father, like son. She goes on and on, calling me the names of the dead, these men who beat their women, and I am afraid to say a word. I'm afraid to meet Jillian's eyes. I apologize to my grandmother, how sorry I am for leaving. Grandma leans in closer to me, I smell her rotted breath. My grandmother who kept a room for me all these years, waiting on me to come back home.

Jillian and I sit by Sugar Creek. The mountains and trees hide the stars, but there is still enough light to see each other.

I tell her about the box of baby clothes. "You want to use them for your film?"

"I think I've got enough."

"You're finished?"

"Yeah."

She tells me she will go back to New York tomorrow. She already bought a plane ticket. She twists her hair with her finger, curling it even more. She's got so much of it, whenever we had sex it used to get stuck in her mouth, stuck in mine.

"What's the film's going to be like?"

"You know. Like my other stuff. It's not traditional."

I know what she means—once she pieces it together, the story of my father's death and my mother's death, my grandmother's fears about her husband killing her, and all the beautiful and sad shots of the mountains, the house, my grandmother's junk, my flat chest, the pictures of my mother who lost her breasts, the baby pictures of me, none of it will add up, there will not be an easy story: I will not recognize myself.

Now here I am, leaving what I know. I got rid of what my grandmother was saving and now I'm selling her land. She used to hang my drawings on the refrigerator. The princess was her favorite, but I liked the one with the angry fists, the invisible one.

"Dean, I wasn't just here for the film," Jillian says. "I care about you."

I think how things could have turned out differently. If I hadn't hit the dog, we could have taken him home with us to our house in the mountains and everything would be different, everything would be fine.

"If I had just stopped a second sooner," I say.

Jillian doesn't reply. Tomorrow she will go, and in a week or two, I will leave too, and no one will be here, except Paul, bitter and lonely, and all these ghosts wandering the woods. When I come back to visit, my grandmother won't know who I am.

The peepers, impossible to see, grow louder. They're all around us. I thought Jillian was the first one who ever saw me, but that's not true. For

236 / CARTER SICKELS

a few seconds the noise suddenly stops. Silence reverberates. Then there's a single chirp and they all join in. My grandmother taught me to look at what was hidden, to see what was right in front of my eyes.

This afternoon, before I left, I promised her nobody would ever hurt her again. She reached out her old claw hand and cupped my face.

"You're a good boy," she said. "A real good boy."

SAVANNAH SIPPLE

Savannah Sipple is the author of *WWJD & Other Poems* (2019). A writer from east Kentucky, her poems have recently been published in *Appalachian Heritage, Waxwing, Talking River, The Offing*, and *The Louisville Review*. She is also the recipient of grants from the Money for Women/Barbara Deming Memorial Fund and the Kentucky Foundation for Women.

WWJD / about love

....

You see her ass in front of you, reach out,
cup her curves in your palm. Latch yourself
there: her hip a hinge, her lips a door
you want to open and visit, not visit,
set up shop. You want to live there. You don't
have to imagine you're male. You don't need
a dick to be loved. Hold on. Her hip a hinge.
Her lips a door. Swing yourself into her
love. Breathe deep [through your mouth]—
let her thighs hold you close.

WWJD / about letting go

....

Jesus would say / *love* / *ask her to not forget* / *hook her*
from behind / *mouth hasped at her neck* / *her thighs*
will miss this / *nuzzle face* / *between lips* /
teach her to drape / *her dreams on you* /
eager / *like legs over shoulders*

Jesus and I Went to the Walmart

....

It was late, and what I really needed was some Epsom salts to soak my
ache. I've been dog-tired since I started exercising every day, and you
know I took on that part-time job cause you can't really make good
money at teaching & living in the city is rough. It costs a lot to keep up.

Anyway, we snuck in on the pharmacy side, past the display of cold &
flu medicine and cough drops. I got my salts and figured I may as well go
ahead & pick up some lady plugs since I was already here & had a coupon
for Tampax Pearl.

I was trying to decide between the active super or the super plus cause
I could tell by the way I was craving a hamburger it was going to be a
bloody time of the month. Jesus gets a little embarrassed by the lady juice,
so he wandered off & next thing I knew there he was in the condom aisle.

He'd cornered some young gun who kept walking past the rubbers,
trying to side-eye the different brands. He'd just about settled on the
ultrathin when Jesus found him, took him by the shoulder, and started
talking about how to please his girl. Jesus held the ultraribbed and had
just said something about clitoral stimulation & remembering this wasn't
a fifty-yard dash when I said, *Jesus, what* are *you doing?* and snapped the
condoms out of his hand.

Honey, [Jesus gets all solemn when he calls me honey,] *you know he's
gonna do it anyway, so he may as well be smart about it.*

Jesus took the condoms, handed them to the boy, said, *don't you knock that girl up.*

Poor feller didn't know what'd hit him. He couldn't get to the checkout line fast enough.

Jesus bought me a burger on the way home, and as we sat outside at the picnic tables, I said, *people around here are either afraid of having sex or afraid of people finding out they're having sex. Why do you reckon that is? Is it cause of religion?*

He took a long swallow and said, *no. It's desire, I think. The only feeling stronger than desire is fear, and most often we're afraid of the things we want so badly.*

Jesus, do you really think that's true?

Of course. Why do you think it took you so long to come out?

Damn. I hate it when he's right.

Catfisting

....

I see you coming a mile away as I sit creek cold
while you drink beer, catch fish with the boys.

I couldn't give a rat's ass about lures,
your rods, or how good you are

at reelin' them in. Your shit-eating grin doesn't work
on me. While you play with your scaling knife,

laugh at your own stories, loud, I'm already thinking
of her—by the time you look up to say *ain't that right* . . .

sweetie, I'm downstream, away from fingers
that hook me, angling for my own mudcat.

Pork Belly

....

Imagine you clutch the carving knife,
slice it under & against your own ribs—
one cut for every time they call you fat.
Take that meat, preserve it with salt
to season your beans—pinto, green.

In your hands, a bucket. The fat
sloshes, hot grease you collect
in coffee cans, glass jars, your dreams
dripping off your meat. This
is poverty: you save every drip.
Tell me, how many people

you trying to feed?

A List of Times I Thought I Was Gay

....

1.
I gave a girl a handwritten copy of Peter Cetera
lyrics and it hurt me when she left them
in another girl's desk.

2.
I wrote a letter to my sports idol.
I wanted to be like her: a girl the boys
feared on the court.

3.
Whenever she made me wear a dress.

4.
I wore shorts & knee socks to the school dance
instead of a skirt. My friends laughed. A cute older boy
asked me to dance and his friends laughed.

5.
In the locker room, surrounded by sports bras
& ball shoes I felt no different. I looked.

6.
I cut myself with a straight razor.

7.
In the kitchen at church camp. I cleaned
dishes in three sinks: soap water, bleach, rinse.
Week after week, for years. I never felt clean.

8.
I wanted to hug someone.
I did not trust myself to hug someone.

9.
Boxing class. My body sore, my muscles
alive.

10.
When I saw you clothed.

11.
And imagined you naked.

12.
When I saw you naked.

13.
When I let myself hug you
in my mind and your arms
found my body, and we were
clothed & naked at once.

14.
I realized, if I wore makeup,
if I wore dresses,
she thought it meant I was straight.

15.

When the youth pastor decried our friend
might be dating a woman, my face flushed.

16.

When I wore my hair in a fauxhawk
then washed it out immediately.

17.

Every time I wanted to buy a new tie.

18.

When I notice your tight
shirt sculpted to your breasts,
your abs, your jutted-out hips.

19.

Every time a friend got married
and I went without a date.

20.

The first time I said
I'll never marry a man.

Then cried
when I realized I didn't have to.

Jesus Signs Me Up for a Dating App

....

Listen, he says, *there's no use wasting time*
on that Tinder bullshit. You ain't interested
in any dick pics, so you may as well pick
the app for lezzies. Find at least one full body
photo. No point in hiding now. Use that one—
the one where you're wearing the necktie
and smiling real big—honey, if that don't
woo 'em, nothing will.

ANITA SKEEN

Anita Skeen is currently professor of literature and creative writing at Michigan State University where she is the director of the Residential College in the Arts and Humanities Center for Poetry and the series editor for Wheelbarrow Books. She is the author of five collections of poetry, coeditor of an anthology, and coauthor of two books of poetry and visual art.

Double Valentine

....

At sixty, my grandmother died
surrounded by three daughters
while I slept, unaware,
on a couch in another room.
You're sixty today, unaware
I'm thinking of you,
about how it is possible
for you to be that age.
A grandmother, too,
and mother of three,
you're surrounded by dogs
and CDs, watercolor tubes,
friends to sing you into
the next decade, not by pills,
a bedpan, a new piano
gathering dust. She died
in the month you were born,
borne away in a blizzard
right out of a Russian film.
I don't know what weather
brought you into life, only
what weather you brought
into mine. The war was on,
chaos around you, at best.

Snow's in today's forecast,
enough to soften stumps
and rocks, cloak the pines.
I loved you both, never
making the connection
until now, how the heart
goes dormant in a season
of cold, how blood
hungers to blossom.

How Bodies Fit

....

In outer space, they orbit, each
keeping its perfect and known distance
from the other, except for renegade
stars which shoot off this way and that
like startled cats. Or on land, think about
the Great Lakes, the way three of them
rendezvous near the Soo, the other two
excluded by Detroit. Think how the body
of the essay slips cleanly between
introduction and conclusion, transitional
sentences tucking it in, or a baseball
snuggles in the soft pocket of glove.
And those six puppies,
see them tumble together in the plastic basket
like lumpy laundry, one brown head poking
through two mismatched paws, seamless
in their reconfigured selves. Or us,
at night in the lull of sleep,
how leg migrates toward leg,
the shifting of tectonic limbs, knee
nudging knee, wave to shoreline,
two islands reunited
after years adrift.

Need

....

In a room, two women sit talking.
A large window, planes
of evening light.

A song they both associate
with someone absent.
Darkness wanders in,

returning the song
to their hearts,
One is home, the other

a long way from it.
A fitting of stories,
a chord.

A touching of hands.
The moon looms like a memory.
The tide comes in.

Something You Should Know

....

I became a poet because I was in love
with a writer of short stories
who loved (she thought) a malcontent
scholar who loved (we discovered)
a beautician named Jackie in Toledo,
Ohio. It is at this point
my life begins. I abandoned my married
lovers for younger ones of the opposite sex,
swore never again to have midnight encounters
with irate wives in local bars, tried to give up
drinking, and promised myself a new start
in a new place. Moving brought me
to the Midwest; a job and a lover
kept me here. The first is now boring,
the second is gone. Better that way
than the other, I suppose. I am ready
for a change. I have rediscovered
choice and I plan to use it:
I am the old hound sitting on the back stoop
barking all night because I want to,
the young girl climbing the tall wooden fence
because it is there, the woman who will take
your hand when it is offered (avoiding
pertinent questions), prune the rings
from our fingers one by one,
drink from the ripe openings of your eyes.

The Clover Tree

....

It's been doing this forever, you say,
when I ask you why looking at the water
rushing over stones in Little River makes me cry.
So you must mean something about endurance,
tenacity, the strength to rush ahead through
impossible impediments. *And grace,*
you add, *it's about grace.* I'm lying on my back
on an old quilt pulled from the trunk of your car
looking up through the leaves of a tree, something
like O'Keeffe must have done before she painted
The Lawrence Tree, but there's no night sky.
You're sitting by the river's edge, close
enough to dangle in your feet, but you don't.
My aunt's name is Grace, I say, being
in associative mode, and that's one
meaning for my name, another way
I learned about irony as a clumsy child
who stumbled over air and broke more bottles
of milk than a passel of hungry cats.
You start to sing "Amazing Grace" soft
enough that I can just barely hear it above
the river's song. I remember the first time
I heard you play it on the harmonica, the first time
of many first times, and of my friend, dead now
fifteen years, who played and sang that song
the way it was meant to be, a spiritual

conversion. Each time I hear "Goodnight, Irene,"
her favorite, tears won't let me swallow.
Wind tumbles in the trees, joining the choir,
when I notice how, without my glasses,
the tree above is a field of four-leaf clover
on this, my lucky day, where I know
what the river knows, and I feel
I could go on doing this
forever.

The Quilt: 25 April 1993

It's the hands I see first, on this panel,
the community of hands reaching toward a name
that could be yours, could be mine,
but happens to be Bob's, the hands simple
as those we drew in the primary grades,
tracing around splayed fingers, stubborn thumb,
a ghostly outline on manila stock.
We cut them out, took them home
to our moms. These hands are fabric,
paisley and denim, tartan and corduroy,
a school of hands swimming toward
Bob's name, hands with their first names
stitched awkwardly in thin thread.
I lay down my own hand, pale one
in the multitude, for enough time
that I feel the hard earth
beneath the weave, a scattering
of small stones. My hand
is the princess resting on the pea.

We move on down the corridor, silent
as those around us. Here's a panel
from Ames, Iowa, one from Kansas, another
from Hawaii, green palm fronds bordering
a blue sea. *This is worse than
the Viet Nam wall*, you say

letting go of your tears. The squares
stretch north and south, east and west,
the four corners of our hearts.
All this color, I think, all this brilliance
about loss. Tom, the next patch says,
then Randy, then Susan.
We say the names aloud, a litany
of stolen light, as we compose
our grief among these postage stamps
of cloth, how we mail our private
and collective message on ahead.

While You Sleep

....

These mountains sleep
side by side, nesting shoulder
along shoulder, knee behind knee,

asking for my hand to reach out
through this cabin window,

to reach toward the blue arc
of the hip, the green lift of the breast,
to lose my hand in the channels
of rivers, my fingers tickling in streams.

In this first light I can barely

call light, how the mist
rises from their curves, how their forms
quicken as I reach
toward them, how they reel in

breath when my hand brushes
trillium and fern, my fingertips
hush over moss. My hand flutters

like moth wing, like falling dogwood,
among the spring leaves,
slips under the rocky ribs of the creek
beds, ascends the explosion of rapids

to my cupped hand. Damp
and pungent, my hand returns to me,
fingers tracing my open lips

as these hills open to rain.

AARON SMITH

Aaron Smith is the author of *The Book of Daniel, Primer, Appetite,* and *Blue on Blue Ground,* winner of the Agnes Lynch Starrett Poetry Prize. He is the recipient of fellowships from the New York Foundation for the Arts and the Mass Cultural Council. A three-time finalist for the Lambda Literary Award, he is an associate professor at Lesley University in Cambridge, Massachusetts.

Blanket

....

Does it matter to you that it's snowing
in West Virginia and people keep saying the word *blanket*?

Over the cars: a blanket and the streets are blank-
eted and the schools are closing under blankets of wet snow.

I'm sitting under a blanket missing every place I've lived—
Pittsburgh's edges, Boston's proper sidewalks, the cold

shoulders and steel jaws of New York.
Do you remember our last walk?

The leaves were sticking to the ground, the park
was orange and oddly warm and people

were laid out on blankets, little islands, little
worlds of what they loved, wanted to love

or no longer loved, but were trying,
for whatever reason, to hold onto.

There's still one story

....

I don't know what to do with:
the little girl in the cage

in the kitchen,

her parents keeping her there
like a dog while the other

kids played and how

a younger brother left,
crawled out the window

and got to the police.

It's not the cruelty,
the shattering we're all

on the verge of,

but it's the girl
who when the police

took her picture

took her hand
and fixed her hair

for the camera.

Twice

....

I was small enough to stand
beside dad while he drove, wedged
between the seat and his shoulder, my small
hand on the small hairs of his neck. The truck
was rust and mud and hunting
clothes, leaves and woodsmoke.
My legs slid against the vinyl seat,
my whole body shifted
when he shifted gears.

———

He came home late from the plant
and only wanted to talk to me, to tell me
a story, maybe ask about my day, about school,
who I ate lunch with, but I didn't want
to talk to him and pretended
to be sleeping when he stepped
into my room—his body
a shadow across my body—
I don't know why I did that.

JULIA WATTS

A native of southeastern Kentucky, Julia Watts has written thirteen novels for adults and young adults, most of which explore the lives of LGBT people in rural and small-town Appalachia. Her novel *Finding H.F.* won the 2002 Lambda Literary Award in the children's/young adult category. A novel for adults, *The Kind of Girl I Am,* was a finalist for a Lambda Literary Award in the women's fiction category, and her 2013 young adult novel *Secret City* was a finalist for a Lambda Literary Award and a winner of a Golden Crown Literary Society Award. Julia's other titles include *Gifted and Talented, Hypnotizing Chickens,* and most recently, *Rufus + Syd,* cowritten with Robin Lippincott. Julia holds an MFA in writing from Spalding University and has spoken at various national and regional conferences, including the AWP Conference, the NCTE Annual Convention, the Appalachian Studies Association Conference, and the Sarah Denman Symposium on Appalachian Literature. She lives in Knoxville and teaches at South College and in Murray State University's low-residency MFA in writing program. She was recently inducted into the East Tennessee Writers Hall of Fame, and her new novel, *Quiver,* was released by Three Rooms Press in 2018.

266 / JULIA WATTS

Handling Dynamite

....

Ronnie comes home black.

Sissy has the tub ready. It took her a solid hour of boiling pot after pot of water on the coal stove, then pouring it into the big galvanized tub. By the time Ronnie gets home, the temperature is just right, on the safe side of scalding. A sheet is strung up around the tub for privacy, even though Sissy never uses it when she has her bath. Ronnie likes to watch her.

Ronnie doesn't like to be watched. A miner's bath isn't like a pretty woman's bath. The blackness has to be scrubbed from the face and hands (the nails stay black). The lye soap is so harsh and the scrub brush so rough that the clean skin that finally does emerge is pink and angry. The water left in the tub is black as ink.

"Ready for some supper?" Sissy asks when Ronnie comes out from behind the sheet dressed in a fresh work shirt and dungarees.

"I could eat a mule," Ronnie says, grinning.

"How 'bout some beans and taters instead?"

It's one of their little jokes. Ronnie always talks about being hungry enough to eat some large animal, and Sissy always offers beans and taters instead.

"Even better," Ronnie says, like always.

Sissy does her part and laughs prettily. Everything about her is pretty. Her wild orange curls and fair skin and freckles. The dresses she makes out of flour sacks are even pretty, the way she sews darts in them so they fit tight around her waist and bust.

They sit at the little table and eat soup beans, cornbread, and fried taters cooked brown the way Ronnie likes them. They drink cold buttermilk. Except in the summers when the fresh corn and beans and tomatoes come in, supper is always the same. But it's good and there's plenty of it.

After she's cleaned the dishes and put them away, Sissy finds some music on the radio. They dance, Sissy's arms around Ronnie's neck, Ronnie's hands around Sissy's little waist.

Most nights they make love. The men at the mines complain sometimes about how their wives never want to do it, but Sissy is always willing, arching her back and letting out little mews of pleasure. Maybe the wives of the other miners are too tired from taking care of younguns all day and just want to sleep. Or maybe the other miners don't know their way around a woman.

In the morning, Ronnie gets into the cart that takes the miners into the mouth of the mine, and a *mouth* is what it is. It swallows them into darkness every morning and doesn't spit them back out until it's dark outside. A wooden sign over the entrance says GOOD MORNING BE CAREFUL—like your wife when she kisses you goodbye and hands you your dinner bucket.

Lots of miners hate the darkness when they first start working, but Ronnie loved it since day one. Daylight feels too bright, too revealing, but darkness is safe and comforting, a soft black blanket.

"Look at that shit-eating grin on Ronnie's face," Buddy says as they ride into the dark. "He must've got some lovin' from that redheaded woman last night."

"Well, you know what they say about redheads," Harold says. He elbows the twelve-year-old breaker boy sitting next to him. "I bet you wanna be like Ronnie when you grow up."

Ronnie just keeps on grinning.

Really, Ronnie loves everything about the mines, the other miners' good-natured ribbing, the work itself even though it's hard. Today, Ronnie, whose smallness is an advantage in the mine's crevices, is lying flat on the wet floor digging into the hard rock with a pick. It's one of the low-ranking jobs, picking like this, but a good picker can get promoted to blast out the coal. It would be exciting, Ronnie thinks, getting to handle dynamite.

For now, though, picking is fine. It brings a steady paycheck plus the jingly funny money Sissy likes to spend at the company store. Others miners complain of aching muscles and permanent colds from the damp.

But Ronnie never complains because life feels as close to perfect as this life can be.

Ronnie shifts on the damp mine floor to better reach a shiny black lump protruding low on the rock face. "Fire in the hole!" a voice yells, closer than it should be. Then comes the blast, then the blackness.

The room is white with no trace of coal dust. Sunlight blares through the white-curtained window. Feeling woozy and achy, Ronnie is wearing a pair of unfamiliar pajamas and lying in an unfamiliar bed.

The door swings open. It's Doc Woods. Ronnie has never had any cause to visit Doc's office but has seen him around the camp.

"Finally decided to wake up, did you?" Doc Woods smiles under his big gray mustache. "That was quite a bump on the noggin you took."

"Am I in the infirmary?" Ronnie tries to stitch together some memories.

"No, three others that got hurt in the blast are over in the infirmary. But I brought you to my house because you . . . you're a special case, aren't you?"

Ronnie looks down at the pajamas and finally understands what they mean. "You took off my clothes, didn't you?"

"Had to. To examine you." Doc Woods pulls up a chair and sits beside the bed. "And I have to say it was the most interesting examination of my career. I thought that gauze wrapped around your chest might be covering up an injury, but that's not what it was covering, is it? And there was that sock you had rolled up . . ."

"Stop," Ronnie says. It would've been better if the rocks had crushed her flat. People would've found out then, too, but she wouldn't have had to live with the consequences. "So you know everything." Ronnie's stomach feels sick.

Doc chuckles. "I don't know everything, but I reckon I'm about to find out. You and I are gonna have a little talk." He leans forward in his chair. "How long have you been dressing up like a boy?"

Ronnie sighs. The biggest piece of the truth was out now. There's no point in lying. "I dressed in my brother's hand-me-downs when I was little. Except when I had to go to school; then Mommy made me wear dresses. I didn't start passing myself off as a feller until I was grown. After I left home, going on three year ago."

"Ronnie—is that short for Veronica?" Doc asks.

Doc already knows too much. There's no reason for him to know the name she was born with. "Ronnie was my brother. He got killed in a knife fight."

"So you took his name?"

Ronnie shrugs. "He wasn't using it."

Doc Wood takes a cigar out of his pocket, lights it, and puffs. "Well, you're brave. I'll give you that." He blows out three rings of gray smoke. "So you and that little redhead you're shacked up with decided you'd make fools of this whole camp, did you?"

"No!" Ronnie says louder than she means to. "Sissy's innocent. We said *I do* in front of a preacher and everything. She don't know."

Doc raises his eyebrows so high they almost disappear into his hairline. "Now I have to say I find this awful hard to believe. If the young lady thinks she's your wife . . . well, then, I'd think you'd be having marital relations."

"I keep on my union suit."

Doc Woods laughs. "Well, that seems like it addresses only part of the problem. You don't have a—"

"I made one. A thing I use. It feels pretty real, and besides, Sissy wasn't but sixteen when we got together. She ain't never been with nobody else, so she don't know the difference." Ronnie feels like crying. Losing her job would be hard, but losing Sissy is the worst thing she can imagine.

Doc Woods shakes his head. He isn't laughing anymore. "So you lied to and corrupted this young girl—"

"I didn't corrupt her. I love her." Ronnie blinks to keep back the tears.

"And you lied to and deceived this whole community. You know what would happen if word got out a woman had been working in the mines? You know how superstitious these boys are. They say if a woman goes in the mines, there'll be an accident soon. And look what happened. I've got three boys—real ones—over in the infirmary, one of 'em who'll probably never walk again."

"And you think I caused the accident because I'm a woman?"

Doc rises to his feet. "Now see here, I'm a man of science. Of course I don't think that. But everybody else in the camp will. And what about Sissy—sweet little Sissy who's been with you more than a year and is probably wondering why she's not got a bun in the oven yet? How will she feel when she finds out her marriage is a lie?"

"It's not a lie." She can't fight the tears anymore.

"And what about Sissy's daddy and brothers when they find out the way you tricked her and defiled her? There are many reasons I couldn't guarantee your safety, *Ronnie*." He says the name like it, too, is a lie.

"But," he says, his tone lightening. "I'm a doctor, and what do doctors do? They cure people's problems. And I've got a cure for yours if you're willing to pay the bill."

"What kind of cure?" Ronnie's voice sounds small and choked, not like her own.

"I'm willing to keep your secret. From your boss, from your girl, as long as you make it worth my time to keep my mouth shut."

"How much?" If she can pay it, she will. She can't lose Sissy.

"I'd say about a hundred a month would keep my lips sealed pretty tight."

"That's half my paycheck." Ronnie can't imagine how she could cut corners so that she and Sissy could live on half her pay. "Look, I know the company must pay you real good. Why would you want to fool around with something as little as a miner's pay?"

Doc Woods smiles. "Oh, extra money always helps. I've got a son starting medical school up in Lexington. Those are his pajamas you're wearing. He'd appreciate an extra hundred." He reaches over and pats Ronnie's knee. "So half your paycheck every month. You can keep the scrip."

Suppertime, and they're sitting over their beans and cornbread. No fried taters, and the corn pone is small. It's been like this the past two weeks as the money's gotten scarcer. "I understand about your ma being sick," Sissy says, "but how much longer you reckon you'll need to send home half your pay?"

"Not much longer," Ronnie says, not looking up from her food. "Just until she's better and her doctor bills get paid off." Ronnie hates chasing a lie with another lie.

"Well, I hope she gets better soon," Sissy says. "For her and for us. But I'd be mean to complain. Your ma's troubles is way worse than ours. I'm praying for her."

Ronnie manages to mumble "thank you." Sissy is a good person. She would never deceive anybody. Ronnie thinks about Doc Woods saying she had lied to Sissy and corrupted her. Had she really? The funny thing was, back when Ronnie wore dresses, that was what felt like a lie.

The miners stand by the mouth, blinking in the bright morning sun.

"Hey, Ronnie," Harold says. "Boss wants to talk to you." He nods over to where Mr. Sturgill, the shift boss, is standing with a clipboard.

Ronnie feels like a rubber ball is stuck in her throat, but her feet shuffle in the direction of Mr. Sturgill anyway. "You was wanting to talk to me, sir?"

Mr. Sturgill looks up from his clipboard. He is a small, mean man. Maybe because he's a lower-level boss, he always seems to be looking to catch you doing something wrong, like he wants to enjoy that little bit of power. "I need you to put a rumor to rest for me." His eyes are beady and dead. "Last night I was playing poker with some fellers. Old Doc Woods was one of 'em, and he was deep into a fifth of bourbon. When Doc's been drinking, he gossips as bad as any old granny."

Feeling sick, Ronnie manages a nod.

"Doc started talking about this interesting case he had. Said one of the miners that got caught in that last cave-in . . . wasn't what he seemed. He didn't name names, but it got me to thinking. You never shower with the other fellers, nobody's ever seen you take a piss." He smiles, but it's not a friendly smile. "Now I might've just been listening to rumors spread by a drunk old man, but I need you to prove Doc wrong."

"How?" Ronnie is afraid she might throw up on the boss's feet.

272 / JULIA WATTS

"Well, there's no need to be vulgar about this," Mr. Sturgill says. "Why don't you just take off your shirt? That'll tell us what we need to know."

Mr. Sturgill isn't the only one watching. All the other miners are, too. She has no choice. With shaking hands, she unbuttons her work shirt, revealing the union suit. Her chest is bound with gauze underneath it so she's flat as a plate.

"Well, I can't tell nothing with them long johns on," Mr. Sturgill says. "Take them off, too."

Once Ronnie had gone coon hunting with some fellers. She had never gone again because she couldn't forget the fear in that treed coon's eyes. Now she is the treed animal. She looks at Mr. Sturgill, then at the other men watching to see what she'll do next. She does what the treed coon couldn't do. She runs.

She runs as hard as she can, not even thinking about where she's going, except away. She runs until she has to stop for breath. She's deep in the woods. Nobody is chasing her. Her running is all the answer they need. She sinks to the ground. Now what? Gossip spreads in the camp quicker than coal dust. She remembers a picture where a whole village turned against a monster even though he hadn't done any harm. She is that monster.

A plan. She has to think up a plan.

The nurse in Doc Woods' office looks startled when Ronnie stomps in, sweaty, out of breath, wearing just her union suit and dungarees. "I need to talk to Doc," Ronnie says.

"He's with a patient."

"Well, why don't you go tell him Ronnie Weaver wants to see him and see how fast he gets out here?"

The nurse disappears into the back room. Doc Woods appears almost immediately.

"You owe me three hundred dollars," Ronnie says.

"How do you figure that?" Doc sounds calm, but his eyes are shifty.

"You busted the deal," Ronnie says. "You said if I paid you half my check every month you'd keep your mouth shut. But you didn't."

Doc Woods holds up his hands. "I held up my end of the bargain until last night when I drank too much. Up until then I stayed quiet, so I owe you nothing."

"You don't owe somebody something when you've ruined their life?" Ronnie says. As soon as Doc Woods opened his mouth, everything good about her life was lost: her job, her friendships, her wife. Gone.

"You ruined your own life when you decided to turn yourself into something you weren't. All I did was tell the truth about you."

"You don't know one damn thing about me," Ronnie says. She had hoped to come away from Doc with some money to help her get away, but she doesn't want it now, even if it is rightfully hers. She strides out of the office empty-handed.

It is still morning. The men are in the mines, the children at school, the women at home. Ronnie walks across the quiet camp knowing she's seeing it for the last time. Maybe she'll see Sissy for the last time, too, unless she's already found out and run home to her mama.

When she gets to the house, somebody has painted DYKES and PREVERTS on the siding in drippy red paint that looks like blood. It seems like if somebody was going to write something hateful on your house, they'd at least spell it right. Ronnie is scared. Not for herself. For Sissy.

She runs up to the porch, unlocks the door, then locks it behind her. "Sissy? It's me."

Sissy is in bed under the quilt, only her red hair visible.

"Are you all right?" She wants to sit on the bed, touch Sissy's hair, but fear stops her.

Sissy nods.

"The people that painted them nasty things on the house? They didn't try and hurt you none?"

Sissy pulls the covers down a little. "They hollered a lot. They tried to get in the house, but I locked the door and hid in under the bed."

"Good girl," Ronnie says. "Do you know why they said them things?"

Sissy nods. Her eyes are red and puffy. "Doc Woods come by this morning after you left and told me. He said it'd be better if I heard it from him."

Ronnie nods. She'd been holding out a little hope that Sissy might not know. Now she feels empty of hope and everything else. "All right then. I'll just get a few things before I go. It won't be safe for me to be here once the mine lets out. You need to go somewhere safe, too, you hear? Like to your mother and daddy's."

Sissy sits up in bed, tears in her eyes. "What if . . . what if we was to go somewhere nobody knows?"

Ronnie feels a fluttering in her chest. She hadn't even considered this possibility. "You mean you and me?"

Sissy nods.

"Even though you know I'm—"

"I know who you are. You're Ronnie." Tears glitter prettily in Sissy's eyes. "Growing up, seeing the way Daddy treated Mama, yelling at her and throwing things at her, even though she worked like a dog for him. . . . I thought that was the way marriage had to be. But it ain't. It can be good. Real good. You showed me that, Ronnie."

Ronnie sits next to her in bed and clasps her hand in hers. "We'd have to go far away."

"I've never been past these here mountains. I'd love to see someplace else."

"And well . . . there'd never be younguns."

Sissy laughs. "I never wanted 'em anyway."

Ronnie laughs, too.

It just takes ten minutes to fit what they can into their one cardboard suitcase. The rest they'll leave behind. The mines don't let out for hours, so it should be easy to get out of the camp without much notice. If they can hitch a ride to town, they have enough money for the train to Knoxville. And from there, they'll just have to see.

SELECTED BIBLIOGRAPHY OF SAME-SEX DESIRE IN APPALACHIAN LITERATURE

COMPILED BY J. TYLER CHADWELL-ENGLISH
FOLKLORELIBRARIAN@GMAIL.COM
EXPANDED BY JEFF MANN

This bibliography is based on published poetry, fiction, and nonfiction dealing with same-sex desires within works that take place in Appalachia. The criterion for the selection is narrowed only to the acts or same-sex desires within the text and is not necessarily reflective of the orientation of the author. However, some texts are included because the author identifies as lesbian, gay, bisexual, transgendered, or queer (LGBTQ) and did at one time live in Appalachia. I have also included authors from Appalachia whose work contains instances of same-sex desire but whose prose doesn't necessarily take place in the parameters of Appalachia defined by the Appalachian Regional Commission as a 205,000-square-mile region following the spine of the Appalachian Mountains from southern New York to northern Mississippi. It includes all of West Virginia and parts of twelve other states: Alabama, Georgia, Kentucky, Maryland, Mississippi, New York, North Carolina, Ohio, Pennsylvania, South Carolina, Tennessee, and Virginia. This research was facilitated by my work with the James H. and Phyllis Wilson Moore literary collection at Fairmont State University's Frank and Jane Gabor West Virginia Folklife Center's Fred Fidura Library.

Selected Works of Fiction

Allison, Dorothy. *Bastard Out of Carolina*. New York: Dutton, 1992.
———. *Trash*. New York: Penguin, 2002.

Alther, Lisa. *Five Minutes in Heaven*. New York: Dutton, 1995.

———. *Kinflicks*. New York: Knopf, 1976.

———. *Original Sins*. New York: Berkley, 1982.

———. *Washed in the Blood*. Macon, GA: Mercer University Press, 2011.

Barker, Gray. *They Knew Too Much About Flying Saucers*. New York: University Books, 1956.

Bishop, John Peale. *Act of Darkness*. New York: Avon Books, 1967.

Chabon, Michael. *The Mysteries of Pittsburgh*. New York: W.W. Morrow, 1988.

Corcoran, Jonathan. *The Rope Swing: Stories*. Morgantown, WV: West Virginia University Press, 2016.

Curtiss, Huston. *Sins of the Seventh Sister: A Novel Based on a True Story of the Gothic South*. New York: Harmony Books, 2003.

Depta, Victor. *Idol and Sanctuary*. Huntington, WV: University Editions, 1993.

Dooley, Sarah. *Ashes to Asheville*. New York: Putnam, 2017.

Drobny, Vasek. *House of the Moon*. Ashland, KY: Blair Mountain Press, 2008.

Farris, Holly. *Lockjaw*. Arlington, VA: Gival Press, 2007.

Fetherling, George. *Jericho*. Toronto: Random House Canada, 2005.

Gearhart, Sally Miller. *The Wanderground: Stories of the Hill Women*. Boston: Alyson Publications, 1984.

Giardina, Denise. *The Unquiet Earth*. New York: Norton, 1992.

Gordon, Jaimy. *Lord of Misrule*. Kingston, NY: McPherson & Company, 2010.

Grubb, Davis. *Ancient Lights*. New York: Viking Press, 1982.

———. *The Voices of Glory*. Greenwich, CT: Fawcett, 1966.

House, Silas. *Southernmost*. Chapel Hill, NC: Algonquin Books, 2018.

Johnson, Fenton. *The Man Who Loved Birds*. Lexington: University Press of Kentucky, 2016.

———. *Scissors, Paper, Rock*. New York: Simon and Schuster/Pocket Books, 1993.

Kelly, E. Layne. *Carcass of the Caterpillar.* North Charleston, SC: BookSurge, 2004.

Knowles, John. *A Separate Peace.* New York: Macmillan, 1960.

Kromer, Tom. *Waiting for Nothing and Other Writings.* Athens, GA: University of Georgia Press, 1989.

LeRoy, J. T. [Laura Albert]. *The Heart is Deceitful Above All Things.* New York: Bloomsbury, 2001.

———. *Sarah.* New York: Harper Perennial, 2000.

Maillard, Keith. *Two Strand River.* Toronto: Harper Perennial, 1996.

Mann, Jeff. *Consent: Bondage Tales.* Maple Shade, NJ: Unzipped/Lethe Press, 2017.

———. *Country.* Maple Shade, NJ: Lethe Press, 2016.

———. *Cub.* Maple Shade, NJ: Bear Bones Books/Lethe Press, 2014.

———. *Desire and Devour: Stories of Blood and Sweat.* Maple Shade, NJ: Bear Bones Books/Lethe Press, 2012.

———. *Fog: A Novel of Desire and Reprisal.* Maple Shade, NJ: Unzipped/Lethe Press, 2011.

———. *A History of Barbed Wire.* Maple Shade, NJ: Lethe Press, 2008.

———. *Insatiable.* Amherst, MA: Unzipped/Lethe Press, 2017.

———. *Purgatory: A Novel of the Civil War.* Maple Shade, NJ: Bear Bones Books/Lethe Press, 2012.

———. *Salvation: A Novel of the Civil War.* Maple Shade, NJ: Bear Bones Books/Lethe Press, 2014.

Maren, Mesha. *Sugar Run.* Chapel Hill, NC: Algonquin Books, 2019.

Martinac, Paula. *The One You Call Sister: New Women's Fiction.* Pittsburgh: Cleis Press, 1989.

McClanahan, Scott. *Hill William.* New York: Tyrant Books, 2013.

McElmurray, Karen Salyer. *Strange Birds in the Tree of Heaven.* Athens, GA: Hill Street Press, 1999.

Meredith, Donna. *Fraccidental death: An Eco-thriller.* Tallahassee, FL: Wild Women Writers, 2016.

Mehta, Rahul. *Quarantine: Stories*. New York: Harper Perennial, 2011.

Pancake, Ann. *Strange As This Weather Has Been*. Berkeley, CA: Counterpoint, 2007.

Phillips, Jayne Anne. *Shelter: A Novel*. New York: Vintage, 2002.

Sickels, Carter. *The Evening Hour: A Novel*. New York: Bloomsbury, 2012.

Skidmore, Hobert. *The Years Are Even*. New York: Random House, 1952.

Smith, Lee. *Fair and Tender Ladies*. New York: Putnam, 1988.

———. *Black Mountain Breakdown*. New York: Berkley, 2012.

Watts, Julia. *Finding H.F.* Tallahassee, FL: Bella Books, 2011.

———. *Hypnotizing Chickens*. Tallahassee, FL: Bella Books, 2014.

———. *The Kind of Girl I Am*. Midway, FL: Spinsters Ink, 2007.

———. *Phases of the Moon*. Tallahassee, FL: Naiad Press, 1997.

———. *Quiver*. New York: Three Rooms Press, 2018.

———. *Secret City*. Tallahassee, FL: Bella Books, 2013.

Willis, Meredith S. *Out of the Mountains: Appalachian Stories*. Athens, OH: Ohio University Press, 2010.

Wyeth, Sharon Dennis. *Orphea Proud*. New York: Delacorte, 2006.

Selected Nonfiction/Memoirs

Allison, Dorothy. *Skin: Talking About Sex, Class, and Literature*. Ann Arbor, MI: Firebrand Books, 2005.

———. *Two or Three Things I Know for Sure*. New York: Dutton, 1995.

Blum, Louise A. *You're Not from Around Here, Are You? A Lesbian in Small-Town America*. Madison, WI: University of Wisconsin Press, 2001.

Dews, Carlos, and Carolyn Leste Law, eds. *Out in the South*. Philadelphia: Temple University, 2001.

House, Silas., and Jason Howard, eds. *Something's Rising: Appalachians Fighting Mountaintop Removal*. Lexington: University Press of Kentucky, 2009.

Jennings, Kevin. *Mama's Boy, Preacher's Son: A Memoir*. Boston: Beacon Press, 2006.

Johnson, Fenton. *At the Center of All Beauty: The Dignity and Challenge of Solitude.* New York: W.W. Norton, 2019.

———. *Everywhere Home: A Life in Essays.* Louisville, KY: Sarabande Books, 2017.

———. *Geography of the Heart: A Memoir.* New York: Scribner, 1997.

———. *Keeping Faith: A Skeptic's Journey Among Christian and Buddhist Monks.* New York: Houghton Mifflin, 2003.

Mann, Jeff. *Binding the God: Ursine Essays from the Mountain South.* Maple Shade, NJ: Bear Bones Books/Lethe Press, 2010.

———. *Edge: Travels of an Appalachian Leather Bear.* Maple Shade, NJ: Bear Bones Books/Lethe Press, 2008.

———. *Loving Mountains, Loving Men.* Athens, OH: Ohio University Press, 2005.

Read, Kirk. *How I Learned to Snap: A Small-Town Coming-Out and Coming-of-Age Story.* Athens, GA: Hill Street Press, 2001.

Verghese, Abraham. *My Own Country: A Doctor's Story.* New York: Vintage, 1995.

Selected Poetry

Allison, Dorothy. *The Women Who Hate Me.* Ithaca, NY: Firebrand Books, 1991.

Anderson, Maggie. *Cold Comfort.* Pittsburgh: University of Pittsburgh Press, 1986.

———. *Dear All.* New York: Four Way Books, 2017.

———. *A Space Filled with Moving.* Pittsburgh: University of Pittsburgh Press, 1992.

———. *Windfall: New and Selected Poems.* Pittsburgh: University of Pittsburgh Press, 2000.

———. *Years That Answer.* New York: Harper and Row, 1980.

Brown, Nickole. *Fanny Says.* Rochester, NY: BOA Editions, 2015.

———. *Sister.* Pasadena, CA: Red Hen Press, 2007.

davenport, doris. *ascent.* CreateSpace Independent Publishing Platform, 2011.

———. *Eat Thunder & Drink Rain.* D. Davenport, 1982.

———. *Madness Like Morning Glories.* Baton Rouge: Louisiana State University Press, 2005.

———. *Voodoo Chile—Slight Return.* Soque Street Press, 1991.

Depta, Victor. *Preparing a Room.* Ashland, KY: Blair Mountain Press, 2001.

Mann, Jeff. *Bones Washed with Wine.* Arlington, VA: Gival Press, 2003.

———. *On the Tongue.* Arlington, VA: Gival Press, 2006.

———. *Rebels.* Maple Shade, NJ: Lethe Press, 2015.

———. *A Romantic Mann.* Maple Shade, NJ: Lethe Press, 2013.

McQuain, Kelly. *Velvet Rodeo.* Los Angeles: Bloom Books, 2014.

Sipple, Savannah. *WWJD & Other Poems.* Little Rock, AR: Sibling Rivalry Press, 2019.

Skeen, Anita. *Never the Whole Story.* East Lansing: Michigan State University Press, 2011.

———. *Outside the Fold, Outside the Frame.* East Lansing: Michigan State University Press, 1999.

———. *Resurrection of the Animals.* East Lansing: Michigan State University Press, 2002.

Smith, Aaron. *Appetite.* Pittsburgh: University of Pittsburgh Press, 2012.

———. *Blue on Blue Ground.* Pittsburgh: University of Pittsburgh Press, 2005.

———. *Primer.* Pittsburgh: University of Pittsburgh Press, 2016.

Steele, Paul C. *Anse on Island Creek and Other Poems.* Charleston, WV: Mountain State Press, 1981.

CREDITS

"Anything You Want, You Got It" by Maggie Anderson first appeared in *A Space Filled with Moving* (University of Pittsburgh Press, 1992). Reprinted by permission of the University of Pittsburgh Press. "Biography," "Cleaning the Guns," "In Real Life," and "My Father and Ezra Pound" appeared in *Dear All* (Four Way Books, 2017), and are reprinted by permission of Four Way Books.

"My Book, in Birds" by Nickole Brown first appeared in *The Los Angeles Review* (2011) and was the winner of A Room of Her Own's Orlando Prize. "To My Grandmother's Ghost" first appeared in *Ellipses*. "An Invitation for My Grandmother" first appeared in *Gwarlingo* (2015). "My Book, in Birds," "To My Grandmother's Ghost," and "An Invitation for My Grandmother" were reprinted in *Fanny Says*, copyright © 2015 by Nickole Brown. Reprinted with the permission of The Permissions Company, Inc., on behalf of BOA Editions, Ltd., www.boaeditions.org. "Ten Questions You're Afraid to Ask, Answered" first appeared in *Bloom Magazine* 4, no. 1 (Spring 2012).

"The Rope Swing" by Jonathan Corcoran appeared in *The Rope Swing: Stories* (West Virginia University Press, 2016).

"The Desmodontidae" by Victor Depta first appeared in *Preparing a Room* (Blair Mountain Press, 2001).

"Bad Habits" by Fenton Johnson first appeared in *Fiction Network* in 1984.

"Not for Long" by Jeff Mann first appeared in *Harrington Gay Men's Fiction Quarterly* 3, no. 1 (2001) and was later included in *A History of Barbed Wire* (Suspect Thoughts Press, 2006; Bear Bones Books/Lethe Press, 2011), and is reprinted by permission of Lethe Press. "Training the Enemy" first appeared in *Pine Mountain Sand & Gravel*, no. 20 (2017). "Yellow-Eye Beans" first appeared in *Appalachian Heritage* 39, no. 3 (Summer 2011). "The Gay Redneck Devours Draper Mercantile" first appeared in *Impossible Archetype*, no. 2 (August 2017). "Three Crosses" first appeared in *Blue Fifth Review* 8, no. 4 (May 2008) and was later reprinted in *Appalachia's Last Stand: The Appalachian Mountains Must Not Be Sacrificed for Cheap Energy*, edited by Delilah F. O'Haynes (Wind Publications, 2009) and in *A Romantic Mann* (Lethe Press, 2013), and is reprinted by permission of Lethe Press. "Homecoming" first appeared in *Bloom Magazine* 2, no. 2 (Fall 2005) and was reprinted in *Loving Mountains, Loving Men* (Ohio University Press, 2005), and is reprinted by permission of Ohio University Press.

"Among" by Mesha Maren first appeared in *Tyrant Books* (23 April 2018), and is reprinted by permission of New York Tyrant.

"Scrape the Velvet from Your Antlers" by Kelly McQuain first appeared in *Kestrel*, no. 30 (Spring 2013), and is reprinted with permission. "Brave" first appeared in *Bloom Magazine* 5, no. 2 (Fall 2015) and was reprinted in *Velvet Rodeo* (Bloom Books, 2014), and is reprinted by permission of Bloom Books. "Vampirella" first appeared in *Drawn to Marvel: Poems from the Comic Books*, edited by Bryan D. Dietrich and Marta Ferguson (Minor Arcana Press, 2014). "Monkey Orchid" first appeared in *A&U* 23, no. 10 (October 2014) and was reprinted in *Assaracus*, issue 18 (Sibling Rivalry Press, April 2015), and is reprinted by permission of Sibling Rivalry Press. "Alien Boy" first appeared in *Bloom Magazine* 4, no. 2 (Fall 2012) and later in *Velvet Rodeo*, and is reprinted by permission of Bloom Books and Sibling Rivalry Press. "Ritual" first appeared in *Assaracus*, issue 18 (Sibling Rivalry Press, April 2015), and is reprinted by permission of Sibling Rivalry

Press. "Mercy" first appeared in *Knockout*, issue 6 (Summer 2017), and is reprinted with permission.

"A Better Life" is from *Quarantine* by Rahul Mehta. Copyright © 2011 by Rahul Mehta. Reprinted by permission of HarperCollins Publishers.

"Richochet" by Ann Pancake first appeared as a chapter in *Strange As This Weather Has Been: A Novel* (Counterpoint, 2007), and is reprinted by permission of Counterpoint Press.

"Saving" by Carter Sickels was first published in *The Collection: Short Fiction from the Transgender Vanguard*, edited by Tom Léger and Riley MacLeod (Topside Press, 2012).

"WWJD/about love," "WWJD/about letting go," "Jesus and I Went to the Walmart," "Catfisting," "Pork Belly," "A List of Times I Thought I Was Gay," and "Jesus Signs Me Up for a Dating App" by Savannah Sipple all appeared in *WWJD & Other Poems* (Sibling Rivalry Press, 2019), and are reprinted by permission of Sibling Rivalry Press.

"Double Valentine," "How Bodies Fit," and "The Clover Tree" by Anita Skeen appeared in *Never the Whole Story* (Michigan State University Press, 2011). "The Quilt: 25 April 1993" appeared in *Outside the Fold, Outside the Frame* (Michigan State University Press, 1999). "While You Sleep" appeared in *The Resurrection of the Animals* (Michigan State University Press, 2002). All are reprinted by permission of Michigan State University Press.

"Blanket" and "There's Still One Story" by Aaron Smith first appeared in *Columbia Poetry Review*, no. 31 (Spring 2018).